A WILLAMETTE HIGH NOVEL
BEBE DUNCAN

EVERYBODY'S HAVEN

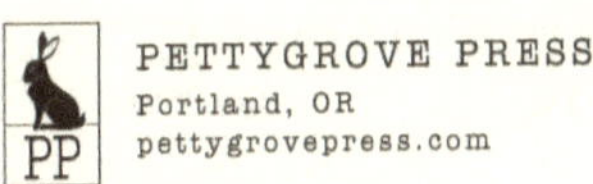

PETTYGROVE PRESS
Portland, OR
pettygrovepress.com

Publisher's Cataloging-in-Publication

(Provided by Cassidy Cataloguing Services, Inc.).
Names: Duncan, Bebe, author.

Title: Everybody's Haven : a Willamette High novel / Bebe Duncan.

Description: First edition. | Portland : Pettygrove Press, [2025] | Series: Duncan, Bebe. Willamette High. | Audience: Young adult.

Identifiers: LCCN: 2025923811 | ISBN: 9798999300140 (paperback) | 9798999300157 (eBook)

Subjects: LCSH: Teenage girls--Psychology--Fiction. | Perfectionism (Personality trait)--Fiction. | Autistic youth--Fiction. | Teenagers--Family relationships--Fiction. | Lesbian teenagers--Identity--Fiction. | Lesbian teenagers--Sexual behavior--Fiction. | Bullying in schools--Fiction. | Neurodivergent people--Family relationships--Fiction. | Friendship--Fiction. | Teenagers--Mental health--Fiction. | Portland (Ore.)--Fiction. | Bildungsromans. | BISAC: YOUNG ADULT FICTION / Social Themes / Emotions & Feelings. | YOUNG ADULT FICTION / Neurodiversity. | YOUNG ADULT FICTION / LGBTQ+ / Lesbian.

Classification: LCC: PS3604.U524 E94 2025 | DDC: 813/.6--dc23

Cover Design by S.J. Dalmar

EVERYBODY'S HAVEN

EVERYBODY'S HAVEN

Acknowledgements

There are many people to thank for their contribution to Everybody's Haven.

A big thank you to beta readers Ava, Miranda, Lara, Miriam, and Amy—your feedback was essential to bringing Haven out in the world (as well as out of the closet), S.J. Dalmar for bringing color and form to this book, Catherine, for your patience as I talk endlessly about the Willamette High world, Althea, who showed me the perfect pair of skates, and to Anita, for going to the rink with me that fateful day.

Everybody's Haven started as a screenplay about adult women. I was wrangling my second draft and suddenly stopped editing and asked myself, "what if they met when they were teenagers?" Cynthia Whitcomb taught me how to draft a screenplay and unintentionally taught me to be a better novelist. Thanks Cynthia!

Thank you to my friends and family who understood when I hid away at the Red Lion and didn't text me to ask where we keep the muffin mix. Love you!

To Anna-phylactic Shock, without you this book would never have been born.

And to the other "Wholesome as a warm slice of wheat bread" woman (you know who you are) who made this possible with a smile.

Contents

CHAPTER ONE

"Why would you want to do that?"

Light peeped through the leaves overhead, the slivers of sun blinding me before dipping back behind the trees or the clouds, leaving the ghost of sunlight over my eyes. I had to admit, when I could focus between sunbeams, the trees were impressive. Everything grew in Portland, but these suckers were on steroids.

Not that I cared. A tree's a tree. But I studied them anyway, trying to identify the ones above me. The Magnolia was easy; it was already flowering. Big pink, plastic-looking Tulip-y flowers. Cherry trees blossomed all along the South Park Blocks, no one could miss those. But those ginormous barely budding things towering overhead could have been Maples, Oaks, or alien invaders for all I knew.

I just wanted my eyes up. Anything was less awkward than looking around at eye level.

But I couldn't miss the flashes of red and green and black and most of all *skin* on the periphery of my vision. So. Much. Skin. Or the flow of humans in the streets and waving hands, signs and banners. There was no avoiding the chanting slogans and the overwhelming scents of spring flowers, hair products, and perfume in the open air.

But I tried. I tried to ignore what was going on all around me.

I didn't try hard enough.

"I still don't get it."

And that was my out loud voice. Crap.

"Haven," Alice started, drawing in a breath to give me The Talk again.

If only I could zip-it like a normal person.

Not that I wasn't the most normal person in sight. I didn't need to look around again to confirm that. But looking just freaked me out, so I focused on Alice. She'd wiped off her glare, no doubt remembering she was supposed to be "opening my mind" and needed to be patient with me. Not that she was any good at glaring. Her eyes were pale gray, the irises barely visible, and she was *not* scary.

Okay, she was a little scary *to me*. For a reason I didn't even like to admit to myself.

I smothered a sigh. Being here was her idea, not mine. And since *I'm* a glutton for punishment I showed. On the upside, I get to hang with Alice on a weekend when she has a day off from Comikaze Coffee. Downside, her latest boyfriend is along for the ride. And I was standing *right next to him*.

I turned and stared at the braided yarn hanging on either side of Finn's face. He *always* wore that stupid knit hat. I wanted to hate him. Hate his black floppy bangs and *Incredible Hulk* T-shirt. Hate his green eyes and the way he rocked on his heels non-stop like he was made of coffee. Hate that look he was giving her.

But, to give the dude credit, I knew he wanted to be right by Alice, instead of me. Holding her hand. Putting his arm around her shoulders. Soaking in her warmth. Brushing her mess of blonde hair away from her face to kiss her. I knew because maybe *I* wanted to do all those things.

And he knew I did.

I sighed. This situation was all kinds of messed up.

Maybe I *could* make a break for my bike, I thought. Not, if I was being honest, for the first time. She was only a few yards away—like I was going to park where she would be out of my sight downtown—and I was fast. Cross-country captain, track medalist, run for the rush of it fast. No way Alice could catch up. She didn't have an athletic bone in her body.

Not that I was looking at her body. Nope. Not at all. I realized I was shaking my head.

"What isn't there to get?" she asked quietly, and I lost my shot at freedom. At least she knew how to adjust her volume. So that none of the groups of shouting, chanting, self-identified sluts heard and beat me to a pulp with their high heels and hand-made signs.

I managed to keep my mouth shut long enough to give my brain a chance to put it diplomatically. Because I just. Did. Not. Get. It. The gathering *and* the point of view. I mean, I should have expected this. It was a *Slut Walk*. What did I think people would be wearing? Puffy jackets, and sweatpants?

Not that it wouldn't have been a better option in April. It was chilly. There was a breeze. There might be rain anytime and there would be mascara streaks and wet skin *everywhere*.

Says the girl wearing shorts and a leather flight jacket, I reminded myself.

Still, I opened my big mouth *again*. "Alice, it's not rocket science. If you don't want to be treated like a slut don't dress like one."

Crickets. Finn inched away and I could feel Alice straighten. Uh oh. The girl already had serious posture. And attitude, even in her fishnet stockings and stupid short skirt. She turned to me and there was no missing the word SLUT, written in cursive across the bare skin below her black bra. "Slut solidarity" she told me.

Because Alice was *not* a slut.

Stupid about boys maybe.

No. She *was* stupid about boys. Hopefully, Finn would be the boy to break her bad streak.

Not that I wanted them to be together, but if she had to be with someone...

"Haven, the point *is* looking like a slut doesn't give anyone permission to rape you, or harass you..."

"Or treat you like shit because you were 'asking for it'," Finn interjected. The sign slung across his chest read "HOW YOU DRESS IS NOT CONSENT".

Alice smiled as she looked across me. At him.

"Well, yeah, I get *that*." Duh.

"Maybe *you* do, but it still happens all the time. Guys excuse forcing a girl because what did she expect looking like that? That police officer basically said women shouldn't dress like sluts if they don't want to get assaulted."

Right. I googled it. The annual SlutWalk started after a Canadian cop screwed up.

I guess.

"But he wasn't wrong. Why go out of your way to get hassled or attacked when guys think slutty clothes are an invitation?"

Alice's jaw dropped. Uh oh. I'd blown it again.

"Because wearing a burqa won't keep you safe, babe."

Some girl was in my face, smirking. And she was *not* wearing a burqa. Her red button-down shirt was tied around her waist so tight she was almost spilling out the top. DERBY SLUT was written there in red. Was that lipstick? It matched her lips, I guess.

"Or the basketball shorts and men's T-shirts you hide in..." she continued, hands on her hips.

"I do not hide," I said. Maybe yelled.

"Or mom-jeans or anything else considered not sexy in our society. If you play along with the 'I need to dress a certain way to keep from getting raped' paradigm you help perpetuate that bullshit and the bad guys win. Not just if you get assaulted, but every fucking day."

I took a step back from her. What? Was she saying that dressing *not* slutty was damaging to women?

What was wrong with avoiding shoes that killed your feet or shorts that left your butt hanging out or tops so tight your breasts wouldn't fit? They were uncomfortable and impractical. How was it even worth the trouble it caused?

Uh oh, I'd used my out loud voice. I could see it on *all* their faces. Because the girl who called me "babe" had three friends with her. Friends on roller skates. Who looked familiar.

In the seconds of stunned silence, I heard Mom's words in my head, "How you dress reflects your beliefs," and how those included freedom from narrow definitions of femininity, freedom of motion, and not valuing brand names or status symbols. Modesty. Humility. How did dressing like a slut promote equality and a just society?

Not like I said any of that aloud. It wasn't the time to thrash out my mom's utilitarian-slash-Unitarian philosophy.

I wasn't that stupid.

The three girls wearing Rose City Rosebuds T-shirts would crush me under their wheels if I pissed them off. More. My bike wasn't just calling me, it was shouting "run".

Alice inserted herself between me and "babe" girl. "Haven, do you know Daisy?"

"Umm, no. Should I?" Did she go to Willamette?

"Daisy King the Derby Queen," said "babe" girl. She stuck one hand straight out like a toddler. The only smart choice was to take her hand. Her grip was no toddler's. Her fingers wrapped like steel around mine before she let go. I was feeling lucky she didn't crush my hand for kicks.

Instead, she laughed.

"I'm in U.S. History with you. And Health and Ecology, Haven Alexander," she lifted one dark brown arched eyebrow, I think, hard to tell with those dark brown bangs.

"As are Sophie," she went on, gesturing to a white girl with buzzed black hair who looked like she could deadlift a Great Dane, "Ellie," she pointed to the tiny girl with purple pigtails who looked maybe Filipina, "and Birgit." Birgit was the total stereotype Scandinavian amazon: tall, white-blonde, and thighs like tree trunks.

Which I was getting a good look at considering they were all wearing those tiny volleyball shorts. Red ones.

I gave them all a nervous nod before shifting my gaze back to Daisy's, the leader of the pack. And whoa! How had I missed that she had the biggest, brownest eyes? Bambi eyes. Her gaze rattled me. Why was she looking at me like that? The smirk was long gone, and it was like she was reading my face. Reading *me*.

It was almost a relief when Daisy turned to talk to Alice, her slick brown ponytail bouncing upward at the end. Defying gravity.

Daisy wasn't bulky or Amazonian or tiny. She looked like a character out of one of Paul's vintage comic books. Curvy and kind of soft and intimidating. Unsettling. I didn't know if I liked her or not.

"She'd make a good jammer, don't you think?" Alice told her.

And now I felt like a side of beef as she and the roller derby girls sized me up. A side of beef they'd probably prefer to carve up than converse with.

"I don't know, can she skate?" squeaked the tiny girl. Ellie.

"She's tall," said Birgit, "That can be a good thing."

"And she's got muscle," said Sophie, and I swear she was going to pinch my bicep to verify, but I flinched away before she could.

"And she would rock the uniform," added Daisy.

What. The. Hell.

"She," I groaned, "Has never skated a day in her life. And doesn't want to. This is all Alice." Alice who was in big trouble. "I don't want to be a jammer or jam tart or whatever."

Daisy laughed. A big laugh. Doubling-at-the-waist laugh. "That was awesome. Jam tart. We should use that. It would make a fantastic derby name." The smile she wore spread over her whole face, lifting those big dark eyes at the corners. It was impossible not to smile back.

"She doesn't know what she wants," Alice interjected. "Cross-country is over and she's bored."

I rolled my eyes. Alice thought I was bored? With my classes and Paul coming back to school? And the SATs. And Constitution Team Nationals coming up. And Track...

Except I wasn't doing Track this year. I was kind of in shock that I'd done it, dropped Track after four practices. Mom and Dad weren't happy about it. *At all.*

Daisy stuck out a hip and crossed her arms, eyeing me up and down. "You should come to try-outs. Give it a whirl. You never know." She chuckled.

Chuckled.

How had I never noticed Daisy in class? She kind of stuck out. In a big way. And it wasn't just what she was wearing. I wanted to be annoyed with her, pushing the derby thing. But it was hard to be annoyed with Bambi. And she *was* inviting me to join her team. It obviously meant a lot to her. I could respect that.

I shook my head, but I smiled, too.

I wasn't even really annoyed with Alice. She was only trying to help. Like I'd find someone I liked at Rugby or Basketball or Derby. Who would *actually* like me back for some reason.

I wouldn't.

I couldn't.

Letting myself even *think* this way was too much to ask.

I stuck my hands in my shorts' pockets, looking everywhere but at Alice. "You know, I should get going. I've got stuff..."

"Oh no you don't," and there she was, in my face, all five-foot-nothing of her; I could see the top of her head. "Come on, just for a few blocks."

And now all six of them were looking at me. No way in hell.

"Alice, look, I can't..."

"Come on," she grabbed my hand and tugged me toward the street, the four girls going first and Finn trailing behind.

Why did she have to be so ridiculously comfortable just grabbing me? I told myself it was because she had to hold onto people when she was drawing on them. That she was practicing for when she was a tattoo artist doing work on jerks she'd rather not be touching.

The truth was it didn't mean anything to *her*.

It shouldn't mean anything to *me*.

I don't know how Alice got me to the middle of the street, sandwiched between two middle-aged moms in miniskirts and a six-pack of maybe college girls wearing shorts, bras, and ink. I looked down at my clothes, hoping I could joke my way out of this. "Hey, no, I'm not dressed for this..."

Finn kept a straight face, but Daisy and her teammates snickered a few feet ahead.

"No one will ever take you for a slut, Haven, no matter what kind of outfit we put you in. You're just going to have to be a slut-supporter. They're welcome, too." Alice glanced at Finn. They were ridiculously into each other even if she said they weren't *together*. I wanted her to be happy. And considering her first two loser boyfriends nearly broke her...

I kind of wanted to punch them.

Alice gave me another yank, and I put down my heels, the rubber of my hiking boots holding fast. Women streamed by as we stopped short. No, I was not marching in a SlutWalk through downtown. Mom might see me on the news. Or one of their friends. Or someone from school. Or church.

And I'd have to go through the whole debate again. *And* explain why I was there. No.

"Not gonna happen," I said.

Alice let go, nodding as I walked backward for several steps.

"Thanks for being such a good sport," she said.

"Thanks for including me even though..."

The "I still don't get it" was silent.

I turned, plastering on a *whatever* face because this whole thing wasn't me. It's not like I *wanted* to be there on a Saturday afternoon. I had more important things to do. Papers to write, tests to study for, a debate argument to polish for Constitution Team. I could probably fit in a run after studying if I got right on it.

I *wanted* to be out of there.

I *wanted* to get on with the stuff I had to do.

I *wanted* to head home.

I *wanted* all these thoughts out of my head.

It was my red 1991 Honda Nighthawk 750 that had other plans. Seeing her blew my mind. My bike. Mine. Thank you, Uncle Jackson.

I shook my hair back from my face and tucked it behind my ears, chin-length strands slipping loose, as always, before strapping on my helmet. I threw a leg over—careful of the dual pipes even though they were cold—and rocked the bike off its center stand. With that first engine rev, my conscious mind was *gone*. I didn't have to think about anything but the road. Feel anything but the rush. Do anything for anyone.

Not Mom. Not Dad. Not Paul.

It was just me.

In a blink I was on Broadway, on Burnside, on 405 northbound and east on Highway 30 toward St. Helen's. Past the industrial area I let her fly.

I watched the speedometer rise and I could feel it. Acceleration. Vibration. The air buffeting my legs and my hands was my doing, not nature's. Mom would have a fit if she knew.

My mood leveled off. She was good at having fits. Like when Dad's brother gave me the motorcycle for my seventeenth birthday in February. *And* when I wouldn't give her back. So, we made a deal. Mom made rules. I followed them if I wanted to ride her. *My* bike.

One of them involved the speed limit.

I slowed down. She wasn't above using my phone to track me. My heavy sigh filled my helmet with warm air. Shooting across her cell screen wouldn't help me at all.

The buzz in my pocket startled me. Speak of the devil, no doubt. I thought about ignoring my cell. Then again, it probably wasn't the only text. They were hard to feel over the vibration of the bike. I changed lanes and pulled over by an open field, nothing but muck and dead plants as far as I could see and only a wall of forest on the other side of the highway.

I was barely at a standstill when I heard the familiar roar and looked up at six motorcyclists racing toward me on the two-lane highway riding two by two. They each gave me a nod as they reached me. I returned "the motorcycle wave" with a smile, then laughed. Duh, I had my helmet on. I saw the words "Gypsy Jokers" on the back of their leather vests as they drove on toward St. Helens.

Huh.

I'd joined a not-so-secret society when Uncle Jackson passed along his bike. I liked it.

Then another motorcycle went by as I rocked my bike onto the stand. An older couple. Their engine was smooth, no custom exhaust system to amplify the rumble like the other bikers had. The Honda F6C Valkyrie's retro cruiser lines and seafoam green custom coat were cool. The couple looked happy. Carefree. And chatted away on the mics attached to their helmets.

My carefree blipped out of existence after I wrestled my phone out of my pocket and saw two missed calls from Mom. A message from Dad. And texts from both. I leaned my head back and groaned. I just wanted to ride for God's sake.

God's sake. Oh crap. I checked Dad's text first.

Did you forget it was the potluck tonight? We have to leave by six.

Yikes. Then Mom's.

Where are you? You never told us where you were going this afternoon.

I ignored Mom's—not like I was going to tell her where I was earlier this afternoon *or* now—and texted Dad a lie.

I didn't forget.

I checked the time. Calculated how long it would take to get home and grinned. I mean, I had to get there. I wasn't going to leave Paul to face a church potluck without me. It was an invitation to speed if I ever heard one.

CHAPTER TWO

"I know I'm an asshole but I'm trying."

"**Y**ou've got this, Paul."

It was like the tenth time I'd said the words in as many minutes. It's a phrase he accepts. Unlike "I know you can do it" which means instant escalation, or "it's going to be okay" which he finds necessary to refute. Because I am no psychic mind reader prophet who can see the future. So how would I know it's going to be okay?

Fair. And watching every word was worth it. He was worth it.

"You've got this," echoed Mom, her hand hovering over his bony shoulder, dying to touch him, but holding back. Because it won't comfort him. It would distract, disorganize, and dys-regulate him. All the dis-es. And that's the last thing we need on his first day back at Willamette High since September 12th.

If I could bring myself to pray beyond "friends are we, friends we will always be" I'd pray that he'll make it through the rest of senior year without hitting another paraeducator—and getting sent back to the *other* school—because Paul hated himself for hurting Naomi.

Not that it was likely, I reminded myself, watching him take another step toward the doors to the school. It was an anomaly. Hadn't happened in years. Easily a decade. Until September.

"I've got this," he said, his voice flat. He'd finally got it through our heads that we should pay attention to his words, not his tone. They didn't always match our neurotypical expectations. Our bad.

"I know you do, Paul," I said, wishing I was sure we'd make it inside the building.

Massive columns flanked the entryway. The school looked more like a red brick east coast college than urban high school. More 1900 than 2025.

Nothing like the single-story K12 he'd attended the last six months. Three hundred students compared to two thousand, the hallways filled with staff trained to assist students like him. At Willamette just going down the hall was like fighting our way upstream to spawn.

But he was doing it. We were in the building.

"Hey, watch out," I snapped, when a freshman nearly clipped Paul. His classroom was one staircase from the front door. Sixteen steps. I could hear him counting under his breath.

I was sweating like crazy by the time we reached Mr. McElroy's room. He was at the door, his teeth just visible under his gray mustache, so I could see he was smiling. He was a constant for Paul through high school.

If my brother missed him, you'd never know it. Mom was all over the special ed teacher, Paul just walked straight to his old desk and sat down. I'd made sure it was waiting for him, following Mom's directions to smooth his arrival. The students would be mostly familiar. Some new since September, some mostly in mainstream classes. All of them somewhere on the Spectrum.

"I love you, Paul. Have a good day," I tried to put it all into those eight words—warmth and encouragement, acceptance of where he was at and confidence that he could do it.

"See you after school, sweetheart." Mom's voice wavered, doubt creeping in.

"We've got him, Kathleen. It's going to be great having Paul in class again. You've got nothing to worry about. Naomi made him a card and cookies. Enjoy your day, okay?"

He knows Mom worries. How could she not?

The last time she stood there was the day she had to pick him up with two police cars parked outside. Paramedics. A fire engine. She didn't know what she'd be facing when she ran to his classroom. They should have pulled me out of class right away. I should have helped.

But he was all right. No police officers had entered the building.

By the time I got there the shattered safety glass was being swept up. But the wire netting in the window frame on the door was totally caved in. Naomi was being checked out by the school nurse and repeating she was fine. Paul was curled in on himself, rocking so fast the chair scooted over the vinyl floor tiles. Mom, the classroom therapist, the Vice-principal, a security guard, and Rick, the other paraeducator, were crouched by him, talking quietly.

But he was okay. That was what mattered to me.

When Mom looked at Paul from the doorway, I knew she was remembering that day.

I wanted to pull her back to the moment, remind her that he did it; he made it from parking lot to classroom without anyone knocking off his backpack or muttering words like "retard" or "spaz". I was ready to punch someone if it happened this morning.

Jesus, get a grip, Haven.

I'd never punched someone, much less at school. I'd never live it down. Different rules applied to Paul at school. I didn't have an IEP and three neurological diagnoses to protect me. I looked back at him, hoping he couldn't read my mind. Stupid, selfish, lucky asshole that I am. Lucky. If he was lucky like me everything would be different for him.

For me, a little voice in my head dared to say.

Shut it down. Focus. This wasn't about me.

My shoulders slumped when the door closed behind Mr. McElroy. Not Mom. She stood taller and I could practically read her thoughts. Her baby boy will succeed, and I will succeed, and everything is wonderful in the Alexander household. God doesn't give people more than they can handle. Everything happens for a reason. Just do it.

"Go ahead, honey, you don't want to be even later for class," she said, her eyes bright.

Sure. She wanted me off her hands so she could run to yoga or swimming or whatever new thing she was doing to keep herself strong and healthy because, according to his therapist, Paul isn't likely to be launching anytime soon. And her sixtieth birthday is around the corner.

She keeps saying it's her fifty-ninth, or forty-ninth, or that sixty is the new forty. But she lives in fear of the future. Correction, *his* future. Watching her, I just want to hug her. I'm strong enough for both of us.

She knows I'll be there for Paul. We've had the talk. We've put me down as his legal guardian if anything happens to them. Gone over the life insurance so I can take care of him without scraping by on public assistance or having to put him in a group home. If that's what's even needed by then. His future is full of the unknown.

"I love you, Mom."

I went in for a hug. Squeezed her so hard I lifted her off the ground and she gave an "oof" and laughed.

"I love you, too, sweetheart."

Delivery complete.

"Pelvic inflammatory disease and chlamydia can cause sterility in women, and they may never even know they have it before the damage is done."

That got my attention as I walked in late to Health. I knew it was her before I even looked. That voice. The girl from the SlutWalk parade thing on Saturday. Daisy. She *was* in my first period class. I'd never noticed her before. *Or* her friends in the desks behind her.

Way to be oblivious, Haven.

But how did she know so much about sexually transmitted infections anyway? I don't think we read about them in the textbook, and it wasn't like Mr. York had written those two on the whiteboard. He'd maxed out on gonorrhea, syphilis, and herpes.

Yuck.

I squeezed into my desk, looking around because who else was in the class I hadn't noticed *all year*. As far as I could tell they were all the usual suspects. Ben Ashcroft, pretending he was paying attention, Renee and Anna slumped in their seats at the back, legs sprawling into the aisle because they were both over six-foot. Great for the basketball court. Not so great for the stupid desks from the seventies we were stuffed into.

Luce was next to Joey, who was taking notes beside me like their life depended on it. They started coming to our lunch table back in the fall, but we hadn't talked much. How must it feel to be treated like a freak by a lot of the school for being who they are?

I didn't get non-binary. Was it like being both genders or neither? Not that I get girls *or* boys half the time. Could I get a pass for not getting any of the above?

Daisy wouldn't give me a pass. I knew that. By the window, she sat perched upright, all tight jeans and fuzzy pink sweater showing skin at her waist, her dark ponytail high. I didn't get the point of dressing like that, other than the ponytail. That part made sense. But what she'd said at the SlutWalk shook me. My shorts and T-shirt won't protect me. Why would anyone harass me?

Wait. Mr. York was giving her a thumbs up. Did I miss something?

"That's excellent, Daisy. How do you know so much about those diseases?"

Two seconds of silence. And then Mr. York turned red. Snickers rained through the classroom. And words.

"How do you think, man?"

"Her last gyno checkup?"

"Slut."

WTF?

"Hey," I started, not sure who to ream first. I looked around, memorizing assholes.

The laughs and jeers got louder and more disgusting before Mr. York got control of the class by smacking his palm on the desk of the worst offender. The cracking sound echoed in the room. He narrowed his eyes at some of the jerks, smiting them with a look. When he went back to the front of the room and cleared his throat to resume the lesson, Daisy jumped in first.

"My mom is a nurse midwife. She sees *everything*." Daisy settled back at her desk, manspreading like she was daring someone to make another comment.

The girl had guts.

I was *starving* by third period. I thought about trying to wolf down a granola bar without alerting Henderson, but before I could dig in my backpack, I heard Knox whisper my name. I ignored him, keeping my eyes on the board. Then the idiot grabbed my toes. My *naked* toes. I whipped my feet out from below his desk, where I usually rested them. Wearing flip flops is not an invitation to touch. Boundaries dude.

I guess I had to spell it out.

A yellow paper landed on my notebook. From Knox. I smothered a groan. Another flyer for Knox's Ska band. I was running out of excuses. I just didn't want him to think I changed my mind about him. The dating thing. Not that he could have been that interested anyway, right? It was just our moms throwing us together. Whatever Alice said in the fall, her "You're kind of a babe" was ridiculous. She didn't mean anything by it.

Not even Knox could think I was a babe. I was all no makeup, blunt blonde bob, five foot ten and built like an athlete, not a babe.

I studied him in my peripheral vision. Should I stay or should I go?

Shit. Now *I* am quoting *The Clash*. Right era anyway. Or so Knox told me. And told me. And told me... He peeked over at me and mouthed "Come on." Like *that* was going to change my mind.

Laurie leaned forward over her notebook, looking over her shoulder at Knox. She was *definitely* a babe: red hair, big boobs, tiny waist, short. And she could run like the wind. She was probably killing it at Track.

'Probably' because I haven't even used the running track after school since March, much less asked how it was going or stopped by practice. I didn't want to explain why I wasn't competing this year. It was no one's business but mine.

I looked back at Laurie, watching Knox. Even I could tell she was into him.

Look at Laurie, look at Laurie.

I was resorting to telepathy.

When the bell rang, I let everyone else cram through the door first. Not that my brilliant plan worked. Knox was still standing at his desk like fourth period wasn't a priority and Laurie lingered, too, putting stuff on her mouth. The fake strawberry smell was gross.

Knox wasn't going to let it go.

"What do you think? No practice for Track," he said.

And I could feel his hurt about *that*. We'd been burning up the track together since we were toddlers. Every competition, we were there. He did not understand why I wasn't doing track this year, and I wasn't about to tell him.

"Nothing to train for, no reason not to go, right?" He bounced his eyebrows up and down. Trying to be charming? He wasn't nailing it. But he was trying.

"Uh..." I floundered—what should I say—and practically dove at Daisy as she crossed the room in front of us. I hadn't realized she'd lingered, too. "Hey! You *are* in my classes."

Brilliant, Haven. Way to state the obvious. She responded with a smirk I totally deserved and a salute on her way out, the buttons on her sweater throwing fractured light on the dirty beige walls. I was an idiot. I pushed the rest of my stuff into my backpack, unable to make up my mind about Knox's show.

I *should* go. That's what friends do, right? They support each other. Even if they HATE Ska music and think their friend looks like a fool dancing on stage. If I had an event, he'd go for me.

When I turned, finally ready to say yes, Knox wasn't even looking at me anymore. He was frowning at the classroom doorway.

"You know *her*?" he said.

Huh. "What do you mean by 'her'?"

He looked, I don't know, guilty maybe?

"She's... she's..." Knox speechless? That was a new one.

"A slut," Laurie said, like it was an irrefutable fact. Period.

Her squeaky voice struck me wrong. I used to kind of like it. It was like a cartoon character voice, and she could be hilarious on the bus after Cross Country meets. It wasn't so funny now.

She called Daisy a slut.

I looked at their expressions. So serious. Zero sense of humor.

My backpack hit the floor as I burst out laughing so hard, I doubled over. I imagined Daisy with "derby slut" written on her body. She'd laugh, too. She could take it like a boss.

But my laughter slowed as they stared at me. And it sunk in that they were honestly dissing on Daisy. And not so happy with me.

"What's so funny, Haven?" Irritation radiated off Laurie.

I *did* laugh at her; fair to be irritated, I guess.

"She. Saluted. You," she went on. "How do you know her?"

"You mean besides being in classes with her for three years?" Same as them. "But back up, let me make sure I got this right: were you seriously calling Daisy a slut? Like, in a bad way?"

Laurie opened her mouth, but Knox got there first.

"I didn't call her that." He looked worried. "It's just, she's not like us."

He should be worried.

"Like. Us. What does that even mean?" I asked, but I had an idea where he was going with it.

It's what Mom said. That some people are 'nice' but they're 'not like us'.

"What are we like, Knox?" I really wanted to know.

In the second before he spoke, my brain echoed his "not like us". Is that how he'd feel about me if he knew I might be different? I wouldn't be *like him,* because I didn't *like* him?

And Daisy was no slut, no matter what she'd written on her body. And even if she was what some might call a slut, it didn't matter. The point was the derision in their voices.

I decided I didn't want to hear his answer after all.

"I'll see you guys later," I snapped, shoving my desk aside on my way out the door. I didn't want to talk to them, or anyone.

Except for Paul at lunch after Calculus. I popped into his classroom where he had lunch to check on him. He gave me about one second of his attention before he was back to showing Luce his latest drawing.

Considering Paul's drawings are like Death Metal CD covers or dark fantasy illustration or anatomical drawings, crossed with that Giger artist guy he's obsessed with, Luce was doing a good job smiling and nodding. She didn't even look over at me when I came in. She was paying absolute attention to him. I only knew it was her because of her crazy, curly brown hair. You couldn't miss it.

I wondered if she knew he always starts in the top left corner and continues without a disconnected line all the way to the bottom right. In ink. Like he sees the whole thing in his head and records it. He's amazing. I gave Luce my biggest smile, even though she didn't see it, hoping she could somehow feel my unspoken "thank you."

My mood crashed again in Ecology, after lunch. Maybe a food coma, I told myself, slumping in my seat—at least there was enough room for my legs with a table instead of those stupid desks—but it was also the schedule. Seven periods in one day?

It's exhausting turning on a dime again and again, even if I should be used to it by now.

Alice scooted closer next to me, her braid swinging as she moved. Her pale skin and the light blonde hairs on her neck caught the light from the window making them gold.

Eyes back to Ms. Allen, perv', I told myself.

Okay, I had to admit it, I still kind of *liked* her liked her.

Which was totally weird because she's all homeschooled, backstage, band T-shirts, red lipstick, and boyfriends. And drawing on her skin all. The. Time. But she's stronger than I am. She wears her emotions on her skin—literally. Mostly happy ones. But in the fall, she was closed off, tortured by the "spark"—as she called it—barely conceived and then lost.

She was vulnerable and I was a judgmental jerk, all up in her business, thinking I knew what was good for her when I had no freaking idea what she was going through.

Alice turned to smile at me, her cloud gray eyes dancing with an affection I don't deserve.

Re-focus Haven, get with it. Ms. Allen was talking about fungi. Edible fungi. On cue our Ecology group partner, Aaron, rolled his hackey-sack ball across the table and it fell into my hands. He reached for it, eyes bloodshot. High as always. I wasn't so cool with it before winter break. Nope. Everything had to be perfect.

Especially me.

Aaron sat up when the word psilocybin was written on the whiteboard. But I couldn't focus, even when Ms. Allen was going on about medicinal use, and legal status, and successful use with traumatized veterans. I was suddenly lost again in Knox's "not like us".

Alice was probably "not like us" by his definition. Girls who drew on themselves all the time were different and that couldn't be a good thing, right? Aaron was *definitely* in that category. Getting baked was for losers to Knox. And Daisy, she was relegated to "not like us" by him and Laurie why? How she dressed? Because she might have different ideas around dating and stuff?

If I started being different about dating and stuff, which I'd totally avoided all these years, was it my turn to be "not like us"?

I wasn't sure I wanted to find out.

No, I was pretty sure I didn't.

CHAPTER THREE

"Would you stop saying that already?"

The industrial clock ticked, ticked, ticked away the seconds, the ka-chunk of the minute hand happening *way* too slowly. I could catch it even over the cacophony of voices, the clink of coffee cups, and the scuffing and squeal of tennis shoes on the linoleum as young kids did one-eighties, slipping through the after-church throng at high speed. Now *that* was fun. Tag among the grownups. Why couldn't I be doing *that*? A groan of envy ripped out of me.

Uh oh.

Mom didn't even stop talking as she gave me the stink eye. Not that it looked like the stink eye to anyone else. Only I knew she was sending me a message with that swift smile. The message was: behave yourself, we're at church, you know better. Her voice didn't slow for a microsecond. She was on a roll.

Mom and Dad sometimes get it that when eyes glaze over, they should stop talking, Dad more than Mom. They knew, intellectually, that there was no need to volunteer every detail of their lives, meaning Paul's life, or snap their fingers for me to perform on command like a show pony. But if someone asked them? It was game on.

Not that Mrs. Perry didn't know what she was signing up for. She wanted to know about our family's latest news after missing church for two weeks, out with Covid-19. The corners of her blue eyes crinkled as she smiled, the right one dulled by a cataract. At least Mom remembered to ask about her upcoming eye surgery before summarizing the Alexander household's activities with abandon.

"I'm looking into the latest research on CBD and autism. I haven't wanted to try that considering Paul's epilepsy, but there have been even more studies recently that suggest success with social interaction and sleep."

Because yeah, Paul doesn't sleep much. He paces. And grunts. It's the lullaby of my life.

Mom laughed. "And you can buy it just about anywhere these days."

Mrs. Perry nodded, still smiling. She doesn't have a problem with hemp products. Pretty much everyone knows she grows weed for her arthritis.

I blanked out on the conversation, my mind wandering, watching the faces around us. Faces I've known ever since I can remember. But I'd prefer to park my ass next to Paul in the stairwell, hidden by the half-wall. I envied him Sundays during Coffee Hour. He got to hide out. I got to stand there like a trophy with my parents' name on it.

"Kathleen, I'm so happy to hear that Paul's back at Willamette and that it went well at the other school. I don't recall the name."

Lewis & Clark was the school. "Went well" was only semi-accurate. Staying there for five more months than the minimum eight weeks required for a behavioral reassignment—because Paul wasn't sure he could regulate himself in the environment at Willamette—was not part of the original plan. But I wasn't going to point that out.

"And that he'll be able to finish at a mainstream high school..."

Mom clams up, not elaborating on how non-mainstream his high school experience is. Every year he's tried some mainstream classes, and every year he needs to go back to the ASD classroom all day. He can handle the curriculum just fine. It's the randomness of neurotypical students that's the problem.

I can relate. People are hard.

"But tell me about Haven," Mrs. Petty went on.

'Hello? I'm right here!' I thought, only just managing to keep the words to myself. Go me.

Mom didn't miss a beat. Blah, blah, blah, Constitution Team Nationals in two weeks. Blah, blah, blah, spring Track going well... I'd let that lie pass. She and Dad somehow thought I'd leap back in and run relays at any moment—and that the coach would let me—so this was only an exaggeration as far as Mom was concerned. Blah, blah, blah, dating her co-captain.

Whoa now!

I think I said it out loud.

"I'm not dating Knox. Just stop already." I looked around frantically—Knox's family is here. He's here. Way to complicate my life, Mom.

"And I'm not captain of girls' Track either," I added in a quiet voice that not even my parents could make out. I didn't like being part of a lie.

Then Mom does that thing. That thing parents do when they argue whatever you say without saying a word? I wanted to scream. And then Dad chuckled. No doubt about the Knox thing.

"We. Are. Friends. Period."

There was no reason for Mom to do this crap. Mrs. Perry doesn't care if I *ever* date. No one here cares if I ever date, or wear pajamas twenty-four seven, or furry ears and a tail. They don't need to believe I'm dating Knox. Her Methodist roots were showing again. That's how Dad describes her traditional streak. She didn't grow up as a Unitarian Universalist like he did.

Mom just shakes her head and slings an arm around my waist, looking up at me like I'm this consternating child but she loves me anyway. I want to cram the truth down her throat but screw it. She's created this story about her athletic, high-achieving daughter with the perfect life. She *needs* me to be successful.

It's stupid. It's not like it's abnormal to have teenagers at their age. Half the Youth Group has parents in their upper fifties or sixties. It's no big whoop.

But then another study gets published, and Mom spends the day in her room crying, and I have to be living proof that aging eggs do not necessarily cause autism and epilepsy and Tourette's Syndrome. That she and Dad were not outrageously selfish by having us in their forties. Like *a lot* of their friends did.

Mom looks at their kids and sees shiny. Social. Perfect.

I could point out a few exceptions in Youth Group.

Like Elizabeth, who's had a substance addiction since freshman year and never met a medicine cabinet she didn't rifle. And Dylan, basically born on the same day as me, has a toddler he gets to see on alternate weekends, because his ex-girlfriend decided he, and his parents, aren't good enough to share custody. Kevin went and joined ROTC at his private school even though his parents are pacifists.

And then there's Rebecca. I saw her across the room, holding a bouquet of flowers someone must have given her after her choir solo. Now *she* was perfect.

Mom pulled her arm away and I noticed Dad was flagging.

Even though he's the one brought up Unitarian, he only comes because Mom needs this. The social circle. The service. Choir. Most of all a community who accepts and embraces Paul. But Dad's wrecked by Sunday. Running for a living as brand ambassador for one of the biggest athletic shoe companies in the world is hard, even if most of his duties are at a desk organizing events. His eyes dart around the room, looking for an escape. I know how he feels.

"Don't you ever get tired, Haven? Your schedule has always been so full. Since you were a toddler."

She's so sweet. Yes, Mrs. Perry, I do, I want to answer. But I don't say it. I leaned in to hug her gently, avoiding the question. "I'm gonna go check in with Paul, okay?"

They look at me like I'm this saint because I want to hang out with my brother. It's stupid.

As I expected, Paul is just fine.

It's weird to me that some people find him uncomfortable to be around. I mean, he's blunt and honest and does startlingly dark art, but he's a cool dude. He peeked at me from under his wild, black bangs as I walked up, his pen never leaving the paper, though his shoulders jerked as I sat next to him. His tics kicking in.

"Hey big brother," I said, wanting to put my arms around him but respecting his space. Space is good. It's nice on the steps. The noise is dimmed by the half-wall, the lighting less intense. If only I could get Paul to lie and say he needs me by his side every coffee hour I wouldn't have to stand next to Mom and Dad and watch them lie. But *he* doesn't lie.

Dad had barely pulled the parking brake before I bailed. I needed pants, shoes, and my helmet NOW. The car drive home had been another push for me to beg, borrow, or steal my way back onto the track team. A nightmare. I rushed past my parents so I couldn't see their disappointment when I told them I was going on a ride. To them it was like I was playing football with

multiple concussions. Like I didn't appreciate being neurotypical.

I did. I so did.

But it's not like no one gets injured leaping hurdles, I
thought, lacing up my shoes, and they wanted me to do *that*.

I got out of the house without another word from Mom and
Dad and jetted out on 84 Eastbound and took the Wood Village
exit to Mount Hood. I passed the Dairy Queen in Rhodo-
dendron and went the extra few miles to Road Thirty-five and
waited for a break in oncoming traffic from the mountain, cars
whizzing by me on the right.

Totally breaking the law.

When I finally turned, the dirt and broken asphalt road was
in bad shape. Worse than December. Though I was in an SUV
then, not my bike. There were times we couldn't get there, the
snow was so high, and we had to go back home.

That was such a bummer.

Now our cabin sat empty at the end of a short driveway surrounded by native plants, almost blocking the view of the front
porch. It was green and newly painted, a project last summer
that kept us from getting bored when Dad had to go back to
work during the week. Not that we got bored that often.

I turned off my bike before the drive, not even past the property line. I couldn't go closer. It would be too hard to leave but
too vacant to stay. It was comics and cookies and fires in the
fireplace, wading in the creek and trekking in the snow. Or mud
or dried grass—according to the season—usually with Mom.

Time we would talk uninterrupted and alone. Time Dad would spend one on one with Paul.

Good times.

The cabin had been dark since December. There was too much going on and the expectation I would be doing Track as usual kept us home in spring. Our plans hadn't changed, even though I told them I wouldn't be continuing Track before spring break. I wasn't going to be Coach Morgan's one-trick pony. Not when it was going to impact the rest of the team's chance to compete.

Mom and Dad didn't have to know about that. They wouldn't get it.

I sighed. There was a lot of denial going on at my house lately.

Denial about Track.

Denial about Paul graduating and what was next for him.

Denial that I was rocking the boat and saying no to Mom's fantasy version of me.

Sometimes.

What would happen if I really rocked the boat? Would we pretend it wasn't so?

I was afraid of the answer, so I turned the key and enjoyed the feel of the bike coming to life, and turned my bike at the next wide corner, heading back to the highway.

I stopped for lunch at DQ, then continued west on 26, hopped onto 84W in Gresham and onto Marine Drive, barely any stop signs in my way. Flying felt so free. The rush lasted only until I reached the Columbia. The light bouncing off the water was blinding, the glare interrupted by old trailers with taped up windows and burned-out cars cramming the side of the road. And lots and lots of tents.

Every time I was on this road, I felt gutted and guilty. Making care packages and box lunches for unhoused people during church services was only a Band-aid. A tiny one.

I wasn't ready to go home anymore. I needed something good in my brain.

Comikaze Coffee's windows were covered in Marvel and DC and posters for local events. Paul loved it there; the comics side partially blocked from the café part, making it quieter, more secluded.

I backed into a spot out front and unhooked my helmet. I checked for helmet hair in the plate glass automatically. Yup, still straight as a stick. Not like Alice cares how I look.

Yeah.

The bells on the door were stupid loud. Nero was behind the coffee counter, partially blocked by the long line of customers. He had a loyal following. Alice told me he decorated coffee foam with skulls. If I had the Volvo I'd get Paul his usual double-shot, extra hot mocha. He gagged at the smell of cheap coffee at church as much as I did.

I saw the second Alice noticed my helmet before she booked it to the glass front door to get a better look.

"That is one fucking gorgeous motorcycle, Haven. I can't get over how you lucked out like that. And that you ride it! Haven Alexander, rebel."

Oh yeah. That's me.

"Do you want a ride sometime? I have another helmet."

Alice bounced on her toes. It couldn't be easy in combat boots. Combat boots... Maybe those would be better for riding than hiking boots. Though I thought the sight of steel-toed motorcycle boots in the entry would give Mom a heart attack.

"And Dad can't say a word since he had a motorcycle for years," she said.

No, I thought, he can't say a word because he *abandoned you* for over two years when your mom died. He doesn't get that privilege. Just saying.

But I wasn't going to say that aloud.

This time.

"Did you ever follow the rules anyway?" I asked, because yeah, that wasn't her prior M.O.

She laughed, showing the narrow gap between her front teeth. Just another way her parents failed her. No braces. No school for years. No supervision while they were doing their thing onstage. They bought her a nose piercing for her thirteenth birthday, for God's sake. What kind of parents do that?

Alice looked anywhere but at me. "You've got a point there. I'm a sucker for danger."

"Not anymore," I reminded her. It took a few seconds for her to meet my eyes.

"Hey, I made it over ninety days without leaping into very bad things."

I had a hard time seeing the humorous side of walking into an ice storm tripping balls and that whole mess with Rowan. I shouldn't have said anything to remind her. I went for distraction.

"Did you know that there's this sign that motorcycle riders give each other? It's like I'm part of some brotherhood..."

"Brotherhood?" Alice raised her pierced eyebrow.

Yeah, not getting into the politics of gender and sisterhood is powerful. I barreled on.

"It's all bikers, except maybe those idiots on crotch rockets who weave in and out of traffic giving motorcyclists a bad name. The other day I got the sign from this old couple on an a-ma-zing Honda Valkyrie. And from these six guys on Harley's. I couldn't make out the words on their vests except 'Gypsy Jokers'."

Alice's mouth dropped open. "Holy shit! As they passed? You waved at Gypsy Jokers? Where were you?"

"Well, yeah. It was only polite. I was pulled off to the side of Highway 30 to answer texts."

"Anyone around you?" she demanded.

"No." I shrugged. "What's the big deal, Alice?"

"Are you insane, Haven?! You pulled off to the side of a two-lane highway, alone, with Gypsy Jokers riding by, and you waved to them?" She leaned over, hands on her knees, her hair swinging as she shook her head. It fell around her face when she stood up. Her very red face. "Do you know much about motorcycle clubs?"

"No…" I started.

"Like there are legal ones and illegal ones?"

"I guess…"

"And that the Gypsy Jokers are second only to the Hell's Angels for criminal activity and violence? They headquarter in Portland with Washington and Oregon as their territory because the Angels have California. I'm talking human trafficking, drugs, murder for hire, rape, kidnapping."

What?

"How do you know all this?"

She looked at her boots. "Well, even bikers like music and they sometimes come in the clubs Dad plays at. He hears stuff."

"Your deadbeat dad is an expert on motorcycle gangs?"

"Hey!"

And now she was mad. I wasn't winning points with anyone today.

"He's not a deadbeat. He always paid for child support. I just didn't know it. And don't say motorcycle gang. It's MC for motorcycle club. You know, just in case any Gypsy Jokers decide to chat you up ON THE SIDE OF A LONELY ROAD."

Yup, still mad.

"I didn't know." I held up my hands. Like, back off hands. Which was stupid, because what was little Alice Carroll going to do to me? Kick me in the shins? Though maybe, now that I was thinking about it, her boots would hurt.

"You do now," she grumbled.

Change of subject time.

"I better get home. Before Mom gets worried. Or pissed. I kind of drove to Mount Hood and back without saying how long I'd be gone." Mom would be looking at the clock constantly.

"It *is* a sweet ride," I heard her say, as the door closed behind me.

CHAPTER FOUR

"Touch my brother and I'll kill you."

Oh my God. Why did he decide to become Mr. Social today, without anyone giving me a heads-up? And who let him come here alone? I was going to kill them. And the bitch getting in his face.

Please don't let her touch him.

This could go bad.

So bad.

Anything could happen in the seconds it would take for me to cross the lunchroom to the food line. I broke into a run. Screw dignity. How much trouble would I be in if I took out Kerry-with-a-K Miller?

It all went down so fast. Paul was trying to draw and hold a cafeteria tray at the same time, the yellow plastic rectangle swinging in wide arcs as his pen moved on the sketchbook in front of his face. People ahead of him dodged it, giving him dirty looks. Behind him, Kerry pointed at his drawing, laughing. I heard her "gross" from twelve feet away. His shoulder spasmed repeatedly. I saw frustration flood him as he tried to follow the rules and stay in line.

Behind Kerry, her BFF Tina muttered "retard" loud enough for the entire lunchroom to hear her and swung her hand up toward Paul. She was reaching over his shoulder, almost touching his headphones. She was going to shove his drawing pad. Maybe him. I wouldn't get there in time.

And then Tina wasn't standing there anymore. She flew backward like she'd been yanked by her hair and Kerry-with-a-K whirled around, leaving Paul's space.

Paul's body was roiling with tics and stims as he looked at the ceiling.

Where was the paraeducator who should have been with him?

I shielded him with my body as much as I could, not easy when he had three inches on me, and held out my arms in case anyone else was dumb enough to get involved.

"Hey bro, want to get a table with me? Is there something you'd like to eat here? I'm proud of you for doing something new." I was talking too much, the adrenaline still shooting through me. If she'd shoved, he might have shoved back in defense or recoiled, slamming into the person in front of him. It was so close.

He processed my words slowly, his tics easing, but still looked up at the quiet place over his head. Ceilings were a safe space, he told me once, the "empty, upside-down room" where he could go when things overwhelmed him. I kept my focus on him but caught the sound of voices raised behind me.

"What the hell?" Kerry or Tina, it was hard to tell when they were both shrieking like a banshee.

"It was an accident." A lower voice. Totally calm.

"You grabbed me!" Yeah, that was Tina.

"I slipped. I just reached out for the nearest thing to hold on to. My bad."

Wait, Daisy?

"I saw the whole thing, that's what happened." I knew that voice, too. Sophie.

"Whore." Kerry.

"Bitch." Tina.

"Dyke." Kerry.

Then silence. The whole room went quiet as the Vice-principal strolled in.

And *that* was when Paul finally spoke.

His "Corn. I want corn," was heard round the room.

"We can get some when the line is shorter. Let's find a table." I led him to the far side of the cafeteria, glaring at the two freshmen at the least occupied table until they relocated. I made sure to position us with our backs to the wall. Not like I was going to take him to my usual table. I could see Tina and Kerry-with-a-K heading that way, then wedging in between two of the baseball players, Trent and somebody I didn't know.

Good thing the lunchroom was noisy again, I thought, I didn't want to hear what those two had to say. Kerry used to be okay, but since she became friends with Tina, she was a pain. Whatever it was they were yapping about, the guys next to them were antsy. After about half a minute, Trent and his teammate looked at each other, then my way, and jetted.

Leaving Kerry and Tina madder than ever.

I refocused on Paul, making sure he knew we were safe, he had his sketchbook, and everything was good. *If* I could use my phone I could get hold of someone in Paul's classroom to come be with him and I'd happily get him some corn, but no.

The stupid cell phone policy we'd had since January complicated a lot of things, though I didn't miss the rounds of rude videos people watched between classes, and I wasn't used to not being able to reach Paul or Mom when I needed to until after school.

Mom was going to freak when she heard about this.

And then I saw the five girls making a beeline for us.

One I was going to kill.

Maim.

Ream.

I took a breath.

Yell at with my eyes.

And following Luce, were the derby girls. With lunch trays. One of them with just a bowl of corn and a bottle of water.

Huh.

Luce got to us first, her whole body practically pleading for mercy, so I knew she *was* the person who abandoned Paul in the lunch line. She didn't usually volunteer until seventh period.

"I'm sorry," Luce started, "so sorry, I got caught up back there with Mary..."

Mary was a student in Paul's class. She was way more social than he was. And very impulsive. I was beginning to get the picture. Still.

Paul looked up at her. "You left me."

I took another deep breath. "So, whose idea was it to come to the cafeteria? Paul's? Mary's? Or yours?" I had to get that straight *before* I boiled over. I needed to *not* boil over because *theoretically* coming to the lunchroom was a good thing for Paul. I didn't want him to think he'd done something wrong by trying something new.

Luce looked from me to Paul. "He was hungry, they were both hungry, and we were having such a good time at the end of fourth period—we had a sub in Spanish and he let me go to Mr. McElroy's classroom instead of just sitting there for forty minutes—so I thought Paul could go with Mary and I when we got lunch and..."

"Where did you go?" Paul spoke over Luce. Something he rarely did. Now.

"Mary had to go to the bathroom," she told him, "And she didn't want to go alone because someone was mean to her the last time she went in there by herself. Was everything all right? You didn't get any lunch."

She had no idea what almost went down.

I couldn't get into it in front of him. That Paul in a church basement full of people he'd known his entire life was one thing. And Paul threatened in a huge room echoing with loud teenagers was another. Luce had no idea of the consequences if he put his hands on someone. Paul already hated himself for hurting Naomi, and if that person's parents decided to call the cops... Jesus.

I had to get it together.

"I didn't know where you were," Paul said. His shoulders started to tic again, his body rocking as he re-lived those moments in line. His vivid imagination had a downside. Memories stuck. Talking about this wasn't helping.

"Are you guys hungry? I can't possibly eat all this." Sophie pushed past Luce and slid onto the bench opposite me.

"Me, either," Birgit said, sitting next to her, kicking me by accident on the way, and pushed her overloaded tray to the center of the table.

Ellie squeezed in next to her. "Not, me. I'm fucking..." She looked over at Paul. "Oh, sorry. Extremely," she stretched out the word, "starving."

Not like he hadn't heard the word before. He was *eighteen* not eight.

And then Daisy sat on the other side of Paul. Right. Next. To. Him. And he didn't flinch. She was careful not to make contact, but still. Wow.

"We've got it, Luce," Daisy said, looking directly at her, "Run on back and let his teacher know we'll walk with him to his classroom when he's done."

I watched the silent exchange between them. Daisy wore a sweet dangerous smile and Luce blinked before telling Paul she'd see him in seventh period. She was out of there in a heart-beat.

Daisy looked at Paul's drawing pad, open on the table.

"Is this the one you were working on?"

His face almost lit up. "Yes."

"You're a fabulous artist," Daisy said, her voice calm and kind. Somehow, she knew what to do. With Paul. She was never like that with me. She was all "babe" this, "babe" that, all atti-tude.

His "thank you" to Daisy let me breathe easier.

I slumped in my seat. Crisis averted. I reached for a French fry from Birgit's tray. Then another. She pushed a full serving closer to Paul. Daisy added the bowl of corn and bottle of water and a spoon. He started eating unconsciously. He was eating in a crowded space with people he didn't know. Damn.

He stayed in the lunchroom for twenty whole minutes.

On the way back to his classroom it was like Paul and I had bodyguards. We were flanked on all sides. Was this a derby thing? I watched how some people swerved out of the way, and some shouldered right into them. Guys mostly. Were they a threat to their masculinity or something? Assholes.

They waited until Mr. McElroy opened the door.

"See you tomorrow, Paul," said Birgit.

"If you ever need *anything* just let us know." Sophie winked at him!

They scattered before I could even thank them. All except Daisy, who leaned against the wall beside the closed door of

Paul's classroom, her feet crossed at the ankle. Like she had all the time in the world and not ten minutes to get to class. I got caught up in the Rose City Rollers logo on her black T-shirt, and the undeniable fact that her tight jeans contained muscle as well as... other stuff that showed when you wore tight jeans.

And she looked like she could kick my ass, even if I was about four inches taller.

"You know, you could do me a favor," she said, widening her brown eyes, if possible, a little more.

So, this is what it was all about. A favor. I crossed my arms. "What do you want?"

"Wait, before you get all pissed," she pushed away from the wall, "That's not why we hung out with your brother. I'm just asking, okay?"

I took a step back. "I'm not pissed."

She hooked her thumbs in her belt loops and studied me as she rocked forward on her shoes. Stupid little girl shoes with thick soles and a strap across the top. She shrugged and curved her lips up at the corners.

"I was hoping you could drive me to practice today. I've gotta stay late, and the other girls will be gone, so..."

"Why do you have to stay late?" I asked.

"Not that it's any of your business but I have detention, okay?"

Huh?

"For what?"

Daisy raised her eyebrows. They disappeared under her straight brown bangs. "There *might* have been an incident in the lunchroom earlier." She looked at her chunky, silver watch, "Like twenty-three minutes ago."

"You got a detention?" What? "For coming over to our table?"

"No," she drew out the word. "There was a misunderstanding in the lunch line, and I might have grabbed Tina's sweatshirt and pulled her. To the ground. By accident. But hey, Vice-Principals don't always notice the narrow line between accidental and on purpose." And those big eyes turned hard. "Or when a bully has it coming."

"You saved Paul on purpose? I thought..." And then I remembered hearing Daisy when I got to Paul.

"That no one else noticed Kerry was being rude, and Tina was pushing it too far? And that you were running all out through the cafeteria? Kind of a sign that something needed to be done right away. I'm not stupid."

"Yes. Yes, I'll give you a ride to practice. Anytime."

She wiggled like a puppy. "Excellent. Meet me at the library at four."

"Meet me in the library at four."

It kept coming back to me in the weight room after school. During squats. And lat pulls. And chest presses.

I didn't even know this girl.

But she'd helped Paul in a big way.

That was a bold ask.

But would I turn down anyone who asked for help?

Probably not.

Then I thought about it more. Yes, I would. Assholes. Bullies. People I was afraid of.

And yet.

I was kind of afraid of Daisy. She was so out there. And didn't seem to care what anyone thought. And those crazy outfits she wore. What was up with that anyway?

I suddenly noticed that the weight room had filled up. Mostly basketball players. The girls' team. The softball team. It was just second nature not to look at the other athletes while they were working out. So why did I start noticing them now? I headed back into the locker room, ignoring the girls stripping and changing around me, more self-conscious than usual.

Dressing after working out was usually whatever, and *now* I was shy about my body? And theirs? Was that going to be weird if I ever decided to, like, *like* girls and have anybody know about it? Would everybody be all "don't look at me"?

Not like I'd be the only one, by a longshot, but it would be *me* and that was different.

Nope. Not going to happen.

Renee and Anna were just coming into the weightroom on my way out. We gave each other the standard jock greeting, ending in the shoulder hug thing. Renee had grown again, she was almost six feet-three I thought, her beaded braids brushed my shoulder.

Anna didn't even bother making eye contact with me. She scoped out the room, her dark blonde ponytail swishing side to side, totally not shy about checking out the guys while they worked out.

All I saw were sweaty pits and stink machines and why were guys allowed to take off their shirts at school anyway? I watched Trent for half a second. He wasn't stripping to the waist. He was scowling on the treadmill, and I wondered if it was because of Tina at lunch or maybe about being dumped by Maddy last fall. He scowled a lot.

"Where's your mind at, H?" Renee asked.

Not like I was going to tell her I was speculating about Trent, because she'd be bringing it up for the rest of the year. And the truth was my mind was all over the place. So, I shrugged.

"I don't know."

Anna finally focused on me; one arm curled around the basketball on her hip. "You need to let loose, girl. Come out with us Saturday. There's a party at Carter's."

"There's always a party at Carter's," Renee said, reaching up to touch the ceiling with her fingertips. I wondered again why she bothered with long nails when she was handling a basketball all the time. It didn't make sense. Now that I thought about it, a lot of the b-ball players wore makeup and jewelry.

Not so much the Cross-Country team. We were nerds that liked to run. Track was another story...

I snapped back to attention. Carter's. Knox's band. Crap. "I don't know," I started.

"You're going," Anna said, shooting her ball at my chest. I barely caught it, the force knocking me backward. No wonder she was already getting scholarship offers Junior year. "Not letting you get out of it."

"You never go out with us. You're going," Renee said. She smiled, all teeth and crinkly eyes and she might even have snorted. "You are definitely going with us." She reached out as if to poke me with a long fingernail, but I dodged.

"Okay, okay," I said, holding up my hands, "But Knox's band is playing. Just sayin'."

They both winced. But nodded. "It'll be worth it," Anna said, "You'll see."

I guess I would. One way or another.

CHAPTER FIVE

"I Just Don't Get It."

"Why are you hanging around?" he said.

I jumped. Knox was *right there*, partially blocked by my open locker. "Jesus. I didn't see you come up. I might have pissed my pants."

"Nice visual, Haven," he rolled his eyes, "Why are you here? Don't you usually book it? You're never here after school since spring break."

Yes, it was an accusation.

"I've got stuff," I lied.

He sighed, leaning against the locker. "Even if you're not going to do track for some reason you won't even tell me…" He leaned in, and I didn't. Move. A. Hair. So, he backed off. "You used to go running with me."

And he wasn't wrong. I did. I ran with him when we didn't have practice or meets. In the fall. And then it got awkward. He made it awkward. Not like I was going to bring *that* up. I scrambled for an excuse.

"It's raining." It was the first thing that came to me but why? It's not like rain would keep me from running. I was a Portlander.

"Good," he snapped.

What the...

"What do you mean by that?" I slammed my locker.

"Because I know your mom won't let you ride that dumb bike when it's raining. I can't believe they let you have it. They practically bubble wrap you and now you own a deathtrap."

Bubble wrap? What did that mean?

"What do you care? You don't have to ride it," I shot back at him.

He pushed away from the locker and paced back and forth across the hall, then stopped right in front of me. "Are you stupid, Haven? I can't..."

"Shut up," I shouted.

"What, I'm not allowed to have an opinion now? Just because you shot me down in December doesn't mean I don't still care about you."

"You don't call people you care about stupid." I clenched my teeth so hard the words could barely squeeze out.

"You do when they're being stupid!" Knox returned my glare. "You've changed. A motorcycle? You? And at lunch today you sat with those roller derby girls. What, are you just dumping your friends now?"

"No!"

"Just don't dump me along with everyone else. Again."

I groaned. "Oh, come on, Knox, I'm not dumping you." Why was I even bothering to reassure him when he was being such a jerk?

"Prove it. Right now." He snapped his fingers. "Let's go for a run. Prove to me that asking you out didn't ruin everything."

"Come on, it didn't ruin everything. We've known each other forever and that was just one day, no big deal."

His strangled cry was freaky. And then the asshat banged his head into a locker. Like a wimp. I knew how to judge a head bang. Paul could put a dent in a metal locker no problem when he was eight.

And then Knox was in my face again. What the hell? I took one step back. Not cool.

"It was not 'no big deal' for me, Haven. You can be so clueless. What did I need to do, send you flowers? You'd have tossed them. Carried your books? Yeah, right. I had to tell you to your face that I liked you when everyone in the whole school knew it except you." He took a step closer. "But the thing is, you did know. And you never even gave me a chance."

He was kind of right. I knew he *thought* he liked me. Telling him I wasn't into him seemed like the right thing to do since he asked me out. At the track. At lunch. And then he took off running. What was I supposed to do? Leave him hanging?

"Knox, you know I'm never going to go out with you, right?" was what I said when I caught up with him that day.

I thought he'd be like "okay" and that would be the end of it. I didn't think he'd stumble and go down, leaving skin on the track. I reached down to give him a hand. He ignored it and scrambled up.

"You *know* I've liked you since middle school…"

I shook my head, hair whipping my face. "No, you *thought* you liked me since middle school."

"Don't tell me how I feel. I *thought* you got this. That we were inevitable. We grew up together…"

"Exactly," I interjected. "It would be like going out with your sister. Ew, right?"

"God, do you have any idea what you're saying? Friends don't treat each other like this." And he left me and his blood behind.

He must have told his mom 'cause she told my mom, and she made me apologize for "being rude" which obviously was a mistake. It would've been awkward for our families if we weren't even friends anymore. But at least he wouldn't slam his head into lockers.

Like he just did.

He ran his fingers through his hair and blew out a big breath. "So, are you going to go running with me or not? You have shoes in your locker, right? Let's do it."

Crap.

"I can't. I would if I could." And he didn't believe me. Not. One. Bit. "Knox, come on. I have something this afternoon. How about tomorrow? No, wait, I'm driving Paul, but we could go after Mom gets home. It's getting lighter in the evenings."

He just looked at me.

"What, so I'm a liar now?"

"I don't know *what* you are anymore," he spat out, and jogged off, kicking the metal trashcan across the hall before shoving the side door open so hard it banged off the brick outside.

Great. I leaned against my locker, sliding down until my butt hit the ground. It wasn't good enough. I slid until I was on the floor. Spread out my arms. Full snow angel, Alice called it. All I knew was the only thing weighing on me was gravity. I didn't have to do anything.

It was bliss for like two seconds.

Then I could feel movement and heard it. Squeak. Squeak. Squeak. I turned my head to the side. Oh.

"*That* went well, babe," Daisy said, and broke out in a skip a few classrooms down. A skip. What was wrong with her?

"Shut up," I muttered, shifting my gaze to the ceiling again.

"No, seriously, I hate when they pull that shit. The locker. The garbage can. The rebounding door. Don't they know it's a trope?" Daisy leaned over me, peering into my face. "You okay?"

I slapped a hand over my eyes and laughed like a maniac. "Make him go away."

She straightened. "Nah, you can take him."

Take him?

Wait, take *her*. I jumped to my feet. "Sorry, I forgot. I never do that. And after what you did at lunch..."

"Time out," she made the hand signal. "Enough about lunch. I know you're reliable. You're Haven Alexander for

God's sake." She shrugged on the black bomber jacket she'd been dragging on the floor and slung a bright red tote bag over her shoulder. "Lead the way."

We were halfway to Oak's Amusement Park in Southeast when she brought up Knox again.

"So, what happened? Did you friend-zone him?" Daisy leaned against the door to face me, propping one foot on her seat like a little kid.

"He *is* my friend. No zoning needed," I grumbled, not happy we were on *that* again.

"Come on, he had that tortured, spurned lover thing going on," she continued.

I snorted. "Tortured? As if."

"As if what, blondie?" she shot back.

"Come on, Daisy, stop it. Blondie. Babe. That's not who I am."

"*He* thinks you're a babe. You *are* a babe. Fact of life."

I glared at her, curled up all cozy in the passenger seat. "You're a weird girl."

She pointed at me. "That is a true story. But you're still a babe."

I snorted. Again.

She tilted her chin up and narrowed her eyes at me. "Obliviousness suits you. You're the total package. Smart. Athletic. Humble. Fantastic sister. Beautiful."

"Knock it off."

And she laughed, low and rough. "Whatever. But believe me, he's not the only person who looks at you like he'd like to eat you."

I slammed on the brakes and the Volvo slid on the wet pavement, the rear fishtailing for a second before the anti-lock brakes caught and we stuttered to a stop at the side of the road.

Another car flew past. Shit. I could have killed us both. When I finally stopped hyperventilating and looked over at her she was a statue, barely breathing, her wide eyes frozen on my face.

Oh no.

"I scared you. Shit. Shit. Shit." I was only just smart enough not to hit the steering wheel. My luck, the airbag would deploy. "I'm sorry. I don't know what happened. I... I... I..."

She thawed enough to speak. "Just drive."

When I pulled up in front of what she called The Hangar, where they practiced, Daisy bailed without a word, slamming the car door with a glare. As I watched her disappear into the building, I realized I didn't even know if she needed a ride home. We didn't cover that because *I was an idiot*.

Not like I'd just dump her there.

I parked in the lot, feeling like a stalker. I could just wait and do my homework; I had my backpack. But I didn't even know how long derby practice was. Mom would eventually notice if I was gone for hours. If I was going to hang out, I'd have to let her know. And why. It's not like I needed permission to go somewhere, but she wanted to know where that somewhere was. Without looking at a phone app.

Yup, I had to do this.

I can do this.

I made my way to the open double doors, blood pounding in my ears because I'd messed up, I knew it, and now I had to talk to Daisy again and she wasn't going to be happy to see me, but I had to find out if she was depending on me for a ride home. When I reached the door the thrum in my ears was drowned out by the thunderous rumble of roller skates and voices inside.

Whatever I had pictured in my mind when Daisy said "derby practice" it wasn't this. "The Hangar" was literally, a cavernous, old airplane hangar but with bleachers and a brightly colored rink. And the walls above the bleachers were plastered with endorsements from businesses and politicians. The women running practice were tattooed and the players were stripping off their street clothes *right there*.

Okay...

So, no locker room for the derby girls?

There were high school girls of every size and shape and ethnicity and color and almost all of them were grinning or wore steely expressions like they couldn't wait to start practice. Or they were already helmeted and padded up and circling the track. The only boys in the building were watching or helping with duffel bags or playing on their phones. Brothers? Boyfriends? Genuinely supportive friends?

Unlike Knox.

I was startled for a second when two girls kissed before one skated off to the bench opposite. Not like making out. Like "have a nice time, honey". In church, girls held hands and hugged and leaned on each other when they were together, but no kissing. This was *so* not coffee hour at church.

I finally spotted Daisy on the other side of the rink. I felt like a fool, waving at her.

And a fool when she saw me. And stood there. Not moving. One bit. Even across the hangar I could see her huff out a breath before she skated over, picking up speed and stopping on a dime right in front of my face. Like she was trying to make me flinch.

I totally did.

"What are *you* still doing here?" She narrowed her eyes at me.

"I didn't know if you had a ride home," I said. It was the truth.

She looked at me, then sighed. "Give me your phone." She pointed the screen at my face to unlock it, then typed in something at lightning speed. "I'm still mad at you," she went on, handing me back my phone, somehow doing even that with attitude, "And I don't need a ride home."

"Okay." What else could I say?

She just glared at me. "Go on then, shoo."

She waved me off, so done. I took a step back but stopped, wanting us to be okay.

"Fine," Daisy said, "I forgive you. Whatever. Just go before I change my mind."

That I could live with.

CHAPTER SIX

"Duh. Why Would You?"

I felt the buzz from my backpack against my bare leg during U.S. History. Oh no! I forgot to turn it off. Weird. No one texted me during school. They knew we weren't allowed to touch our phones. No one texted me much, period, except my family. Or Alice.

I looked around the room, leaning forward so I could see around Knox. He only leaned forward, too, his eyes focused on Henderson, gripping the front edge of his desk so hard his knuckles went white. He hadn't made eye contact with me once since the stupid trash can incident.

I turned around to see if Alice had snuck her phone out, but she was just drawing on her arm.

Please don't let it be about Paul, I thought, slipping my hand into my backpack and sliding out my phone behind my palm.

This was stupid. I could be suspended. The cell phone policy was draconian, even if they let us keep them now instead of locking them in a pouch when you walked in the front door.

That had been a logistical nightmare.

I unlocked the screen anyway.

It wasn't about Paul. I didn't think.

You can make it up to me.

The I.D. said DQ. Who was DQ? I glanced down to see if another text was coming. Nothing. Texting *who is this?* would take too many letters so I settled for *how?*

"Miss Alexander. I expected better from you."

My phone was in Henderson's hand before I could push the lock key. Crap. He looked down at me to make sure I knew what was coming and was adequately quaking. I bet he'd make up stuff if the text on someone's phone was nothing to sneer at. He liked to sneer.

"Hmm, 'you can make it up to me'," he quoted. Out of his mouth it sounded skeevy. "And the question is how will she make up what to whom? Note the use of 'whom' as the protagonist of the sentence is Miss Alexander herself, unlike the question 'who' is texting her. Let's speculate."

Double crap.

"Did she fail to show up for an appointment? Refuse a favor? Publicly humiliate an admirer?"

I stared at nothing. Ignored Knox. Ignored the laughter because now I was a big joke.

He tapped the edge of my phone on my desk, then tossed it and caught it like it wasn't a nine hundred-dollar iPhone!

"Nothing from you?" He leaned down to look at my face, his coffee breath warm on my skin. Gross. "So be it. You will find out the answer to your scintillating question at the end of the day when you've served your detention. Though," he tossed and caught my phone again, "You should be getting suspended. But I'll let it pass." He shoved my phone into his back pocket.

I was *not* the only person in the room cringing.

"That was super shitty," Alice said, coming up next to me in the hallway after class. "Why does he get away with that?"

"It *is* the school policy."

How many times had *I* reminded people to put their phones away as a peer counselor? Too many if this is how it felt.

"But not reading the text out loud!" Laurie said on my other side, her long red curls bouncing as she walked. "Totally a violation of your right to privacy."

I guess I was forgiven for hanging out with people who weren't *like* her. She even acknowledged Alice with a glance before heading off to Latin. But then she did a one-eighty, spinning on her toes. Ballet was forever.

"You came up at Track again yesterday The new coach was ragging on you about being a quitter. Coach Johnson really talked you up before she left, she said, and then you suddenly don't even bother to show up."

Oh. Of course, the new coach was ragging on me. So was Laurie.

"We'd better win some events this year or we are going to be fucking fed up with you."

Not forgiven.

I guess she didn't need a response because she walked away before I could say a thing. Eventually, maybe, I should say what happened. But it was petty of me. Selfish. I wanted us to win. I just didn't want *her* to win. Coach Morgan.

I hesitated outside the lunchroom after fourth. Did I sit at my usual table and ignore Knox's cold shoulder and resist the urge to whack Tina and Kerry with my backpack if they dare to show up again? Get pizza down the block and avoid everyone? Before I could come up with a third option, the derby girls were right there.

Ellie was leader of the pack this time.

"We want to talk to you about your brother," she said, jerking her head toward the door to outside. "Come sit with us outside by the pool house."

Where the smokers and stoners sat at lunch. Just off school grounds, near the leash-free area in Willamette Park. The school was surrounded on three sides with tempting off-campus spots for *a lot* of things. The area by the public pool, closed for the school year, was the designated "waster" zone, according to Knox. And my friends. And me. Before...

Things were never as simple as they looked.

But hang out by the pool house? No. Way. I was terrified every year that some baked student would sneak in when there was no water in the pool in the off season and take a header onto concrete. Or a skateboarder would hop the fence and do the same. I didn't even walk by the pool house if I could help it, which wasn't easy with the parking lot so close.

"I get it," Ellie went on, thinking she was reading my mind. "Not your scene. Sophie's trying to quit smoking. We're on her ass about it."

"And we don't want her there on her own," Birgit said, "People are always calling her a dyke."

Sophie shrugged her thick shoulders and ran her hands over her buzz cut. "They're not wrong."

Birgit hip-checked her but Sophie didn't move an inch.

"They mean it like an insult," Birgit insisted.

"And it's against the school guidelines on harassment and bullying and hate speak." Oops. I opened my big mouth. They didn't need me to spell that out. Or that school rules didn't apply there anyway because it was technically off campus. By about twenty feet.

Fortunately, they ignored me.

"And the gestures they make, ugh, I just want to," Birgit didn't finish and clenched her fists. She could be formidable if she wanted. But she seemed like a softie.

"Don't forget we need to talk about how you're going to make it up to me."

Daisy. The text was from Daisy.

DQ?

How did she get my number?

And she read my mind. Nailed it, in fact.

"D.Q. Derby. Queen. You gave me your phone yesterday, babe."

I remembered *now*.

"Don't call me that," I muttered.

She just laughed.

And I still didn't get it. Why did she *do* that? I'd slammed on the brakes and scared the crap out of her because she was saying that stuff. But she still said them. Why? Did she say those things to everyone?

I was so in my head I only realized we were in front of the pool house because of the smell. Weed. And smoke after Sophie pulled out a pack and lit up.

"I don't get it. Why am I here, sucking in second-hand smoke, when you could have just told me what you wanted inside?" Yup, I was whining.

"My fault," Sophie held her cigarette over her head, waving away the smoke. "I'm going to quit. I mean it. This time."

I turned as the smoke drifted my way. Aaron from Ecology gave me a friendly wave from a packed picnic table, totally high on mushrooms probably. I'd find out next period.

I was shocked to see Eric and Mark from the Ultimate Frisbee team smoking. They were primo athletes. Why would they do that to their bodies? I fought down my compulsion to remind them of school rules. They *knew* the school rules. *And* we weren't on school property.

Still, they took off in seconds once they saw me. At least I interrupted their smoke break.

I watched them head back toward the parking lot. And saw three people headed our way. This wouldn't be good.

I stepped in front of the derby girls, in Tina's path. They were my friends, sort of. I wanted to protect them from the look on Tina's face. It was ugly and they didn't deserve that.

The guys hung back a little. Anthony used to sit at our table before his teammate harassed Joey and got kicked off the basketball team. And was no longer welcome. Rutger thought he was a badass, his boxers showing above his baggy jeans, his hair to his shoulders. Nothing but a rich and spoiled brat I'd dealt with since fourth grade.

Tina pointed a scrawny finger at Daisy and tried to pass me. Not happening.

"Out of my way, Haven. I don't have a problem with *you*. This is about *her*."

I heard Daisy's dramatic sigh behind me, so I looked back. Her arms were crossed over her chest; her hip cocked to one side. Uh oh.

"Guys, hold on, I can help you work this out," I said, following the script I'd been trained on. "Or we can take this to the counselors' office."

"Out of the way narc," Rutger growled. "Run along and protect your retard brother."

"Not cool," Anthony mumbled. "You don't want to go there, dude."

Hell yeah. Did the idiot want to get kicked off the wrestling team? Not that I was in the mood to report him; I was one inch away from whaling on the next person to insult Paul.

"This bitch you're taking up for hit on my boyfriend last night. Offered to suck his dick. As if he'd want that skank anywhere near him. She was getting back at me because of her detention."

"Hey," I started, but Daisy put her hand on my shoulder to stop me.

"I've got this. First," she said, enunciating carefully, "the detention was worth every minute. You need to think twice before picking on Paul Alexander. And as for your boyfriend, he came on to *me* last weekend and asked me to suck his pathetic dick. As if."

I had nothing.

"And you, pretty boy," she said, pointing at Anthony, "not happening again."

Tina whirled on the tall guy behind her. "What?!" And I saw it, the vulnerability underneath her mean as she laid into him, practically chasing him back toward the school. Rutger just stared at us for two seconds too long before he turned to follow them.

Tina wasn't the only one who said, "What!?"

The same word came out of my mouth.

"What?" I repeated. Did Daisy mean she *had* done that? I did not get it. I did not belong here. This was way over my head. "We can talk later. Okay?" I almost thanked them for 'inviting' me. What was the protocol here?

"Hold up." Sophie stamped out her cigarette and put the butt in the garbage. "Sorry for that shit."

I had no idea how to respond. It wasn't her fault.

"Look," she went on, "we want to know more about your brother. What's he into? How does he like to be approached? Are there triggers we should avoid?"

My mouth opened. Shut. Opened again. "What?"

Why was that the only word that came out of my mouth?

Birgit shifted on her burgundy combat boots.

Alice would like those I thought. And then, since when do I notice shoes?

"I've got a nine-year-old cousin on the spectrum, and he's got all these sensory issues. Doesn't like to be touched. Flips out at certain sounds. And we can't so much as whisper the word 'Disney' because he's been traumatized by the whole mom dying thing. We just stick with Scooby-Doo when he's visiting."

Ellie jumped in after Birgit. "And we know Paul's not a kid. It's just, we don't want to make him uncomfortable."

"We think he deserves a really great senior year, you know?"

Sophie was serious. They all were. Only Daisy hadn't chimed in.

"What do you mean by that?" I asked.

Sophie opened her arms wide. "We want to adopt him!" Her brows pulled together. "No, scratch that. We want to hang out with him at lunch. He needs friends here, after being gone most of the year."

God. My eyes were swimming, and I never *ever* cry. I turned so they couldn't see me wipe my eyes on my T-shirt.

How could they see that Paul wanted friends when no one else did? No one but his therapist. And me. All the specialists and appointments and small classes he had over the years made making friends almost impossible. Just because he didn't talk to people much didn't mean he didn't want to.

But. It sounded too good to be true. "Paul is not a community project. He's a person."

"That's the point," Sophie went on, pulling out her cigarettes but pausing. "He is. We like him. And he's not judging us."

"Why?" I asked. Why would he judge them? But they misunderstood.

"Because we're decent human beings who think your brother might be a cool dude to know? Like that's so impossible?" Daisy looked like a pissed off kitten.

"It's not like we're all assholes," Ellie said, looking up at me. "Only Sophie."

Sophie stood up straighter, putting her pack of cigarettes back in her pocket. "Hey, what the fuck?"

"And he doesn't expect blow jobs," Ellie added.

Lalalala... I *almost* put my fingers in my ears and *definitely* wanted to shower my brain.

"Whether you like it or not, we just became his best friends at this fucking school." Sophie grinned.

"Right. So, details, girl," Birgit said.

Before I could say anything, like to ask Paul, Daisy pulled me away and around the corner. By the arm! "Details can wait you guys," she called back before facing me. "About making up for scaring me to death."

Holy mental whiplash. And it all came crashing back. How could I have done that? I was not an irresponsible driver. I don't think I'd done an unsafe thing in my life—besides riding my motorcycle, and that was debatable. Telling her so seemed pointless when I'd already shown Daisy I couldn't be trusted.

"What do you want?" I said. Anything seemed reasonable.

She squeezed my arm but let go when she saw me staring at the spot where she touched me.

"I want you to be my personal Uber," Daisy said, shifting her weight.

This made no sense. After how I messed up.

"Let's get this straight," she went on, not even giving me a second to respond. "What happened was an anomaly."

Did everyone know what I was thinking?

"You are super responsible. I know that." Daisy shifted again.

"I don't mean all the time. The Uber thing. Just, like if I don't have a ride home when the bus stops running. Or from a party or someone's house. I don't want to depend on people who are drunk or high."

I just managed to not say "Duh."

She avoided my eyes. "Sometimes you go out with people, and you think they're cool? And they flake or get fucked up?" She twisted her fingers together. "Never mind, forget I said anything. I can get a real Uber."

She was never this nervous.

"Don't your friends drive?" I asked, "It seems like you're always together."

She laughed. "None of us have a driver's license but Ellie, and she can't drive anyone under eighteen for another month. And cars cost money. None of us have any. Ellie is just using her brother's car while he's overseas."

"The Volvo isn't mine. My dad works in Hillsboro and Mom needs a car to drive Paul. He can't drive because of his epilepsy. They're borrowing this one for me from my aunt. They can't drop everything and drive me to meets and stuff." That was before I got my motorcycle, but they didn't want me driving that.

"I don't want to drive. But you know how it is, sometimes it's not safe out there."

Huh? "Out where?"

I could feel her holding back something snarky.

"Like walking home alone at night? Or taking the bus or the Max train? I mean, I *can*, it's just, you know?" she went on, watching me for a reaction. Apparently, I didn't give one because she added, "When guys sit down next to you on the Max when there are plenty of seats and ask how old you are. Or get off at your stop. And try to get you to talk to them. Come on, you know what I'm talking about."

Oh...

"No one ever looks at me like that. I mean, maybe once every six months someone might yell something when I'm running on the track. But..."

She made a "T" for time-out. "Let's not get into that right now."

In the brief pause I said, "Yes."

"I know. I just said we won't get into that."

"No, I mean yes, I'll be your on-call driver. When I can," I added.

Daisy's eyes got big. Bigger. "So, if I needed a ride to practice this afternoon, like at four-thirty, you'd do it?"

"Can it be four forty-five?" I could just get there after detention.

She nodded. Then Daisy King the Derby Queen skipped around the corner to her friends. "Guess what? We've got a ride to practice today!"

What had I gotten myself into?

Ms. Lamb held out my phone at four forty-two but when I took hold of it, she didn't let go.

"This is a first, Haven. A detention. Using your phone at school. You want to talk about it?" Ms. Lamb asked, giving me "the big eyes" she was famous for.

Wait, now that they were trained on me, I realized her eyes were almost *exactly* the same color as Daisy's. Maybe that was why I trusted Daisy so much, so fast. You couldn't *not* trust Ms. Lamb.

But no. Not going to get into it now. I tugged just a little. "I can't talk now. I've got to go."

Her grip tightened. She wasn't going to let me off the hook.

"Okay, but I only have a minute. An actual minute. I'm giving someone a ride."

As soon as Ms. Lamb closed her office door behind us, I felt trapped. The framed slogans all over her walls stared at me. I was down with the positive messages. But it was like they were shouting at me. *Just Do It. Say No to Drugs. See Something Say Something. Believe in Yourself.*

Ms. Lamb spun her chair toward me, her office so small our knees almost touched. We both had long legs. Everyone in the world knew she'd made Olympic Trials in basketball.

"I heard about what happened in the cafeteria yesterday. All in all, the whole incident was so well managed there was hardly a reason for staff to step in. It was nice to hear that someone beside you had Paul's back. That's new."

"It's the first time anyone was stupid enough to bring him to the lunchroom," I grumbled.

Oops. I blinked at Ms. Lamb. She was not fond of the "S" word.

"Luce meant well. She only started volunteering with Mr. McElroy in December and never worked with your brother before then. She feels terrible for letting him, and you, down like that. And goodness knows she has enough on her plate." Ms. Lamb shook her head somberly.

What happened to Luce?

"And he was doing great," she continued. "You should be so proud of him."

"I am proud of him." She was right, it was incredible. And I wondered if he would have mastered the lunchroom by now if he hadn't been reassigned in September.

He probably wouldn't have met Daisy, I thought, and looked at the clock. Four forty-seven.

"And," she continued, "he stayed in the lunchroom with you and the girls until lunch was nearly over. That's really something. Did you tell your mom?"

I shook my head. Ms. Lamb was right. I *should* tell her. But then I'd have to fill her in on who they were and... I wasn't sure I wanted to.

She nodded. "It's okay not to tell her. You're not Paul's keeper. You're his sister. You're allowed to let other people help him stretch his boundaries."

But not at the cost of harming him. Ms. Lamb couldn't know how much he suffered after he lost it with Naomi.

"Mom is trusting me to watch out for him," I told her. It was the truth.

"It can be hard to have a sibling with a disability. Your life is structured around his needs much of the time. It's just the way it is." She leaned closer, so we were eye to eye. "But it doesn't have to be like that here. You are allowed to focus on you. It's good for you to have needs. Can you work on that for me?"

I shook my head. I swear she suppressed her sigh.

"I know how you love to overachieve, Haven, so consider this an assignment. Bring me a list of at least ten needs to talk about when we meet again." When I looked at her blankly, she said, "Five. Give me five. Okay?"

What could I do but nod? Even though, yeah, my needs? Give me a break. I stood up and opened her office door. "I need to jet. Thanks Ms. Lamb."

"Say hi to Daisy for me, will you?"

She really *did* know everything.

CHAPTER SEVEN

"Why Do I Have to Be So Perfect?"

My T-shirt stretched over my boobs in a weird way. I squirmed on the area rug, trying to get comfortable. Mom must have slipped some girl shirts into my drawer. Again. They just didn't fit right. I shifted my shoulders and tugged at the bottom. I still felt like I was being squeezed all over. If I had to wait another five minutes, I'd bolt upstairs and cram this shirt somewhere Mom would never find it.

Hurry up and wait was not a foreign concept on Sunday mornings. Dad paced. Paul hunched over the kitchen table, rocking fast with his headphones on and playing on his phone. I hit the floor.

Not on the ocean of hardwood wall to wall. No, I dropped onto the island of carpet in the living room. Flat on my back. Fingers gripping the carpet. Eyes closed. Held up by the earth. Giving in to something bigger than me.

Without ants. Or pebbles. Or itchy blades of grass. Luxury, indoor pile was my jam. I was drifting into gravitational heaven when I went and opened my stupid eyes.

That brought me down to earth. The best spot in the whole house had to be facing my personal wall of weird. A monument to making the grade. An ode to achievement. Framed, matted, and hung with the bottoms aligned with a T-square.

Thanks Dad.

The Honor Roll certificates. The "perfect" report cards from last year. The Cross-country and Track and Field ribbons. The debate winner medals. There were times I felt like I lived in a trophy case.

If it sucked for me, how did it make Paul feel? He never said anything about it. It was hard to know what he kept in his carefully categorized mind and what was deemed junk and deleted. I just hoped it didn't hurt him, knowing they were all about me. I was such a chickenshit for not asking.

I closed my eyes again, wishing I was on my bike. My early morning ride was cut short by drizzle. I didn't need Mom talking brain cells. Again. Not like I was ever going to forget what she said when Uncle Jackson brought the bike over.

"I hope that it rains every single day for the next six months or until you get over this selfish rebellion. I can't have someone else... I can't have you getting brain damage!"

It was like a slap.

"Paul is not brain-damaged," I'd hissed. How could she? What if he heard? He, Dad, and Uncle Jackson weren't far.

"I know," she'd whispered, tears already falling. "I didn't mean it."

Lately she reminded me not to take my brain and body for granted every time I grabbed the keys to my bike. Sometimes, I thought maybe I *was* being selfish. But God I loved that thing.

Mine.

Yes! I heard movement in the other room. She was finally off the phone, and we'd get going.

Or not.

"Terry Cooper called," Mom said, standing over me like she'd teleported from the kitchen.

Oh. Crap. I scrambled up. If this was about what I thought it was, I was in trouble.

It was.

"Seriously, Haven," she started in, "a detention?"

She spat out the words, like having "a detention" was something major. And disgusting. Thank you, Terry Cooper, for being a snitch.

"I know you're disappointed," I started. Mom didn't let me finish.

"Since when do you use your phone during class? You never break rules. And the cell phone policy is there for a reason."

She looked toward Paul at the table, pretending he wasn't listening to every word. I knew what she was thinking. That he was exempt from the rule. He could have his phone. A lifeline just in case.

I was a different story.

"This is so unlike you, honey." She was morphing from disgust to confusion to hurt in a heartbeat. I leaned my forehead against hers, knowing she was right. It *was* so unlike me.

"I thought it might have been about Paul," I said softly.

It was the right answer. I could feel her body relaxing.

"That makes sense," Mom said, pulling back, "Who was it? Why would they reach out to you during school hours?"

I calculated how much to tell. "It was from this girl, Daisy. She's in a couple of my classes. She wanted to ask me something."

"She should know better than to text you during class..." *And* Mom was building up speed again.

"It *was* about Paul," I interjected.

Guaranteed distraction.

"About Paul? What do you mean?"

I had this.

"She wanted to know if Paul would like to sit with her and her friends at lunch. Like a regular thing."

"The lunchroom?" Her brow furrowed.

Maybe I didn't have this.

"Is this about what happened Wednesday? When Luce left him with those girls?"

Oh, Mom. Seriously?

"What do you mean by 'those' girls? It was Luce who left him in the lunch line. Daisy and her friends had his back."

"Mr. McElroy told me they were kind of different. Not that there's anything wrong with being different."

Could she hear herself? Mom's suspicion of "different" was lifelong. She was just parroting what was said at church. Or maybe what she wanted to feel? I could hope.

"They're not *that* different," I snapped, and the guilt was real. *I* thought they were weird when I first met them at the SlutWalk. "They're nice. They're... They're friends of Alice."

Mom's face lit up. "I remember her. That little blonde girl. It was so nice of her to come over on Thanksgiving. It's too bad she didn't try my pumpkin pie. I'm sure it would have changed her mind."

Alice hated pie. All pie. Why did Mom think she needed to change her mind? Who cares?

"It was so kind of you to take her under your wing. She seemed like she needed a friend."

No, Mom, I needed her. As a human shield. To save me from another holiday meal with you throwing me at Knox like a piece of meat to a dog.

Not that I said any of that out loud.

"I heard she's a troubled girl. I never asked—did you meet her while peer counseling?" Mom asked.

Troubled? Great. Which Booster parent told her that?

"Just because she's not a neighborhood clone, that doesn't mean she's 'troubled'. And she's my friend," *friend*, "So, she's obviously a good judge of people." *Girl* people.

Mom laughed. "Anyone can see you're the best. But," she went on, "I assume you told that girl, that Daisy, that Paul won't be going to the lunchroom again. It's not worth it."

Ugh. Again, the calculated risk-benefit ratio of every moment of my brother's life. Did any possibility that he'd lose it outweigh his potential for trying new things? I figured if he succeeded in the lunchroom, with the derby girls' help, who knew what else he could do? He was *eighteen*.

"I get it, Mom, I do. But he did it and it went great." No need to go into the whole fiasco with Kerry-with-a-K and Tina, "He was there for twenty minutes!"

And she went rigid.

"And you knew it was happening? He should have gone right back to his classroom! How dare you make decisions like that? It's your brother who pays when mistakes are made."

Hello, Paul was in the kitchen! I clamped my mouth shut to keep from screaming it.

"It's not like I don't know my own brother. And seriously, he couldn't have been in better hands. No one messes with those girls."

And *that* was the wrong thing to say.

"Why wouldn't anyone mess with them? You're not reassuring me, Haven."

Sigh.

"So, they're on the roller derby team. They've got attitude and kind of a tough reputation because it's a really physical sport. Like rugby! Mostly people give them space because Daisy's bossy."

That was one way to put it. Another was "confusing as hell."

"Roller derby?" I could just see her brain ticking away. If *I* knew it was a thing, *she* should. "Your brother hung around with roller derby playing girls other students steer clear of?"

When she said it like that, it did sound sketch.

"Look, when Luce left him on his own, that b..." I stopped myself just in time. "Girl, Kerry, was rude to Paul when he was drawing in line. And her friend, Tina, reached out to push his sketchbook away..."

Mom gasped.

"And I was booking it to get there but before I could stop Tina, Daisy yanked her back. She got detention for it."

Mom was practically hyperventilating. "That's exactly what I mean. Why weren't you there in the first place?"

Because I'm not f-ing omniscient!

"I didn't know he was down there. He always has lunch in his classroom!"

Mom wasn't getting it.

"Look, the point is that those girls stayed with Paul until Luce got back. And they talked with him about his art, Mom."

She tilted her head. Not buying it. The truth.

"They did. They could see how talented he is. And the next day they were all over me about what he liked and disliked and how to interact and who does that? They are offering him friendship on his terms."

The abrupt change on her face almost broke me. "Friendship? Do you really mean that?"

"Yes. Really." And I really hoped they would come through. If I had to drive them all to practice every day until Paul graduated and even next year that was a small price to pay.

CHAPTER EIGHT

"Why Would You Want to Do That?"

What was I thinking? I could have been bingeing ESPN with Dad, my hands smothered in hot sauce, eating wings from The Smokin' Oak on the couch. Standard Saturday night fare. But no, I was in Carter's overcrowded basement ADU, surrounded by smoke, strangers, and too many students I knew getting wasted. While being assaulted by Ska music.

And I had to use Knox as an excuse for going out since I was still grounded for the phone thing: I was going out to listen to his band! Support his music! It was going to bite me in the butt big time!

Thank you, Anna and Renee, for talking me into this.

And now only Anna was outside when I pulled up on my bike. No Renee. No Carli, who swore she was going to join us.

"Where is she?" I grumbled, rocking onto my center stand.

"'You never go out with us. You're going.' Renee said. And she's a not even coming?"

Anna heard the last part and checked her phone again.

"Wait," Anna said, scrolling down. "She sent another text. Oh, no. Trust me, we don't want her here." She mimed throwing up and shoved her phone back in her pocket. "Something came up all right." She took a long drink of her beer and then nodded slowly to the music as we muscled our way through the sea of people.

I was going to kill Renee on Monday.

Steal her favorite sweatshirt.

Break the tips off her long fancy fingernails.

In that order.

As if.

"Are you even going to drink that?" Anna leaned down to shout in my ear a little later, swinging her empty bottle in my face. The girl had some freaky long fingers.

I just handed her the beer Knox thrust into my hand before taking the stage. I guess he figured if I gave up Track, I was open to all the vices. Then again, he *knew* I was on my bike—he saw me get off it when I was complaining to Anna about Renee blowing us off—and should know I would *never* ride under the influence.

"Defensive driving is key for motorcyclists." Uncle Jackson had drilled it into me from the moment he mentioned his old motorcycle and my birthday in the same sentence.

"Thanks," Anna drew out the word, from snarky-ness or too much beer, I couldn't tell. "I forget you don't drink. That would be too..." She closed her eyes to concentrate. "*Wild* for you." Then she laughed.

Because me being "wild" was *so* funny. She wobbled as she pushed her long dark-blonde hair out of her face. We shared the hair-in-our-eyes problem. I had to shove mine back all the time. Somehow *my* hair was Mom's department, and she thought this "bob" thing was "cute". At least Anna could put hers in a hair tie.

"Aren't you, like, with that guy?" Anna said, moving closer to the wall by the stage.

"Hell no," I said. People turned to stare and even Knox stopped skipping around with his microphone to look.

So, I talk loud. Sometimes. It's not a character flaw.

"I don't date," I mumbled. Not happening. Nope.

Anna snorted. "Who said anything about dating?"

Jesus. That's what Alice said to me in the fall. Before things got bad for her. Fat chance I was hooking up with anyone either.

There was plenty of that going on around us already.

I recognized a lot of people from school when they came up for air. Or wove through the crowd spilling beer. Or danced in front of the makeshift stage. Stupid Finn in his stupid hat. I didn't see Alice with him. Basketball players, off the hook since the season ended, gathered at the keg with baseball players who should know better than to get wasted. Baseball season was in full swing.

So to speak.

And Badger Moore was practically humping Luce's leg across the room. I wasn't wasting sympathy on her. She could take a Badger space invasion after leaving Paul in the lunchroom. Not that I felt good about not intervening. Luce *was* nice. Then I saw Finn making a beeline for his cousin. He'd get Badger to back off.

Girls were gathered around the keg as well, hanging all over the basketball players.

Why did intelligent girls hang all over assholes who'd forget they knew them on Monday? I didn't get it.

Though maybe the girls didn't care if they were forgotten. It saved them the trouble of ghosting the assholes themselves. Or so I'd heard in the bathroom at school.

Trent held up a wall close by, shrugging off the girls wanting a piece of him. Politely. *He* was no asshole. I watched him for a minute. He looked like he always did, short hair, letterman jacket, jeans, but haunted, if that was a thing. I didn't get why he was so heartbroken. They dated. Maddy cheated. Game over. It seemed pretty simple. But he didn't look like it was that simple.

And his season, our season, was sucking because of it.

Hell of a sports photographer though.

I looked back at Anna. Her normally wide shoulders curved inward. Too relaxed. An Uber was in her future because I was taking her keys.

"This party blows," she slurred, setting another empty bottle on the windowsill. She'd raided 'the good stuff' from Carter's personal stash. "Can we go soon? I'm meeting with a recruiter from San Diego tomorrow."

Now *I* was the one dragging *her* to this dumb party?

But I wasn't going to be an asshole.

"Basketball or crew?" I had to yell the words so she could hear me over the metal band that took the stage after Knox's. Anna could row like a beast.

"Crew. University of Washington is my top pick, but San Diego has better weather, you know?"

No, I didn't know. We didn't travel. It was too unpredictable for Paul when he was younger. He needed predictable and same then. Same bed. Same food. Same routine. I wondered if he'd like to travel now. Things change. He was changing. A week with the derby girls showed me that.

"Oh my God. Would you look at that?" Anna sneered, her beer breath wafting over my face as she leaned her arm on my shoulder. I waved the stink away before following her line of sight.

What? Oh... Disgust and some feeling I couldn't identify swamped me, giving me goosebumps. Wrong. It was all kinds of wrong. Why did she let him do that to her?

Daisy. Up against the opposite wall with some guy's hands on her and his tongue in her mouth. Her arms rested on his shoulders, limp. Was she even into it? I didn't want to look. I couldn't *not* look.

"She's such a ho'," Anna slurred, and laughed.

I stepped away from her and she stumbled, caught herself, and gave me the death glare.

"Shut up. It's none of your business what Daisy does," I snapped. "And she's not a ho'."

"I forgot," Anna said, tilting her head drunkenly, "She's like your brother's bodyguard now, her and her friends. They're a traveling circus freak show, Haven. Birgit's all right, she'd be boss on crew. But that one girl? With the buzzed head? Total dyke."

Did Anna not feel the *shut the fuck up* radiating off me?

"How does Paul feel about being their little charity case? Are they getting volunteer credit?"

I whirled on her and the music, the people, the smell, were gone. "I mean it. Shut up. Were you always this much of a bitch and I never noticed? Never, ever, call my brother a charity case again or I'll..."

"What? You'll what?" She squared up to me, arms out, "Bring it."

God. Anna was drunk and could do three-hundred-pound leg presses and bench one-sixty. Messing with her was not smart.

But my smart was offline. All I felt was anger. So much anger. Scorched earth level. Something had to give. I sucked in a big breath through my nose and blew it out.

Anna tipped her chin, six-foot-plus arm span spread, so I couldn't pretend this wasn't happening. I grabbed her jacket off the floor and started toward the door and out of her reach. In her state I could move faster. I didn't exactly wait for anyone to get out of my way.

"Hey, Trent?" I said, when I got near him, "Could you take Anna home?" I tossed her jacket to him when he nodded.

He looked past me, to Anna, "Won't be the first time." He'd known her forever.

"Hey! Where are you going?" came a husky voice just behind me.

I tried to ignore Daisy. I needed to get the sight of her public make-out session out of my mind. Wait, was that her finger going down my spine? What the hell? I swung around.

I hadn't been able to see much of her behind the jerk eating her face. Now that she was standing there, it was hard to ignore the polka dot top thing that barely hid her bra. She had a small red heart drawn on her bare left shoulder. Alice's work? Why *that* was what I said is anyone's guess.

I pointed to her shoulder.

Daisy dropped her chin to see where I was pointing, the movement slower than it should have been. "What?"

"This," I said, for some stupid reason touching the heart. Her skin was warm and damp. I rubbed my thumb along the drawing, but it didn't smear. I jerked my hand away. What was I thinking?

She laughed. Laughed. "What's so funny?" Why did everyone laugh at me?

"It's a real tattoo, babe. What do you think I am, six?"

"You're not eighteen." Fact. That was the legal age. Alice told me.

"No," she said, drawing out the word like *I* was the six-year-old, "But you can get one at sixteen in Canada." She wiggled, a smug look on her lips, bare of her usual cherry red. I hated the reason for that.

"That's stupid," I snapped. "What did your parents say?"

For a second, I thought, 'Uh oh, I called her stupid' and that she was going to be pissed. But no. Her smugness only grew. "My mom took me to get it." She put her hands on her hips, cocking one to the side, and batted her big dark eyes at me. People really did that?

Her words took a minute to sink in. "Your mom took you to another country to get a tattoo?"

"Yup." She wiggled again, so pleased with herself.

I think my mouth literally hung open in shock. Moms do not do that.

That shock was blown away by Daisy's next move.

She kissed me. On the mouth. Total contact. Like not a peck either. No, there was maybe a full two seconds that felt like forever of lips-to-lips before she went back onto her heels and beamed at me. Smugness times one thousand.

Thoughts crowded faster than I could single them out.

Did that just happen?

Why did she do that?

Did anyone see?

What was she thinking?

Wasn't she just making out with some guy?

Was this some stunt she thought was funny?

And then—so *that's* what a kiss felt like.

I was speechless. I'm sure my mouth dropped open again. When I was finally able to focus, I saw that a lot of people *did* see. Like Laurie. And Anna. And Trent. And Knox…

Oh shit, this was going to get right back to Mom and Dad. Shit. Shit. Shit.

I swung my gaze back to Daisy, who was looking less smug, side-stepped her, and blew through people clogging the exit, getting sloshed with beer every two steps. Hello to stripping in the laundry room before Mom got a whiff. Great.

"Wait," Daisy called after me.

No, I wasn't going to wait.

But I could hear her following.

Why was she following?

I didn't stop. If she had an excuse to make, let her run. I wasn't going to make it easy when she had just made my life so hard.

"Haven! Come on, stop already," she called. I made it to the front of Carter's house and could hear her shoes slide on the pebbles along the driveway several feet back.

"No," I yelled, reaching my bike. Why had she done this to me? I thought we were friends.

Daisy grabbed my arm, and I tried to shake her off. No such luck.

"Haven, please, just give me a sec', okay?"

I reluctantly turned toward her. My anger or confusion or irritation or whatever cooled a little when I saw the apology in her eyes.

But that didn't sit right either.

"Hey, I'm sorry if I offended you or crossed boundaries or pissed off your boyfriend…"

"Jesus," I snapped. "Knox never was and will never *be* my boyfriend."

"Whoa, I know, I was joking," she threw up her hands and stepped back, "I'm sorry."

We both knew what she was really talking about.

"Then why did you do it, if you're so sorry?"

Not what I meant to say at all. But being so sorry about kissing me kind of stung.

She crossed her arms, wrapping herself tight. "Don't you ever just want to kiss somebody?" she said quietly.

"And you didn't get enough with that guy?" I shot back.

She looked like she didn't even know who I was talking about. Was she high?

"The one who was glued to your face," I added.

Ding. The light went on. "Oh, Josh? That was just whatever. It seemed like a good idea at the time. For like five minutes. He was a lousy kisser."

Seemed like a good idea at the time…

I didn't *think* I said the words aloud, but I guess I did.

"What?" she said, "I wasn't going to have sex with him if that's what you thought. Like you've never thought, hmm, I feel like making out right now. They'll do." And she pointed to an imaginary boy, like she was picking someone out of a lineup.

Or on a menu.

"No," I said.

"No?" She tilted her head and peered at me. Like I had to be lying.

"No." Why did she keep asking?

"Not even a teensy bit?" Daisy asked, putting her hands on her hips. Her vulnerability gone; now she was teasing me.

"Drop it already." I turned away to grab my helmet.

"Wait," she said, and I could hear anxiety in her voice this time.

"What?" I snapped, throwing my leg over the seat, refusing to look at her.

I saw her step closer out of the corner of my eye. "My ride left. Can you be my Uber driver? Please? I know it's not to or from practice, but I need a safe ride."

I pressed my forehead against the handlebars. "Can't you ride with Finn and Alice?" Alice had to be in there somewhere if Finn was. "Or ask Trent? He's taking Anna home."

"Alice's dog is in the back seat of his truck. I'm allergic. Like *so* allergic. And I don't know Trent. That would be weird."

And Anna thinks she's a ho', I thought. That couldn't go well. Especially now that Anna probably thought Daisy was a bisexual 'ho'.

Who kissed innocent jocks.

For the hell of it.

"I thought you traveled in packs," I muttered, and then remembered what Anna said about the derby girls being traveling circus freaks. I didn't want to come off like her. Now or ever.

"Never mind. Forget I said that," I told her, finally lifting my eyes to see her face. "But... I only have one helmet with me."

"I trust you. Even without a helmet you're better than walking. My cousin dumped my ass for some guy and blew out of here."

I turned toward her fully. She was twisting her hands. Like she knew I'd let her down.

"So, call a real Uber or your mom or dad. That would be safer still," I said.

"No cash. No card. Mom's on a twenty-four-hour shift. Dad's forty minutes away." She grimaced. "And I didn't go see him the last three times he asked so I'd feel like shit calling him for a favor."

"That's what parents do, Daisy, give us a ride if we're in a bad situation. He wouldn't want you riding on the back of a motorcycle without a helmet."

She squirmed. "It's not just the seeing him thing. He owns a bar, and this is the busiest time of the whole week. *And* he's always telling me to bring money when I go out. Just in case."

I thought of the driver's license in my back pocket. Why didn't *I* bring my debit card or some cash? I didn't even bring keg money 'cause I don't drink. "Look, I could walk with you, so you won't be alone. How far away do you live?"

"A couple miles. But then you'd have to walk back here alone."

"Yeah, but that's different."

She threw her arms up in the air. "Do we have to argue about everything? We've talked about this. You are female. You have a slit between your legs. That's all that matters to creeps. And besides, you're beautiful and you know it."

I was so stuck on "slit" I didn't tell her she was full of it about me. "Fine. Whatever. But you're wearing the helmet." Because hating myself forever if she got hurt outweighed the fact that my mom would kill me if she found out.

"No. That wouldn't be..."

"Do you want a ride or not?"

I was surprised when she didn't argue and put on the helmet. Before I could blink, she'd climbed on and positioned herself behind me.

"Have you done this before?" I could feel the shake of her head.

"Keep your legs away from the tail pipes. They get hot." I kicked out the foot pegs for the rider, grateful that Uncle Jackson had them installed because they weren't standard.

And then she wrapped her arms around me.

What was I supposed to do with *that*?

I mean, it was for safety.

But it didn't feel like that.

I tried to shake off the tension. I could do this. I just hoped I didn't get pulled over by the police for not wearing a helmet.

It would be just my luck.

But I was doing this.

I patted her hands over my stomach once. "Okay, hold on. Lean when I lean. Don't readjust in your seat while the bike is in motion. And watch your leg when you step off. Avoid the tail pipes! It's like riding a horse, but I'm holding the reins."

Word for word what Uncle Jackson told me to say if I ever had "a bitch on the back." Not sure why he assumed it would be a girl, not a guy, but maybe there wasn't a term for that.

"Riding a horse. Gotcha." She scooted closer. "Not that I've ever ridden a horse," she said, barely audible over the rumble of the bike.

Neither had I.

Or ridden without a helmet.

I felt naked. And grateful for the empty roads. With Daisy holding on to me this was a different kind of ride. Being responsible for another life. I didn't like it.

"Thanks," she said, when we'd gone about a mile down Prescott. "I really, really appreciate this."

"You're welcome," I said, turning slightly so she could hear. "It's our deal, right? You ask, I say yes."

Oops. Awkward. I was grateful she couldn't see my face. If only she couldn't have heard me.

"You say that to all the girls," she barely got the words out as she giggled. Giggled!

Innuendo. This was not good. Not going to touch that one. Change of subject.

"So, your mom. Twenty-four-hour shift. What does she do?"

"Catches babies," Daisy said.

Oh, yeah, she said so in Health class. "Does she like it?"

"What's not to like? Blood, amniotic fluid, poop, vaginas galore. And then baby. Plop."

Uh, that was more than I wanted to know about giving birth...

"I did it again, huh? Rendered you speechless. You shouldn't make it so easy." There was that laugh again. A big one. That shook her torso. Against my back.

Okay, I told myself, ignore that she's right there behind me. It's just a ride. I'm being her driver. Being a friend. A friend that she kissed because I was standing there. Stroking her stupid tattoo.

It was still weird.

"And your dad owns a bar?"

"A tiki bar. I practically grew up surrounded by fake steam and the smell of pineapple. Oh, and rum. Lots of rum," she said, emphasizing the "lots".

Huh. Fake steam, pineapple, rum, tiki bar, dad, babies, plop, mom. Daisy was making a little more sense maybe.

"This is it," she said, "Turn right here."

I pulled into a narrow driveway by a small dark house. I turned the key, the night suddenly silent, and steadied the bike while Daisy swung her leg wide to avoid the tail pipes.

"Thanks again," she said, teeth bright in the half-light as she passed me my helmet, "And sorry." She wrinkled her nose.

Sorry for what?

Oh. That kiss out of nowhere.

I wanted to ask her "why me?" But I knew why. I was just there.

I shrugged. What was done was done. I'd be hearing about it until June. Or until I graduated next year. Whatever. I'd deal.

Daisy said, "We have a bout tomorrow at the hangar. At noon. You should come. You and Paul. He might like it." She backed up toward her house, watching me all the way, as if waiting for my answer.

Why did she ask me and Paul? He wouldn't like it. Too noisy. Too many people. Too much.

But I said, "Maybe," anyway, and made sure she was inside before pulling on my helmet. It smelled like her.   Riding solo, I told myself, I could go faster. It was the best feeling.

But the feel of Daisy laughing against my back? That wasn't so bad either.

CHAPTER NINE

"What's the Big Deal, People?"

Monday, Health class was everything I expected it to be. A shit show.

I groaned when I walked in. The white board was still filled with the ABCs of STIs. And today was Herpes Simplex. The oral jokes started before I even got to my table.

None of them funny.

"You guys are disgusting, and your jokes suck," I grumbled.

"No, you suck."

I walked into that one.

Mr. York could hardly control the class on a good day. Now every description of how herpes was transmitted was accompanied by kissing and sucking noises. How it was preventable came with "look before you lick" and "suit up". Herpes' incurability came with a "bummer" and "guess you'll have to finger fuck because who knows where Daisy's been."

Hurrying on to genital warts was a total waste of time. Human Papillomavirus shots at twelve reducing the risk of cervical cancer went almost unheard because of the groans and noises cascading at the words "genital warts". I heard, "Every guy's thinking about getting sucked off at twelve but who wants a shot?"

Never mind the dozens of "sucks to be you" aimed at Daisy and me.

Mr. York gave up and dismissed class early. Chicken.

I glared at him. So much for enforcing the no sexual harassment policy.

I glared at everyone. Except Daisy and the other derby girls. I was between laughing and crying when they walked past me. But Daisy was fearless, walking with her head high, making Queen Elizabeth waves on her way out the door.

Damn.

Not like we weren't expecting this crap. My phone blew up on Sunday morning with warnings about social media and pictures online—thank you Celeste and Alice—and mean texts from people who didn't even hide who they were. I spent every moment at church worrying about whether the gossip was spreading there, too, or if Knox was being a decent human and keeping his mouth shut.

Score one for Knox's humanity, I guess. Because I didn't hear a word about me.

Other than Mom's usual fantasy narrative about her perfect daughter.

Not.

Second period AP English was bizarre. Anna Loewe sneered at me and Renee wouldn't look my way. Which was stupid because half the girls' basketball team was gay. Not that I was. Or

Daisy. But if they were okay with half the team, why get weird with thinking I was that way?

It answered that question I'd been asking myself: what if?

What if I liked a girl?

Other than Alice, I reminded myself. Like, a girl who liked girls.

What if she liked me back?

And now I know the answer.

I'd be looked at like an alien popped out of my chest and I was all about the sex.

I barely thought the last word.

It was too weird. People are thinking about me. And Daisy. Like that.

It was so... personal.

And awkward.

And not true.

We were supposed to be reading another old white guy's wish-fulfillment fantasy masquerading as literature with a capital "L"—not shy about sex *at all*—but Hemingway couldn't keep me from the thoughts spinning through my blown mind.

People were assholes.

Half the people I thought were my friends, weren't acting like it.

And now I knew what it was like for Alice when I outed her as a cutter. Or whatever that was when her pen left that nasty scar over her heart. *This* is what it felt like to be stared at, whispered about, pointed at, and get perved on in the hallway. And first period.

"Your T-shirt and basketball shorts won't protect you," Daisy had said.

They sure weren't.

Blood throbbed in my temples, and I could feel the tightening between my eyes. I ignored it. I didn't have room for a migraine with everything running through my head.

There had to be a quote for this situation posted on the walls at church. "We shall overcome"? "This too shall pass." Something by Gandhi? Or John Lennon?

It could be worse, I reminded myself. Alice had to go through being called an anorexic, suicidal, emo, whore. All I had to deal with so far was name-calling, not so subtle suggestions, requests to watch me and Daisy "do it" and being looked at like I was a stranger by some people I'd known most of my life.

Not that everyone had been like that so far.

There was that guy from choir who popped out and sang "I Kissed A Girl" with a voice like an angel.

And there were the purple-haired pierced people. I pulled out one of the thirteen-hundred or so flyers for the LGBTQ+/Straight Alliance that fell out of my locker before classes. Super supportive, sure, but seriously? Like I would fit in. Plus, the not being gay part.

Liking one person didn't make me gay.

And there was *nothing* between me and Daisy.

By U.S. History third period, I decided there were three answers to *What the fuck was that Saturday night?* more effective than "None of your business".

My options were:

A) disavowal: "I don't know what the heck that girl thought she was doing. She's crazy." But I didn't want to throw her under the bus.

B) complicity: "we're doing a social experiment for a paper on how tolerant high school students really are, because you know neither of us is a lesbian." Which sounded a lot like "some of my best friends are gay" So no.

C) the truth: "I don't get why, but who cares?"

Okay, so I cared. I just wasn't sure in what way I cared.

Not that everyone was being Captain Obvious. The Hipster Twins didn't show an interest in anything but vintage cameras, drinking out of glass jars, and pushing their thick black glasses back in place. Breaking up hadn't changed a thing about their routine.

Aaron didn't look like he knew about the gossip. Or anything, based on his red eyes. At least they were open...

Knox was back to pretending I wasn't there. That was fine with me.

Daisy's eyes were glued to the board. She leaned on one elbow, looking relaxed. What was *she* telling people? If we were going to get out of this drama, we had to get our stories straight. I should have texted her earlier, I knew that. But I felt guilty about skipping her roller derby bout.

Not that I'd ever been to one before.

But she'd asked and I didn't say no.

I'd kind of left her hanging.

Not that she would care if I was there or not.

But still.

Now my head felt like a bowling ball, the skin of my scalp prickled, and my eyeballs ached. Just what I needed. Before I knew it, I'd be vomiting in a trash can and lying in a darkened room in the school clinic. I needed caffeine and painkillers. Now.

A wad of notebook paper hit the back of my head and bounced to the floor. I hesitated for one heartbeat and then dove for it. Henderson would love to read it out loud. I crumpled the paper tight in my hand and shoved it in my shorts' pocket. I could feel people watching. Feel Knox looking my way for half a second and then back at the board.

If I'd only told him "Hell no" to seeing his band, none of this would have happened.

Basically, I told myself, it was his fault.

All I wanted was my simple life back. Rewind. Do-over. Wipe out Saturday night.

Oh no.

Points of light floated in front of my eyes. I had a minute max.

The legs on my desk screamed on the linoleum as I shot out of my seat, knocking it into the next aisle. I strode toward the door, pain radiating from every part of my head now—even

Henderson could read the signs—and down the hall to a spot I'd found when this happened before.

Mom always said you can't hide from a headache, but I tried. I attempted those breathing exercises Ms. Lamb showed me so maybe my head wouldn't feel like it was expanding and contracting like an indecisive balloon. I could do this.

After I rushed to the bathroom and puked my guts out.

My head throbbed like an idling engine that revved every time I moved. I slid my chair soundlessly up to the table and pulled out the contents of my lunch bag one by one, ignoring my sandwich. The thought of crinkling Saran Wrap made me shudder. Water, caffeine, three ibuprofen, and fifty minutes in a darkened room had helped some. I opened my yogurt and licked the lid like always, leaving me eye to eye with the whole table.

Nine pairs of eyes. On me.

"What?" I snapped. A ghost of a smirk crossed Dog Meat's face before he looked away. He *would* find this amusing. Joey looked like they were going to speak but stopped when I narrowed my eyes at them. Maddy was vibrating in her seat, dying to ask questions. I groaned and leaned on one elbow, facing the firing squad, grateful that Knox was a no show.

"Okay. Let loose the third degree. Just ask quietly. Please. My head."

Joey winced. Maybe they got headaches, too.

Maddy pointed across the table at me, her frosted pink nails refracting light. "You look like you got cut from Cross Country, not kissed by a hottie."

The flood gates were open.

Next to me Kevin put out his fist to bump. For what? Kissing a hottie, like Maddy said? Trent grinned like a fool with his shoulders hunched in his letterman jacket, barely holding in a belly laugh—it was good to see him smile. And Sarah and Grey looked at me like I was their toddler taking my first steps.

What was wrong with these people? I'd thought I'd be safe from comments sitting at my usual lunch table instead of with the Derby girls and Paul like I did last week. No such luck.

"I'd hit that," Kevin said, lifting his chin toward Daisy across the lunchroom.

The urge to hit *him* had me leaning in, angling my shoulders like I was gonna take him down. Stupid basketball jock.

"Better suit up first," Trent said.

"Really? That's what you have to say?" I wanted to say a whole lot more.

"Trent, I wouldn't," Dog Meat said.

Trent turned on him. "Shut the fuck up. We all know what, and who," he shot a glance at Maddy so raw it hurt, "you'd do." He slammed his tray, sending a plate flying across the table and to the floor. He was gone.

Dog meat wrapped his arm around Maddy. She was crying.

"Too soon, man," Eddie muttered, not meeting his friend's eyes.

Love was stupid. Trent's pain. Maddy's crumpled face. The concern in Sarah and Grey's eyes. So much drama. I had enough drama. I started to pack up my lunch. Then Joey met my eyes, theirs zeroing in on me. Did I do something wrong?

"What?" I threw my arms out, my voice boomed off the cement walls, louder than the babble and clanking plates all around me. Everybody looked. Everybody.

Crickets.

Then Eddie nodded toward my sandwich. "Gonna eat that?"

Thank you, fellow Constitution Team member for saving my ass.

"Go ahead." I shrugged, and it was like nothing happened. The babble resumed. Plates clattered. Athletic shoes squeaked. Kerry-with-a-K's laughter rose shrilly from the next table. I leaned back in my chair, letting my legs splay, tension easing out of me.

Miraculously, my headache dimmed.

Someone knocked into my shoulder from behind. Hard. I looked to my left and watched him walk on. Rude. I couldn't see his face, but he looked familiar. I saw him stop at the Derby Girls' table and lean into Daisy's space.

It was the slobbery asshole from the party. I stood up, ready to move, ready to get him out of her face. Then I reminded myself her teammates were right there, ready to back her up. He wasn't going to hurt Daisy. They wouldn't let him.

Then it hit me that I was watching the derby girls, instead of my *brother*. Paul was sitting right there, across from Daisy. The guy was invading Paul's safe zone, and that was not okay with me.

I was halfway there when Daisy pushed the guy back, speaking quietly. I couldn't make out her words. Ellie and Birgit rolled their eyes, but Sophie's fingertips were touching Paul's on the table. I slowed my steps. Me freaking out wasn't going to help Paul.

I could see the guy's face now. Josh. Daisy said his name was Josh. He glared at her.

"Whatever. You don't suck dick *that* good, Skank," he spat out.

He turned and saw me and headed in another direction.

Asshole, I thought.

Then my stomach flipped. Did Daisy really go down on that jerk before kissing me? Gross. I stared at her lips where they lifted in a one-sided smirk. How could she smile after what he said?

Daisy's smile vanished when she met my eyes. "What's wrong, Haven?"

"What's wrong?" I repeated.

Unbelievable.

"What wasn't wrong?" I wanted to say, "He called you a skank. He said you did *that*. He got in your face." But I didn't even know where to start.

Paul's blank expression came to my rescue before I said any of that out loud. Blank meant he was feeling threatened. I needed to chill.

"Oh," she said, her mouth going round as she saw I was looking at Paul. Daisy reached across the table toward him but didn't touch his hand. "Paul? You good, sweetheart?"

She called him sweetheart.

I could see him calm as I struggled with Daisy's response. She thought I was concerned about Paul. *Only* about Paul.

I don't get it, I thought, don't you care about what just happened?

Oh.

And that was my out loud voice.

Her eyes snapped back to me, one brow raised, disappearing under her bangs. "No big, Haven, drop it."

No big.

I did not get it. Did nothing get to this girl? This asshole got in her face, and she dealt with it. She waved like a princess after getting harassed in Health class about the stupid kiss. She even joked about the crude things people said to her while I drove her, or all of them, to derby practice.

I looked at her and the thing that got to me the most was wondering if she really did go down on that jerk before kissing me. I didn't want it to matter. But it did.

Her expression shifted while we looked at each other. She didn't look as sure of herself. Was what happened sinking in?

"Do you play video games?" Paul said, looking at Daisy's back.

She turned and smiled at him. "Hells yeah, I do. What do you play?"

"I have all the *Halos*, *Battlefronts*, *Zelda* games, and *Ninoku-ni*. I got them from my cousin. I don't play them anymore. Do you play *Psychonauts*? It's from two-thousand six. It's about crazy people and it just came out on PC and the next game, Rhombus of Ruin, came out on VR but I heard it's bad and I can't do VR because I have seizures and now Psychonauts 2 is out. The graphics are intense."

Wow. Go Paul.

"I've heard of *Psychonauts*. I have an older stepbrother who used to play it, but I was little, so I didn't understand what it was about. Raz was cool though."

Paul nodded. "Raz is cool. He goes in brains. *Psychonauts 2* is better. Do you want to watch me play?"

"I don't think Daisy can come," I said, preparing him for a 'no', "She has practice in the afternoons."

Where I was going to drive her.

If she still wanted me to.

Maybe the kiss thing would put her off.

Then again, nothing seemed to bother her.

My scalp tightened. And released.

"What does she practice?" Paul asked.

"I thought Haven would have told you." Daisy looked at me like I was in big trouble. "I play roller derby. So do Sophie, Birgit, and Ellie."

"I know that. But you play derby. That's not practicing. I practice chess."

"I don't know chess. My dad tried to teach me, but I sucked at it. But I don't have derby today! I can totally come over."

Ellie looked over at me where I was *still* standing and said, "The coach is out of town with Wheels of Justice."

"One of the teams. The World Champions. Five times! They have a lot of bouts on the road," Birgit added.

World Championship roller derby teams?

"Hey now," Daisy said, reading my mind as usual, "it's the fastest growing sport, girlfriend."

Girlfriend? I looked around but no one had heard her.

Daisy rolled her eyes. "It's just an expression. You worry too much. And Paul, I would love to watch you play video games."

He pounded his fist against his thigh and rocked.

She'd made him so happy.

And then she made a huge mistake. She put her arm around his waist and side-hugged him. Only for a second. I took a step closer, watching Paul for any sudden moves, for his face to betray fear or defensiveness. But nothing. He just looked away.

He. Just. Let. Someone. Hug. Him. This was big.

Mom was going to love Daisy.

And nothing was going to keep me from seeing that.

CHAPTER TEN

"I Still Don't Get It."

A one-word text from Dad after the last bell rung—so I could look at my phone without risking repercussions—changed that.

Migraine.

He didn't even need to specify that Mom had the migraine, not him. She got them a lot. Mine were mini migraines by comparison. This wasn't the first time we'd synchronized our headaches. Maybe it was like periods? But I already felt fine, just a little fuzzy at the edges of my brain.

Brain! Raz. Psychonauts. Poor Mom. She wouldn't see Daisy watching Paul play. She was down for the count. No doubt lying in a darkened room moving only when she had to heave.

I jetted to Paul's classroom after seventh and Daisy was already there. What did she have for seventh period? I didn't really know much about her. Except that she was walking with him toward me. And he was talking. And smiling.

Smiling.

I could barely hold in all the happy.

But I would. Those moments, I held them tight. The moments when Paul let go and laughed or smiled so wide it lit up everyone in the room or when he made Mom happy by saying "I love you."

They weren't Christmas, or birthdays, or special occasions, which were usually overwhelming for him. They were yogurt splatting the ceiling at our cabin after a spoon mishap. They were the tub overflowing and soaking in the hallway carpet and Paul standing there on his sock feet, his face lit up with delight. They were moments of grace. When he would express affection spontaneously.

"Hey," I said, breaking out of my thought bubble when Daisy and Paul reached me, "Mom has a migraine."

I could see what Daisy was thinking as soon as her expression changed.

"No," I hurried on, "You can come over."

"Are you sure," she said, "If she's not feeling well..."

I interrupted her. "She'll be upstairs. She won't hear a thing."

Paul repeated, "Won't hear a thing."

Daisy only looked more confused. "Are we sneaking in or something?"

I was saying this all wrong.

"No. I mean we won't disturb her. It's cool. I promise."

Paul mouthed "It's cool".

I had no idea if it was going to be cool.

But as soon as we walked into my house it was all kinds of cool. My brain fuzz went "poof" when Paul told Daisy, "Come downstairs with me," and *reached for her hand!*

Pulled back at the last second but still.

I bolted after them, missed the last step, caught the banister in one hand and swung in a wide arc before landing bad. My left ankle didn't pop or anything, but it was not happy.

But I was. Paul was letting Daisy sit beside him on the loveseat in front of the TV. He *never* shared it. He was syncing his laptop with the flat screen and the look on his face was open and excited. The throb in my ankle was nothing with all the feels flowing through me.

I wanted Mom to see this.

But, as I limped over to the armchair opposite, it might be good she wasn't here. Any little thing could tip the balance. I wanted to take a picture, but it was so not worth ruining this.

Daisy's mouth was moving a mile a minute with the volume on low. Paul stared straight ahead, but he was talking back. I could make out the back and forth. He was making conversation instead of monologuing.

All the years of ABA, and speech therapists, and special ed experts coaching him and he never mastered talking *with* instead of talking *to* for more than a couple sentences.

And he was doing it.

Daisy turned just a little, took in my tears and the smile I couldn't stop if I wanted to and I swear she looked like she felt... not the same, but that she *got* it.

"I'm done with you now," Paul announced almost an hour later.

Between watching the swirling colors of *Psychonauts 2*, studying their faces as they talked, and seeing my ankle swell, the time flew. When she shifted to stand their shoulders bumped and he didn't recoil. He'd tolerated touch again. She was magic.

"Thanks, Paul. That game is rad." She beamed at him even though he didn't look up. When he was done, he was *done*.

I followed her up the stairs to the main floor, waiting a whole two seconds before tackling Daisy, lifting her up in a hug, and shaking her side to side. Just when I realized she probably didn't want to be jostled around or squeezed to death, she surprised me.

She hugged me back, wrapping her arms around my neck and holding so tight she shook and all I could think was "she got it, she got it, she got it" and how grateful I was, and that her lips smelled like cherries, and it wasn't so bad.

It took a second for her to release me even after I set her on her feet and pulled my arms away. That second was confusing. Why did she hold on? Is this what friends did? I didn't hug my friends. Or anyone but Mom or Dad. Suddenly, I felt all kinds of awkward, and Daisy didn't say anything and that wasn't normal.

At all.

But I was sure, as we got into the Volvo to take her home, that now we'd have "the talk". The one where we got our stories straight. Where we'd laugh about the way people had nothing better to do than make a big deal about a dumb kiss on a Saturday night.

Nope. Nada. Not one word since she climbed in and crammed against the window like she couldn't get far enough away from me. The only sound was the windshield wipers' steady rhythm and wet pavement. I couldn't keep in a sigh as we turned onto her block. Daisy had done nothing but look out the window. Was she watching the raindrops race down the glass? Or waiting for me to speak first?

She never needed prompting before. Ever. When I drove her to derby, just the two of us, she told exaggerated—I hoped—stories about her life with her mom, on the track, at the tiki bar, teasing me because I was so uncool.

This was more like the time I scared her to death by slamming on my brakes. Had my hug scared her? What did it say that she could kiss me on the mouth, in front of everybody, but that *me* hugging *her* freaked her out? When *she* hugged me back. I didn't get it.

When I pulled into her driveway, Daisy hopped out and slammed the door, ignoring my "Thanks for coming over to hang out with Paul" before she disappeared inside her house.

I just sat there with the car running in her driveway, trying to reason out what happened. Even Alice made more sense than Daisy did, and she was like a thousand-piece puzzle.

Alice.

Alice!

She could translate this stuff.

The wood steps creaked under me. That part was the same. Even if the boards had been replaced and painted since January, the creaking remained. But the whole house was now dark blue and white, the landscaping was tidy, and a rocking chair sat on the porch between the two doors.

It was still weird. A bungalow shouldn't be split in half to make a duplex. At least Alice's grandmother lived in the other half now, instead of a total stranger.

I raised my hand to knock and stopped. This was a mistake. So, Daisy clammed up. It didn't have to mean anything. She could have had a stomachache or was peopled out or she was hungry. I didn't even think about making snacks! Mom would be ashamed of me.

That was when the door opened, and Alice stood there in a black *Ramones* T-shirt.

"How did you know I..." I started saying but she interrupted.

"Grendel let me know someone was on the porch. What are you doing here? Don't you have practice in the afternoons?"

Oh, right, I hadn't told Alice I quit track.

"Or is this a driving Daisy day?" She swung the door wide, the smell of dog greeting me before Grendel plodded by, surprisingly mellow considering the whole pit bull rep. I followed her in.

"I don't know. No. Yes. Sort of?"

How did I even start?

Alice held up her palm and I stopped. She called out, "Hey, Dad, Haven is here, we're going to hang in my room."

A deep voice rumbled from down the hall. "What? Are you asking my permission these days? I didn't know I had *the power*."

Was that a Darth Vader impression at the end?

"As if," Alice chuckled, "Just, you know, being polite."

"Just sayin'."

Alice rolled her eyes and turned toward her bedroom. I glared down the hall before following her, unable to see anything but his booted foot. Maybe she could get over his abandonment when her mom died, but I couldn't.

"Haven, what is up with you? You never drop by," she plopped down on her bed, "How come you're here?" Her eyes followed me as I sank down. "On my floor."

I stretched out on Alice's fake sheepskin rug, gripping the edge with my fingers. Forget dignity.

"You know I love floors." I stared at the sparkly ceiling. At Grendel staring down at me before coiling up at my feet.

She climbed down and sat next to me cross-legged. Waiting. For maybe thirty seconds.

"Do I really have to drag this out of you? This is about Daisy."

I stiffened. "Why would it be anything to do with her?"

I was about to hoist myself up, but Alice touched my hand to stop me.

Her hand.

My hand.

But it didn't feel like anything. This time.

"Come on, what's up really? You had to have a good reason to come here because you hate my dad."

"I don't..." Denial was automatic. But a lie. "No, you're right. I do hate your dad."

"And you came anyway even though he was likely to be here this time of day."

I snorted. Because normal people *work* this time of day. Responsible people. They didn't disappear at six for sound checks and spend their nights playing in punk tribute bands instead of being there for their daughters. He had no business shredding, or whatever it was bass players did, when Alice was home alone.

Not that I knew what "shredding" was, but Knox said it one time.

"Come on Haven, I can see those wheels turning. He's here now. He's doing dad stuff. Promise. His take on it anyway."

Even Alice had to admit he wasn't exactly a stereotypical father with his shaved head, full sleeve tattoos and the height and weight of a pro football player.

"Enough about Dad. What's up? What did Daisy do that was so confusing you had to come over here when you're usually out running the world or something?"

What was the deal with picking on me? It was Daisy who was acting weird.

Which, somehow, I said out loud.

"Now we're getting somewhere," Alice sat up straighter, "What happened?"

I got all the way from the asshole getting up in Daisy's business in the lunchroom to the miracle of Paul sitting beside her playing *Psychonauts 2*—Alice mouthed 'Wow'—but stumbled at the part where I space invaded Daisy.

"I just had to hug her, you know? I should have asked first. Silence is not consent and all that…"

"You were paying attention at the SlutWalk," Alice interjected.

"Shut up," I growled, "She didn't seem to mind and hugged me back. I let go and she was still holding on, so it seemed okay but when I drove her home, she got all silent and just stared out the window. What does that even mean?" I let my body relax, so gravity could take over.

Alice sat there, obviously thinking before speaking, unlike me.

"Okay," she said, "my guess is that after all that emotional stuff, Josh, and Paul, and you getting all huggy on her, she probably ran out of social."

"But she usually talks. A lot."

"She had stuff to process. I think she gets how special it is to really reach Paul."

I thought she did, too.

"And there were all the homophobic comments you both got all day. That had to be draining for both of you."

"Nothing seems to bother her. People say stuff and it bounces off like it's nothing." How did Daisy do that?

"Maybe."

"But the hug, you think that's why she went all silent on me?"

"She can't have minded the hug because she hugged you back, even if it surprised her at first. Did it give her ideas about you being interested in her, do you think?"

"Wait, what? Why would she think that?" I sat up. Grendel lifted his head to look at me. I disturbed his nap.

"Let's see," Alice counted on her fingers, "You let her be close to your brother, who you protect with every cell in your body, you invite her over to your house..."

"No, that was Paul."

"Fine. You drive her to practice..."

"Because we have a deal about that."

"Which Daisy would continue if you never gave her another ride to practice and you know it. Then you hug her out of the blue and I'm not sure I've ever seen you hug *anyone*. It's not like you've ever hugged me."

You know why, I thought. I wasn't going to hug someone I thought of *that* way.

It was too weird.

Because she didn't think of me that way.

"Give Daisy a break. She's probably confused about why you didn't make a big deal out of the kiss and then you hugged her and..."

"So, now Daisy thinks I like her or something? That's why she freaked?"

Ouch.

Not that I wanted her to think that. That I liked her. Or something.

"I wouldn't call being quiet 'freaked'. See how she is tomorrow, and if something is up, ask her."

Easy for Alice to say.

"I still don't understand why she kissed me. She said it was because she just wanted to kiss somebody. But why me?"

Alice just repeated. "Ask her."

CHAPTER ELEVEN

"Did You Really Have to Go There?"

"A girl?" Dad asked, incredulously.

"I heard a girl's voice," Mom insisted.

"Why would a girl be here?"

Dad and Mom. The clueless one-two punch of investigative parenting. Because Paul already *said* why the girl was here. Listen, people.

"To watch me play *Psychonauts 2*," Paul had stated, skirting by the dining table, and scooping up a handful of carrots and his bowl of plain pasta. He preferred eating downstairs most days but today he settled near the conversation.

Which was like waving his arms shouting, "Ask me more!" in Paul-speak. And they didn't even give him a chance.

"I think you imagined it, Kathleen." Dad gave his 'nice guy grin', dismissing both Paul and Mom in one sentence.

I kept my mouth shut. Barely.

I'd only just got in the front door from Alice's when I heard them. I was still reeling from my rollercoaster emotions around

Daisy, and unsure of Alice's advice, and was *not* going to join Mom and Dad's debate if I could get around it. Every second since I stepped through to the kitchen, I was contemplating turning around.

And since they were in the dining room and couldn't see me, I reasoned, I could probably get away with it. I took a quiet step back.

"David, I did not imagine it. I had a migraine not an acid trip. Come on Haven, I heard you come in."

Crap.

I walked over and plopped down in a dining chair opposite them.

"Who was here?" Dad asked.

Paul started humming one of the tunes from *Psychonauts 2*. Talk about an acid trip.

"You guys, it was Daisy, from school. Paul really asked her, and she really did come over and watch him play the game."

Dad perked up. "Good work, Paul, inviting a girl over."

I wanted to roll my eyes *so* bad.

"Not like that," I said, "I told you about Daisy a week ago. She's one of the roller derby girls who hang out with Paul at lunch. His *friends*. When Paul asked her to come over, she did."

Dad lowered his voice, "Paul *really* invited a girl over to hang out?"

Why was Dad asking me again? I told him. Paul told him. It's not like Paul lied!

"Honey," Mom turned to look at Dad and there was that shiny hope in her eyes. "That's big. Do you think he likes her? More than as a friend?"

It felt like a kick in the gut. Now she was going to start matchmaking Paul? With *Daisy*?

That was not going to fly.

Before I could jump in, Dad went right to the heteronormative point, "Is she pretty?"

I didn't even skimp on the eye roll.

"They're friends, you guys! What does it matter if she's pretty?"

"It might matter a lot to Paul. He's a teenage boy. It's natural he'd be drawn to someone he thought was attractive. And was a nice person of course."

Nice save, Dad.

There was no question that Daisy *was* pretty. Not like Laurie with her red curls and freckles. Or Alice, with her gray eyes and pale skin and blonde hair. Maybe my folks wouldn't even classify her as pretty because they couldn't see beyond her tight jeans and low-necked sweaters. I could hardly see beyond them at first. Hardly see *her*.

A girl with big brown eyes, almost black hair, warm tan skin, and a wicked smile. Who *saw* Paul. And kissed me for some reason that still didn't make sense. And freaked out when I hugged her!

And they were looking at me. Waiting for an answer.

"I don't know," I shrugged, "Like I'm an expert on pretty girls."

Not. Going. There.

Dad didn't even listen to my answer. He'd moved on.

"She's *kind* of an athlete. She roller skates anyway."

I had to groan at his "anyway". Like, maybe she bowled or played badminton sometimes, maybe took long walks. Not a total sloth.

I felt a little smug that she could probably kick his butt. I almost opened my mouth to tell him so but thought better of it. I almost opened my mouth to tell him what Daisy said—that it was the fastest growing sport in the world. But I didn't.

He wouldn't get it.

"We should meet this girl if she's spending time with Paul," Mom said. "You can ask her to come over on Saturday, Haven."

Yeah, no. I was in no hurry to watch Mom shove Daisy at Paul.

It was beyond gross.

And I couldn't ask her to come over. We'd have to be talking to make that happen.

How Daisy got a ride to practice for the next two days I had no idea. She wouldn't even make eye contact. And texts? Nothing.

Thursday, I glanced at her table during lunch for the millionth time—not like I was going to force my presence on her by sitting with them—and Sophie was mid-story, Ellie and Birgit listening, and Daisy...

Daisy was quiet, sitting stiffly beside Paul, who was eating French fries, hearing everything through his headphones.

"The Kiss" was old news. Mr. York finished the section on Human Sexuality and was on to Community Connection, aka volunteering, so the jokes were less crude in Health. The GLBTQ+/Straight Alliance stopped stuffing flyers in my locker and my tablemates looked at me with sad eyes.

What the hell did that mean?

And Alice kept mouthing "ask her" during Ecology.

Enough.

I felt like a stalker parking the Volvo by the Hangar when I didn't have a legit reason to be there. I didn't expect a warm welcome. Birgit and Sophie and Ellie didn't exactly shun me at school, but they followed Daisy's lead. Fleeting side-eye was about all I got. Not even a nod.

The bleachers inside were mostly empty, just the same kind of friends, family, or boyfriends, girlfriends, or whatever kind of romantic friends as last time. Same tattooed coaches with clipboards hauling stuff. Same bizarro collection of sponsors' banners overhead. A sock store. *Willamette Week*. Zinnia's Tattoos.

Even though I didn't see anyone changing out of street clothes into practice gear I looked away from where some of the players were getting ready and parked my ass on the bottom of the bleachers halfway down the Hangar and buried my hands in my pockets.

I wasn't there to stare at Daisy or make her feel weird. But, when she was done with practice, we were going to talk about the hug. And her silence. And that kiss.

Holy shit!

I threw myself back, smashing my shoulder blade into the second row up as a girl flew past, barely missing my legs and shot off the rink, went down on her padded knees, and slid a good eight feet. Players were suddenly whizzing by at ridiculous speeds and there was zero barrier between them and the stands. They could wipe out a whole row of ticketholders.

And I could be wiped out any second considering the aerial ballet move happening four feet in front of me as a girl with a star on her helmet pirouetted out of reach of a mob who'd been crowding her. She landed on the toe of one skate on the line and then hurled herself forward full speed ahead.

Wow.

I expected physicality. Elbows driven into the other team. Hip-checks as the jammers—the players with the stars I remembered—took off. Booty blocks, Birgit had mentioned them one day, when she was trying to explain the game. And stuck out skates to trip the opposing team. Even though it was an illegal move according to Ellie.

I didn't expect athleticism like this. When I came in before, after I scared the crap out of Daisy and didn't know if she needed a ride after practice, things were barely underway. Now I could see what derby really was.

I needed to go to a bout.

I hoped Daisy would be okay with that.

Big brown eyes met mine across the rink. She was sitting with five other players in red shirts. I didn't know what I expected. But it wasn't the wide smile that broke across her face, or the princess wave she gave me as she leaned into the girl next to her and said something. The girl looked at me like I was an interesting species. What did Daisy say to her?

It wasn't like she could skate on over and talk to me. This was practice.

I focused on the players on the rink. Red and purple flying by. I spotted Birgit, her height and blonde braids making it easy. Then Ellie, with her black hair and tiny frame. She was *fast*. I didn't see that coming.

Sophie was in the middle of the group blocking the purple team's jammer, her wide stance intimidating. But the jammer kept coming, ramming into her and the other blockers holding the line, then sprinted to the side and lost control, flying out of bounds, landing on her knee pads, and skidding. Again.

I was beginning to get it. Falling was a big part of the sport. Jumping and falling, or tripping and falling, or being knocked into and falling. They had to be black and blue. All of them. Maybe that was why most of them wore tights with their shorts.

Though ripped tights didn't cover much. And there were some of those.

And then I saw Daisy, the star cap pulled over her helmet, moving faster than Ellie, her arms out to block the other team, a swing to her body I hadn't seen on any other girl. She made it look... unreal. Magic almost. Her strong legs propelling her forward and side to side, crossing her skates to push to the rim faster than I could keep up.

I jumped when the bench shook next to me. A woman around Mom's age sat down, dropping a big woven bag onto the bleacher between us. She rested her arms on her knees, a long skirt pooling below the bench. Long, dark brown hair hung straight down, half-shielding her face. Was she a mom? An aunt? A coach? There seemed like a dozen of *them* on the sidelines now.

The shrill blow of a whistle and the players came to an abrupt stop. A guy on the next set of bleachers leaned forward, and I realized someone was injured. I stood to see who had taken a hard enough hit to stop the game. Was it totally wrong that I was relieved it was a short blonde girl who was limping to the side?

And not Daisy.

I was an asshole. And selfish. Pastor Sabin would be so disappointed in me.

I felt even worse when I saw the girl crying.

I leaned my arms on my knees like the woman next to me and cradled my head. Great. Now I'd picture Daisy, Ellie, Birgit, and Sophie limping to the side of the track. Every time I dropped them off.

If I got to drop them off.

"It's okay, Terri always cries when she's frustrated," it was the woman next to me, "It's not that she's really hurt. After you get hip-checked a dozen times and wipe out in the first five minutes, you've just gotta cry."

I looked at her again. "Does that mean you play? On one of the women's teams?"

She laughed, her mouth wide and open, bending at the waist. When she stopped cackling, she said, "No way. I'm a derby mom. My daughter is over there, on the red team. Killer Queen."

Oh. Crap. Daisy's mom.

Now I had to figure out something to say better than 'your daughter does derby like a boss.'

Or 'your daughter is confusing.'

Or 'your daughter is making my brother's life better.'

Nope. I came up with, "You're not worried about her getting hurt?"

I was. The skaters whipped around like hockey players weaving through breaks in the other team's defense. Or making breaks happen. Half the team had already wiped out, sliding off the track or causing a stumbling traffic jam. I didn't know how anyone played without getting a concussion, even with the helmets.

Daisy's mother eyed me up and down. "You play a sport?"

"I'm a runner. Why?" I had a bad feeling about this.

"Does anyone get hurt in your sport?" She wove her fingers together, thick with silver rings.

I nodded. Not like I would lie to Daisy's *mom*. "Sometimes. If you take a wrong step."

"And football or soccer or basketball—do people get injured in those sports?"

"Yes, ma'am," I said. Her intense look was kind of scary.

She recoiled. "Ma'am? You called me ma'am? That's a hoot." She laughed so hard she almost cried. "You are funny. Sorry for getting worked up. It just ticks me off that people are *so* concerned about girls getting hurt in derby when there are all these other ways people get hurt in team sports. Sexist hypocrisy all the way."

Yeah, I guess, is what I said, not daring to jump in with what I was thinking: those skates looked like they could crush a skull.

"Who are you here to watch?" she asked.

Saying "your daughter" would just come off weird.

"I go to school with Sophie and Ellie and..." she was looking at me funny.

"Derby names, please, when you're in the Hangar."

Okay...

I studied the shirts speeding by. It took a few circles before I got it.

"So Fine You're Mine, Give 'Em 'Ell, Git-er-done, and Killer Queen." I felt like an idiot saying them out loud. Some of the names out there were intense. Anaphylactic Shock? Toxic Haste? Big Bang Fury?

"Oh, you know my daughter! She is an amazing jammer. She must get her bravery from her father. No way I could do it."

Right, Tiki Bar guy.

"How long has Daisy been playing?" I asked.

"She's been doing derby since she was a Rose Petal, maybe ten?" I must have looked lost because she added, "The younger girls' team. These girls are the Rose Buds. And then if they're into it, they can become Rose City Wreckers—the rec' team—when they graduate. And if they're *really* good, there are the competitive teams and the travel teams. I don't think Daisy will do that though."

"Does it pay badly?"

I was serious, but you'd think I made a joke. A big one. Even the skinny guy on the next bleacher was gawking and snickering. Asshole.

"What? There are sponsors, right?" I waved toward the banners above us, noticing more businesses. Breweries, radio stations, wait, my dad's company sponsored the team, too?

Daisy's mom patted my leg. "Honey, the sponsors pay for the Hangar, the outfits, the travel costs for the teams that compete out of town. It's a nonprofit. There's nothing left to pay the players with all the youth and community programs. They all do it because they love the game."

I got that. I liked competing. But for me it was about running itself. The feeling of the earth under my feet pushing me forward. The rush of fresh air hitting my face. The sounds of the other runners catching up or falling back. The opposite of carpet-nirvana and just as good.

"I'm sorry, I never introduced myself, I'm Ruby King," she said, giving me a friendly grin. A Mom grin.

And I almost called her Ma'am again. "Nice to meet you, Mrs. King, I'm Haven."

"Ruby, please. I haven't been a Mrs. in ages. You should meet her father. He's a piece of work. Bet you can't even imagine me married to the guy." She did that double at the waist laugh again. The same laugh as Daisy's.

"Is he here?" I looked around. There were a lot of people I'd call "a piece of work" on the bleachers. Pretty much any of them qualified. The guy who laughed at me for starters.

Ruby shook her head. "He works all the time when she's not in school, so it's hard for them to meet up. He makes it to a game sometimes. Some practices. She sees him whenever she wants, it's not a custody thing, it's just that he's usually at the bar and she ends up doing homework or messing around on her phone in the backroom if she goes to see him. Not exactly the best father/daughter time."

I nodded, pretending I got it. I was lucky. Dad and I had running and sports on TV. At least we used to. Since getting the bike, I didn't run as much, and when I did run, he hadn't gone with me. Ever since I dropped track, he turned me down when I asked him if he'd like to run with me. Was he punishing me? I wondered. Or did he just not want to hang out with a quitter?

I knew he wouldn't get why I quit. He was all about winning. But at what price?

Another whistle blew. Once. Twice. Three times. Players skated in every direction, some toward the bleachers, others toward the back benches, grabbing gear. I'd never get to talk to Daisy, now. She'd be going home with her mom.

And then I saw the toes of a pair of red skates. I looked up slowly, realizing that Daisy was wearing volleyball shorts and fish-net stockings with holes in them. I had time to wonder what her mom thought of that when I saw Daisy was beaming at both of us.

"You guys met! This is the girl I was telling you about, the one I kissed at that stupid party and gave me a ride home."

I froze. This was where her mom turned on me. And killed me. Or looked at me with loathing. Or something. Something other than what happened.

"Oh, thank you! We talked and she'll never do that again."

The kiss. She was talking about the kiss. She was *talking* about *the kiss*. "Oh, okay. Me, either."

Ruby King looked at me funny, "That's good." And she patted my leg. Patted. My. Leg. "You can keep her honest."

My mouth was gaping. I knew it.

"Not that she really needs any help keeping on the straight and narrow. Daisy's a responsible girl. Always carries ID and money to get home so she doesn't have to rely on some inebriated asshole. I don't know how she forgot." She looked up at Daisy, "You *won't* ever do that again will you?"

"Never. I swear." She held up fingers in what might have been a Girl Scout sign... hell if I knew.

"And thank you," Ruby turned my way again, "For giving her a ride home. Your parents must have been upset you rode without a helmet."

Never even considered telling them.

"Something could have happened, and I'd never forgive myself if one of you got hurt."

So... she wasn't upset that Daisy was on a motorcycle. And we were all going to ignore the kiss part. I could live with that.

What I couldn't live with was Daisy not letting me drive her to practice anymore.

I guess that was a conversation for another day.

Ruby stood, pulling her skirt out from under her sandals. "Are you riding with me or the girls?" She nodded toward Ellie, Birgit, and Sophie, still talking on the penalty bench. "Is Ellie's cousin still here?"

"Yeah, he's outside doing his calculus homework. Not a derby fan." Daisy looked anywhere but at me. But she *spoke* to me. "Are you driving your folks' car or your bike?"

"My folks' car." She couldn't be planning on riding with me. Could she?

"Awesome," she held out a hand for a high five and I high fived her back on autopilot. "I'll go with Haven. If you're sure you don't mind, Mom?"

Ruby shrugged. "Fine with me. See you at home, love." And she folded Daisy into her arms, and brushed Daisy's bangs to the side to kiss her forehead. There was a scar there. A thin one from her hairline to just above her right eyebrow. I tensed, my mind going bad places. Had someone hurt Daisy?

When Ruby left, the awkward crept in. Daisy sat down next to me to untie her skates.

I meant to say, 'are you sure you want to ride home with me?'

What came out was, "How did you get the scar?"

Daisy sat up fast to face me. "Really, that's what you have to say? I haven't talked to you in days, and you want to know about my scar?"

"I... I..." guess I'd screwed up again.

And then a huge smile lit up her face, making a dimple in one cheek I'd never noticed before. "That's what I like about you, Haven, you don't hold grudges, and you care about people." She pointed to her forehead. "It's not what you think. I broke a glass when I was four. With my forehead."

I blinked.

"It seemed like a good idea at the time."

It seemed like a good idea at the time. I'd heard her say that before.

But.

"I do hold grudges. There are things I can't let go." One of my many flaws.

Daisy bumped my shoulder with hers. "There are things we shouldn't let go. Like those bitches in the lunch line that day. Grrr."

Okay, Daisy going all growly? I couldn't help but snort.

"No, I mean it. They better watch out."

"You're kind of terrifying, you know," I said.

And she was, just not in the way I was implying. Sure, I hated being on her bad side, Tina and Kerry-with-a-K should watch out. But even when Daisy and I were okay, she scared me. She was so alive, so in-the-moment, and knew who she was.

She blew out a noisy breath beside me. "I'm sorry for freaking out, Haven. It was just too…"

"In your space. I'm sorry…" I started.

"Real," she went on as if I hadn't spoken. "The intensity, I didn't know how to handle it. It was like you'd crammed every molecule of joy and gratitude you felt into the hug, and I didn't deserve it. I just watched a friend play a video game, Haven, not cured cancer. It was a lot to take in."

Yeah, I knew it wasn't curing cancer, but it was a big deal to me.

"And it was the best hug I ever had in my life, and my family, we're huggers. I had to think about it, you know?"

I knew. I was still thinking about it, too.

This time it was a friendly silence on the way to Daisy's house. She was relaxed and curved toward me instead of away. Until we pulled into her driveway. Then she pulled her knee up on the seat and sat up straight.

"Look, Haven, about the kiss. You don't have to dance around it. If you want to make sure people know you were just an innocent victim of circumstance, that's okay."

She was giving me an easy out.

"But that makes you into the bad guy. There doesn't have to be a bad guy. It was just a kiss."

My first kiss. Like ever. Never in a million years would I have imagined it would be from someone like Daisy. Someone who said things that made me want to crawl into a hole or sent my eyebrows skyward, wore whatever she wanted no matter what anyone said, and was kind to Paul.

So awesome. Daisy was awesome. And totally unexpected. And watching me.

"You're all right, Haven Alexander."

"Yeah, yeah," I said, but were we okay? I had to ask.

"Yes, Haven," she smiled at me, almost a shy one, "We're okay."

CHAPTER TWELVE

"Who Cares What I Wear Anway?"

I t was the third pink polo shirt that set me off.

We'd been in Eddie Bauer for fifteen whole minutes on Sunday afternoon, standing in the "girl" section, with Mom showing me things I wouldn't wear even if they fit, which they wouldn't. I was tall. My shoulders were wide. I'd rip anything with gathers or trim or whatever it was Mom kept showing me. And how many kinds of pink were there anyway?

"Are you going to show me anything that isn't pastel, Mom?"

Okay, that was a little whiny, I realized, but enough with clothes that looked like they belonged to a newborn.

Or anyone else but me.

And I saw right away that she wasn't in the mood for my opinions. Her back stiffened and I swear she steeled herself for battle and sucked in a calming breath. Before turning to explain reasonably why I was wrong.

At least she paused pitching pink at me.

"Honey," she started, "you can't always wear athletic shorts and a T-shirt, as comfortable as they are. There are times when you must wear something special. Dressy. You know this. Paul's graduation ceremony is coming up," Mom tapped a wooden hangar twice and mouthed 'knock wood'. "You want to look nice for his big day, don't you?"

I groaned, pushing away the light blue cardigan Mom held up.

"That thing wouldn't even cover my waist! Don't they have a tall section somewhere? And Paul's graduation is more than a month away, why are we doing this now?"

Now, as in, a gorgeous May afternoon, blue skies, and zero rain. I could ride my bike far away from clothing stores and the city and Mom.

She met my eyes. Dead serious. "Because I knew you'd be difficult and wanted to get this off my shoulders."

Ow.

Low blow.

But this was ridiculous. How could she think I wasn't going to come through for Paul anytime, anywhere? How I'm dressed at his graduation? He. Did. Not. Care. If he wasn't wearing sweatpants it would be a miracle.

"I think it's time for me to buy my own clothes."

The words just fell out, unplanned, and barely loud enough for Mom to hear above the eighties' song flowing through Eddie Bauer. Karma something.

But she caught it.

"You hate shopping. And you'd come home with the same thing you wear every day."

Saying 'So what?' would probably not help.

I blew out a calming breath of my own. "Maybe it's time I figured out what *I* want to wear." I couldn't believe I was saying it. I didn't care about clothes. It was the trying to make me *not me* that I cared about. "I'm seventeen. I should know how to dress myself don't you think?"

Not that I had any idea what I would buy. That wasn't the same thing I wore every day. Maybe Alice would help. Or Daisy...

No, that would be weird.

"But I know your style, honey. You want basic, nice, good quality clothing that can be worn every day, even the slightly dressy stuff for church. Modest, free moving, neutral." She beamed at me. "I know you better than you know yourself."

"No, you don't!" I shouted.

Or wanted to.

But it would hurt her feelings. She thought what she said was sweet.

Not kind of creepy.

The store was full of basic, nice, modest, free moving, and neutral. And okay, I might resemble that description, but coming out of Mom's mouth? Ew.

Then, I noticed better colors on the opposite wall. The "guy" side, I guessed and headed that way, reminding myself that "guy stuff" and "girl stuff" didn't mean much. They were totally blurring. Half the girls I knew wore guy stuff. Grey with her dad's dress shirts, Sarah and her long wool men sweaters from Goodwill. And Joey dressed like a twelve-year old boy.

Only cooler.

Or so Maddy told everyone, after she dragged Joey to the mall for an ambush makeover. This mall probably. Huh. I wonder where they shopped. I tugged my phone out of my pocket to text Maddy but stopped. Because Mom was following me, holding some blouse-y thing and looking at my phone.

"What are you doing, Sweetie?"

"I got a text," I lied, put my phone away and looked at some long-sleeved T-shirts in front of me then moved on to the next rack.

The fall clothes were already showing up in the mall. And it wasn't even June.

"I like these sweaters," I said, pointing to a rack of plain V-neck sweaters that looked super soft. The sign read "merino wool". Like I would know what that was. "And look, Mom," I pointed at a sale rack, "those are dressy."

And shorts. And khaki. Dad wore khaki to work. The shorts would be appropriate for graduation. If they had my size...

"Those are men's clothes, Haven. They won't fit your woman's body." She might as well have added a "duh" with that tone.

I looked down. Minus the boobs I was pretty much curve-less, and a sports bra minimized that. I held out my arms, gesturing at myself. "I don't think that will be a problem."

"Oh honey," Mom sighed. "Okay, sweaters, yes. But no on the shorts. They're built for people with a penis." She whispered the last word.

She had me there.

But.

"So, what does this mean then," I asked, and walked back to the "girl side" and grabbed a pair of thin jeans off a rack to show her, "the label says they're 'boyfriend jeans'. Do they have room for a guy's junk?"

Mom's mouth dropped open.

"What's the difference if these," I walked back to the other side and grabbed a pair of jeans that looked almost the same, "are for guys? The fabric is more durable. And look at the pockets—they're bigger!"

So they might be baggy in the crotch. That would only make them more comfortable. I hated it when things were tight there.

Not that I had any intention of wearing either of them. I was all about the shorts.

She glared at me, snatching away both pairs of jeans. "Come on Honey, you don't want people to think you're a lesbian."

The pause before I responded felt huge.

I waited for Mom to qualify her statement with "not that there's anything wrong with that" or "not that it should matter" or maybe even "*do* you want people to think you're a lesbian?"

Nothing.

I turned my back on her before I answered, pretending the "girl" T-shirts were worth looking at.

"Mom, who cares?" I said at the wall. "I mean, half the girls at school are gay or bi or pan, plus all the nonbinary and trans kids. Just like at church."

She was silent for a whole minute before finally saying grimly, "Look, life will be harder if people think you're gay. And as for the kids at school and church, if they want to sign up for that kind of trouble, that's up to them and their families. You're not."

Between the words "sign up for" like it was a choice, and "you're not" like I had no choice, I didn't know what to say. My eyes felt watery. I blinked, looking up at the ceiling to force back tears.

I couldn't help imagining how she would feel if I *was* a lesbian. Or bi.

Or liked someone.

Maybe one person.

Who was a girl.

"I don't know why we even got into all that," she said. Like it was nothing. "We're here. You need new clothes, and this store is your best bet."

No, I *almost* pointed out, there's a sporting goods store right downstairs. T-shirts, athletic shorts, Adidas flip-flops, boom! But I wasn't sure I could take what she'd have to say about that.

She went on, "Anywhere else will be full of tight shirts with low necks and shorts that show everything, and you don't need that kind of hassle either."

Either, as in, getting hassled for looking like a lesbian or hassled for looking like a straight girl who liked uncomfortable clothing? There was no winning.

I turned around and looked at her. Tears gone.

"Is *that* why you always buy crew necks for me? So I don't get hassled? I thought it was a Unitarian thing. Like not being a showoff. No designer labels or manufacturers who pay workers like crap."

I mean, not getting hassled was nice and all but I thought it was about something bigger. Not that I was supposed to hide my boobs.

Mom shrugged and wagged her head, a yes/no/maybe kind of response that left me hanging.

"Yes," she said cautiously, "it is about those values. And how you present yourself reinforces how you'll be treated. If you emphasize your breasts then that will be what others notice, Honey, not your beautiful brain."

Mom smiled and reached out, but I shifted away.

"And yes, I don't want my baby harassed. It's better not to call attention to yourself with tight clothes or long hair," she looked lovingly at my stick-straight hair to my jaw. "You don't want to look like..."

What was she going to say? A slut? A lesbian?

"Fresh meat." She made air quotes. And laughed nervously.

She thought she was daring. Scandalous.

It was gross.

"You know what, Mom?" I looked her right in the eye, "I think it's time I took over my hair, too. I want to grow it out. At least enough to have choices."

Meaning put it in a hair tie or not. But "choices" felt like a loaded word.

And I'd said it out loud.

Mom looked at me like she didn't know me. I wasn't sure she did.

CHAPTER THIRTEEN

"Why Can't Everyone Just be Normal?"

As soon as we walked in the door Mom was grabbing her yoga gear and told me she was going to the studio for her "sanity".

Back at you, I thought, as I tugged on my running shoes and changed into more appropriate shorts. I *always* wore a sports bra so no need to change that.

I waved at Dad, who'd turned me down when I asked him to join me, as I headed out and was up to a steady speed before leaving the block.

The jolt of impact.

The sound of my shoes hitting the ground.

My heart, steady but climbing.

My breath, conscious and controlled at the beginning, setting the pace.

I almost stumbled when I realized I'd forgotten my earbuds.

No music.

Shit.

Should I go back? Instead of being stuck with my thoughts.

But the thoughts were already rushing in faster than the air hitting my face and arms and legs. Faster than I could run.

Mom didn't know me. She didn't even *think* she knew me anymore.

Two blocks down.

But if she did, would she love me?

Too big a question.

I passed Knox's house. He hadn't been to church. Was he out of town?

Knox. Were we ever going to be friends again?

We used to do everything together. Why did it have to change?

I passed the park. A running path wasn't what I wanted. I wanted the pounding of the sidewalk.

Birthdays. Christmas. The cabin. Fourth of July. Knox was in all those memories. And that was over.

Paul. Paul hadn't asked about Knox. Did he wonder why he didn't come over anymore?

Paul. The derby girls. Daisy.

I turned at the next block, slowing as I ran down the ridge, so I didn't fall headlong.

Like Alice almost did. In an ice storm. High. She wasn't like that now. And she had Finn.

The sidewalks leveled off. I passed Peaceful Yoga. I hoped Mom was cooling off better than I was.

I ran faster. Pushing myself away from Mom.

She was trying to protect me.

By making me bland.

I was bland. Blonde and bland.

The dappled shade from the trees along Grant Place reminded me of the SlutWalk. The huge trees overhead. The patterns on the sidewalk. But it was quiet except for the sound of my feet, a car radio in the distance, and the snip, snip, snip as a woman trimmed a bush in her yard.

Bland.

Why did Daisy say I was a babe?

Daisy was not bland.

Daisy *was* a babe.

I took a few deeper breaths. Blew them out slowly.

And according to Mom's standards "fresh meat".

Meeting each other face-to-face might not be such a good idea.

For me and Daisy both.

After my shower I checked my phone again. Another link to the reels on Instagram. Mom was totally going to hear about this from some stupid Booster parent. According to the texts I got all weekend, Daisy and I were Willamette High's newly elected poster girls for Pride. Again.

And the videos were nothing. A short clip of us toe-to-toe talking at the Hangar, another of me talking with her mom on the bleacher, a third of us walking to the Volvo. Totally platonic.

But "The Kiss" was only a week old, so the rumors were back in action bigtime. And so was the video that asshole took at the party. Being shared. And shared. The texts poured in. The ones from Laurie bugged me the most. We used to be friends.

What the hell do you think you're doing hanging around with that girl again?

Seriously, Laurie, "that girl"?

Don't you care what people think?

This is what you dump track for??

"This"? What the ever-loving fu...

I'm telling your mom.

I'm serious.

She so would. Even though it was wrong, unfair, and inaccurate. I quit track weeks ago. Before I knew Daisy. It had nothing to do with Daisy. Or anybody on the team. And *everything* to do with Coach Morgan.

And I was not going to tell Laurie about *that*.

Not that keeping my mouth shut was doing me any favors considering who bumped into me, literally, on Monday morning. T-boned me, in fact, holding a clipboard, as I was coming away from Paul's classroom after drop-off. Not subtle at all.

I was not in the mood to deal with her. She might look like a perky tennis player who'd bulked up, all tanned skin, blonde ponytail and determined smile during practice, but she wasn't. *She*, I noticed for about half a second, was wearing khaki shorts that maybe I could have fit into and was seriously pissed off. Still.

"We might not go to state because you dropped out," Coach Morgan started, low enough that no one else could hear,

"Coach Johnson told me you were a team player. I guess she was wrong."

I pushed my hair out of my face. "I am. I'm all about the team. Are you?"

She looked confused. Of course she did. It's not like she *knew* I heard her.

"You're a natural born leader, Haven. And you and Knox work well together to get the athletes psyched up, organized, trained, and on task, I saw it during Cross-Country, and according to my predecessor you were the same for Track. But not this year."

For one thing, I could have told her, Knox was barely looking my way, much less talking to me. We would not be good co-captains. For another, no way was I going to add gold stars to this woman's resume.

But I went for the lie. It was becoming a habit.

"I'm sorry," I said, not at all sorry, "But I wouldn't be able to keep my grades up if I did Track. Latin is kicking my butt."

Only a little lie. Latin *was* kicking my butt, but I'd make time for Track if she wasn't a backstabbing, self-centered asshat who only wanted the W and not for the good of the team.

I thought about telling her what I heard, but I didn't want to give her the oxygen.

"And next year?" she pushed, "Are you doing Cross-Country for the whole season or dropping out after four practices?"

"I don't know," I said, "Is everyone on the team getting a chance to compete? What percentage is on the active roster?"

"What are you talking about? Everyone competes in Cross-Country."

"Which is why I love it."

"Yes, fine," she interjected, "But you were born for Track, Haven."

"And I love my teammates in Track," I went on, like she hadn't spoken. "Don't they all deserve a chance to shine?"

"Come on, Haven. Only the best athletes get to compete. You earn your spot in Track."

I thought about telling her I heard her. I really did.

But getting into it now? Before Health? There wasn't enough time.

The first bell rang.

Decision made.

"Oops. Gotta go," I said, looking straight into her eyes.

She kept eye contact. "We'll talk again."

Yeah, we would.

It was gray outside during Health and AP English, so it wasn't hard to focus. Even though I was still pissed off. The sun finally came out during third period. Making everyone want to be anywhere but in a classroom. Mr. Henderson was fuming by the time he got the class to focus. By fourth period I was having life regrets.

I should have ridden my bike.

I should be running this afternoon.

I should lie in the sun during lunch. Have a moment alone. Commune with the earth or whatever. Shake off the Coach Morgan ick.

But I also didn't want to disappear from the lunchroom without knowing Paul was good.

Then I would go. Find a sunny spot far from everyone. And not think about anything.

Or so I thought.

I forgot that the purple-haired pierced people might be back. At my table. In the flesh. I swear there were balloons last week and a whole posse; this week it was just CeCe and a couple of earnest students with dyed hair and political T-shirts. There weren't even any fliers in my locker this morning or I'd have been prepared for this.

They'd pretty much given up on me while Daisy gave me the silent treatment. But now, according to Insta, we were talking again. So, CeCe was back. Right where she was a week ago, in a chair next to the head of the table—my spot—her friends a little way back. They had the non-intimidation we're-all-cool thing down.

As if I'd be intimidated by this tiny person with a fauxhawk, practically vibrating in her seat, the holes in her jeans exposing a whole lot of skin.

Thank goodness only on her legs, I saw, when I sat down. I could still see some boxers as I made myself comfortable and gave her my full attention. Cartoon kittens. Last week it was sushi.

She seemed nice enough if *way* over-caffeinated.

I wondered if she'd invite me to their Friday lunches in the old French classroom again, tell me about the latest guest speaker. Remind me the lunches were for queers of all kinds *and* their straight supporters. And wink at me again.

I was getting tired of people thinking they knew me better than I knew myself.

Last week, when I didn't jump on the offer, CeCe and her two purple-haired, pierced people, two Soccer players, a drama geek, Connie from Cross Country, and the president of the sophomore class just left.

Now I figured we had to go through the same routine.

"CeCe," I looked her in the eye, "it's super cool you want me to join your club, but I'm not gay." Not enough to go to French classroom.

Her leg jumped in place as she sat facing me. I felt bad.

I almost did the stupid 'a lot of my friends are gay' to prove I wasn't an asshole in disguise. Instead, I said, "I'm sorry."

I wasn't even sure what I was apologizing for. Letting her down? Not being who she wanted me to be? Rejecting her offer of friendship? Being a coward.

She sighed.

"Okay, Haven. But if you just want to come hang-out, you know where to find us. We're fun people." She stood up, still looking at me. Like *she* was sorry. Weird.

They *looked* like fun people when they came by last week. I mean, not like the usual people I hung out with at school, not nice, basic, neutral, modest or whatever. Knox would probably think they were "not like us". But they were willing to put it out there. To be themselves. Like Daisy did. I had to admire that.

"Thanks," I muttered, touched, and guilty for letting her down.

I looked away from CeCe and her friends' backs, suddenly aware that CeCe was, ironically, wearing a pink polo shirt, and saw Knox frown and push away his tray. I don't know why he even bothered coming to this end of the table if he couldn't stand looking at me.

But Maddy was beaming at me for some reason. And Grey was giggling. And Trent gave me the chin tip. What the hell?

Joey was thoughtful enough to say something.

"I think someone wants to talk to you," they said, barely holding in a laugh.

I felt a finger poke my shoulder.

I turned and looked up into big brown eyes.

And whoa. That was a lot of skin below her neck and in my face. And everyone else's, I realized, ready to ream the first asshole with something to say about it.

Yup. Mom would absolutely consider Daisy "fresh meat". Not a nice, neutral, modest, or as far as I could tell, comfortable piece of clothing on her. But if she wanted to rock a pair of pants that looked like leather, a sleeveless sweater that showed her bra and short boots with bat wings on them—because how could I not look—that was her business.

"Hi," Daisy said, leaning in with her hands on her knees, which didn't make the boobs in my face thing better, "I don't have practice today. Can I come over after school?"

"What?" I couldn't have heard her right.

"Can. I. Come. Over. Today. After. School."

I had the insane—and maybe kind of hysterical—desire to laugh. She sounded like a preschooler but looked twenty. Putting her words together took a second.

Oh...

"Paul asked you over. Yeah, it's a good day," I said, which was another moment of insanity because wasn't I freaking out yesterday about the idea of Mom and Daisy in the same room? What was wrong with me?

I did my best not to focus on the purple lace poking out underneath the pastel pink sweater. The sweater did *not* look like baby clothes on her. I focused instead on her tan face, her round cheeks, long nose, and red lips. The tiny wrinkles at the corner of her dark eyes. I swear her pupils were bigger than other people's.

"No, Paul did not ask me to come over. But I'd love to try a round of Halo with him." She turned halfway and waved at him where he sat next to Sophie. Then she straightened, rocking on her heels. "I just thought we could hang out."

And I sat there. Mute. Kind of still stuck on her face. Dad *would* think she was pretty.

Daisy gave me a look. "So... Haven? Is the answer yes or no? 'Cause you look like you're not sure."

"Umm, yeah, I mean, you can hang out," I said, suddenly aware of my audience. Welcome to the Haven and Daisy show. I was surprised I couldn't hear laughter down at the end of the table.

She raised one eyebrow. I think. "Are you *sure*?"

"Yes!" Oh God. Mental face palm. Could I have said it any louder?

"I'll meet you at Paul's classroom then?"

I nodded, not sure what else to say.

"Okay, babe, see you there." And she skipped off, rubber soles squeaking and bat wings flopping. "Hey Paul, guess what, I'm coming to your house after school."

Forehead meet table. Yes, they were my friends, but not one of them was ever going to let me forget that Daisy had just called me "babe". They didn't even have to say anything. I could feel their thoughts.

"I don't bug you about your relationships, I mean friend-ships," I said, giving all of them a glare when I sat up. Knox was gone. When did he go?

"Freudian slip," muttered Kevin.

I glared at him, ignoring the laughter from the other guys.

"She just says stuff like that."

"Right," Trent said, pretending to mean it.

"You all suck, you know that? How about we hassle someone else for a change?"

"We're not hassling you," Joey said, but they were smiling all the same.

"Oh yeah, we are," Dog Meat said with a laugh.

Assholes. Only two and half hours of school to go.

CHAPTER FOURTEEN

"Who Said I Wanted to Go?"

I just stood in the doorway, watching Daisy zip off her bat boots, toss them into the shoe basket, and follow Paul toward the basement room like she lived there. It felt *different*. What was up with that?

But she left me behind like I didn't matter. So much for hanging out.

I was so confused...

Snacks. I should get snacks. I totally forgot last time. Mom would have been ashamed of me. This time she was going to be mad.

I got out the stepladder and raided her secret stash of Twinkies and Ding Dongs from the cupboard over the fridge, then grabbed carrots, fish crackers, three bottles of water, and a load of sugar snap peas for Paul. As I tried to figure out how to get it all downstairs, I reminded myself to replace Mom's Hostess hoard before she noticed. We all pretended we didn't know because it was her special thing. Like the only unhealthy thing she put in her body.

I *had* to remember to hit up a 7-11 tonight...

I didn't miss the bottom step this time and got the pile to the coffee table safely. It was worth Mom's potential wrath. Daisy pounced on the Twinkies as soon as Paul paused the game. And Paul knocked into her as he dove for the fish crackers. *And he didn't mind*. They were like... normal.

Not that I will ever use that word out loud again.

"Thank you, thank you! These are heaven." Daisy took another bite and considered the Twinkie like it was something fancy on *The Great British Baking Show*, only with finger licking. She looked up at me, her smile up to her eyes, full of life and joy and the world tilted.

I stood there too long, too quiet, too focused. She patted the love seat beside her. I almost did it. Shoved myself in the gap between Daisy and the arm rest. But that would be weird.

Right?

I sat down where I stood and grabbed a Ding Dong, peeling off the edge of the chocolate cake carefully. Avoiding Daisy's strange look.

"The floor? Seriously?"

I frowned. "I like the floor."

I heard a sigh. "Whatever you say. Ready Paul?"

I looked up. Daisy was looking at the screen, moving the controller, and caught up in the game. I might as well make myself comfortable, I muttered under my breath, stretching out next to the loveseat on my back. I closed my eyes to Daisy's laughter.

"Can I get another bottle of water, Haven?"

I opened my eyes and looked up. Daisy was leaning over me. How long had she been there? And... the words wouldn't come. Her long, dark hair swung forward. It was kind of hard to speak when she was standing there.

She tilted her head. "Are you okay?"

Umm. "Yeah. How long have I been asleep?"

"An hour. Approx. Paul's killing it at *Portal* now."

I was way too comfortable to move. "You should try this," I said, feeling stupid as soon as the words were out. I suggested she lie on the *floor*. It wasn't even carpeted.

"Okay," she said, not skipping a beat. She was horizontal before I registered that she. Was. Going. To. Do. It. When she was settled with her hands on her belly, she turned her head toward Paul. "I'll get up and watch more in a few."

I looked at her exposed neck. She had a mole just under her hairline...

"Are you falling asleep, Haven?"

Daisy's foot nudged mine. She'd turned so she was looking *right in my face*. I suddenly felt very awake. And speechless. I think I got out "Umm" aloud this time.

"I went upstairs to find the bathroom. What was up with the framed montage over the sofa?"

Oh. "I know. It's weird."

"It's not weird. Your parents are proud of you," she said.

"I guess."

"I noticed the glass case by the front door. You were in Little League, too?"

Yeah, she was teasing me now.

"Weren't you?" I could tease, too. Take that.

"Hell, no. I played the flute once. And won an essay contest. Oh, I was in a bowling league in middle school before the place had to be shut down because of Covid. I kinda miss it. I was pretty good. And the shoes were fab'."

"I like bowling."

She grinned at me, her breath warming my cheeks. I don't think I'd ever felt that before. It wasn't like getting breathed on. More like breathing with. And before I could think that through, she poked a finger to the tip of my nose, said, "Boop," and jumped up. I could hear her say, "Can I have a turn?"

And Paul said yes.

I heard a voice from the top of the stairs, "Haven?"

Oh crap. How long had Mom been home? I jumped up and grabbed the wrappers off the table and crammed them into my pocket before jetting upstairs.

"Mom?" I found her in the kitchen, hoping she wasn't digging for Twinkies, and I was in trouble big time. Hoping she was in a good space. Because meeting Daisy mattered.

She was leaning against the counter, all casual. Then stated the obvious. Because from where she was standing, she could see our front entry directly. And the batwing boots poking out of the shoe basket.

"There is a girl in our basement with Paul."

I'd have expected a smile to go with that statement. Isn't that what she wanted? Instead, she looked... thoughtful.

"It sounds like she and Paul are having a good time."

"I told you before, Daisy's great." Mom didn't respond so I added, "And totally trustworthy." Code for 'not going to freak out if Paul did something unexpected'.

She turned toward me, resting her arm stiffly on the counter. "And not the point, Haven. You're not supposed to be home. You know, I forgot and went to your school and lo and behold, no Paul. No car in the parking lot. And then I remembered you'd dumped track weeks ago. For what? To do nothing? To drive those girls to practice? To bring that girl here? For Paul?"

And there was the magic word. Paul. If I played that up, I'd probably get a pass, and she'd drop the Track thing for the moment. It would also be a lie. She wasn't here *only* for Paul.

But damn, part of me wanted to beg Mom for forgiveness for quitting Track. Be a good little pony and do all the tricks. Run, Haven, run. Jump, Haven, jump. Go faster. God.

"Look, this is important, honey..."

'Honey' that was a good sign.

"You need all the extracurriculars you can get."

Those words were not a good sign. I knew this speech by heart.

Maybe I could cut it short. "You know volunteering is more important on applications," I interjected, "And the ACT."

She took the bait.

"You should start volunteering in the nursery for first service again. You did well enough on the ACT. Could have been better if you'd studied more..."

In the fall. On top of classes and being co-captain of Cross Country and peer counseling and starting my college application essays because Mom said you can never start soon enough. Yeah. Sure.

"But things like Track Team count. We need all the scholarships you can get. A four-point GPA isn't good enough anymore. I didn't mean for it to be this way, but we can't take the chance."

Nope, didn't take the bait.

"I hate that you do this, Mom. Pull the 'I'm so old' card. You aren't any older than the other moms..."

She cut me off, "I get the senior discount at Fred Meyer for God's sake."

"And you do yoga and have friends and learn new things," about autism and epilepsy and Tourette's, "and that's what keeps you young. There is nothing wrong with you."

"But you know why this is so important."

"Stop. Don't even go there." Oops. That was my out loud voice.

She growled. "Don't even go there? Do you think I want to go there? Do you think I want to be worried about the future all the time and wonder if your brother will end up homeless because he can't take care of himself, and you aren't able to get a job that supports both of you? Our savings will only go so far."

I felt the weight on her shoulders spread to mine.

"I don't even know what is happening with you lately."

Me, either. Why couldn't I just tell her that? Use my out loud voice for *me*.

Her face softened. Maybe I could.

She sat down on a kitchen chair, and I sat next to her, tapping her knee with mine. "This is a different Haven I'm seeing lately."

Yes, Mom, I am different. And I don't get it at all.

But I had to try. "Mom, I'm..."

"Haven, can I get that water?" Daisy was there. Framed in the doorway. In all the flesh. She looked from me to Mom. Waiting.

I jumped up. "Mom, this is Daisy, my friend."

Paul came up behind Daisy, a tic bringing his shoulder to his jaw. He stood close to her. And Mom didn't miss it. "My friend, Haven."

Mom smiled tentatively. "Your friend, Paul."

And my moment was gone.

Being Paul's "friend" made everything okay. Mom stopped looking at Daisy like a specimen—'cause she totally had been—and started looking at her with interest. I couldn't take it.

"Hey," I made an obvious glance at my smart watch, "I think it's time to take you home. You had that thing, right Daisy?"

She played along like a champ. "Right."

She did a great job at "nice to meet you" and "see you again soon" and a half-hug for Paul that he didn't return but didn't seem to mind. Mom's eyes lit up as she took it in. I grabbed my keys, slapped my pocket to make sure I had my wallet, and ushered Daisy out the front door before Mom played up the Paul angle again.

Daisy and I just looked at each other before getting in the Volvo. What was there to say? Mom had picked a side, and it wasn't mine.

CHAPTER FIFTEEN

"I'm an Asshole."

It was a sucky day that was suckier by the second.

First, it started pouring as soon as I got to school. On my bike. Mom was going to flip. I was stuck walking or getting picked up until the rain stopped. Or lose my bike until school was out.

No way.

Second, Paul saw something distressing on a student's cell—*YouTube* at school? Really? The Special Ed' kids *did* get to have their phones on but jeez—and banged his head on his desk. No injury or anything, just enough to have to call his emergency contact to notify them. And if Mom or Dad don't answer their phones, that's me. Got that news in second period.

Nothing gets the heart racing like being sent to the office because of "an incident".

And now the fire bell rang.

Henderson yelled directions as students just grabbed their stuff and took off. From what I could see they were heading out of the building however they could. The heck with the safety plan. The hallways were thronged with students strolling, running, skipping, walking, and shouting. And the staff were shouting back.

'What would happen if there really *was* a fire?' I thought as I made my down the hall, ignoring the shoulders and backpacks in my way. Or an earthquake? Or a school shooting? Did no one read the evacuation protocol posted at every exit? Which was a stupid question because obviously not.

I kind of had a thing about evacuation protocols.

I trusted Mr. McElroy to get Paul's class out. They had easily accessible exit doors almost no one used, and they weren't on the main fire drill route. Naomi and the rest of the staff would take care of them.

So long as some asshole didn't ram into them on his way out.

Since it was a sucky day, I wouldn't be surprised.

Outside, I barely had time to pull on my hoodie before rain was dripping down my hair and onto my T-shirt. I headed for the football field where we were *supposed* to gather. If we had to stand out there for more than five minutes, I'd be sopping wet.

Which was going to happen. Since half the school decided to skip out and leave campus instead of assembling. "The Lecture" from Vice-Principal Michaels was any time now.

And *she'd* have an umbrella. Because *she* knew the fire drill was coming.

I was surrounded by freshman and sophomores. No Juniors or Seniors. No one I knew. Not even Knox, who was all about the rules.

Until I felt someone behind me and *her* voice broke into my thoughts. Daisy.

"Hey, Haven."

And I remembered; she'd texted me that she didn't have practice, so I didn't need to drive them today. That was why I rode my bike.

I grumbled because look how that turned out. I turned about to ask her what was up.

And had zero words. Because she was *right there*, and I was looking at *a lot* of wet skin.

I blinked. And blinked again. Because I didn't know what to say. I thought I ought to say *something*... Like offer my hoodie maybe. Because the rain was making her jeans that much tighter, and the stupid biker jacket she had on wasn't even to her waist and did nothing to stop raindrops from streaming down her neck toward the deep V of her not-so-fuzzy-anymore sweater.

And she didn't seem to care. Even though she was obviously into her "look". Girls all around us were squealing about their hair and makeup and clothes but not her.

I did not get girls. Especially Daisy.

Her shoes squelched on the fake turf as she shifted her weight. "I'm starved. Do you want to go to my house and raid the fridge?" She waggled her eyebrows at me—she must have gotten a trim because I could see them under her bangs now—like she had the mother of all refrigerators at her place.

My "no" was out of my mouth before I even gave it a thought. What would Henderson think if I didn't show up again? What would everyone else think if I didn't show up and neither did Daisy? I'd be hearing about it at lunch for days. And I was already going to be in big trouble with Mom for riding my bike this morning and not checking my weather app.

What were we going to do, walk to her house in the rain?

"Come on," she said, tilting her head and looking me in the eyes. It was unnerving. She was unnerving.

"I don't want to get marked absent if I don't get back before the drill is over."

"True. But homemade macaroni and cheese. Like *really* good mac and cheese..."Good try Daisy.

"Henderson would love to give me another detention." And Mom would hate it.

"Well," she drew out the word, "I'm calling in a favor because I'm not going to make it through the day if I don't eat. Now."

"Calling in a favor." She had to use those words.

And I owed her. Only yesterday Paul had been at the derby girls' table, talking with *all* of them—I could hear his voice from across the lunchroom, he was jazzed about something—while I argued with Knox in the doorway about quitting Track and Daisy calling me "babe" and never even made it inside until five minutes were left of lunch. And they were still there. The longest he'd made it through the hour since he started sitting with them.

I didn't sit with them most of the time because he'd be quiet when I was there. A sibling thing, I guess. And I didn't want to take that from him, even if it felt weird, like I was ignoring him. Them. Her.

Even if I didn't feel like I owed her, she was my friend.

I couldn't believe I was even considering this.

I *did* have my spare helmet.

"Please?" She gave me Bambi eyes. It wasn't right. Her mascara was smudging a little; it only made her eyes look bigger.

"Fine, but it won't be fun in this rain," I said. "And I'm dropping you off. I can't afford to skip."

She sang the words, "Your loss," and turned and wove straight through the sea of people crowding the football field, sure that I'd follow her.

It was a quick shot to her house, maybe five minutes, so I could get back maybe before anyone noticed, I thought. The sun broke through the clouds right as I rode up her driveway. It blew me away the first time I saw it in daylight. Daisy's house was purple. Like Crayola "Blue Violet" purple. It still kind of wigged me out.

My house was all about the Colonial Blue. Boring.

Daisy shoved me in the shoulder after she swung off my bike. "So, my mom likes purple. Are you coming in or what?"

I looked at Daisy, then at her front door, a wild sunflower color.

I shouldn't.

Absolutely definitely shouldn't.

But as Daisy pulled off her helmet, her hair wet and dark over her shoulders, thick and wavy at the ends, I had a hard time looking away. Without her ponytail she looked younger. Like a teenage girl. Not a pin-up or someone in a comic book.

I didn't know what to do with that. She'd taken out her hair tie the other times she rode on the back, but I didn't really notice then. She was just different this time.

Was I coming in? I blinked a few times, getting my brain on track. And walked after her without a word.

"Thanks! If you wait a minute for me, I can ride back with you." She smiled over her shoulder as she threw open the front door, like she already knew my reaction.

Whoa. Holy sensory overload. Every wall was a different color, and art was everywhere and there was stuff. So much stuff. Stacks of books and magazines. Metal desk trays overflowed on the coffee table and on a shelf by the front door. There was a small blue folded sheet on top of one of the piles.

Daisy's grades. I could picture her mom opening the envelope.

Daisy was more like a real girl all the time.

Was it just me who was noticing?

She threw her wet jacket onto the couch and continued walking. I picked it up, afraid of the fabric getting ruined, but Daisy came back, plucked it out of my hand and threw it down on the couch again.

"Don't worry. I live here," she said in a whisper, "the couch can take it."

I followed her toward the kitchen, weaving around furniture and potted plants. It was like the Botany class green house. I spotted all the specimens I cited in my final paper last year: African Violets and Ficus and Cyclamen and Orchids.

Daisy stopped in front of the kitchen, blocking the entrance with her body. "Don't judge," she said, and stepped aside to let me walk in.

Yellow green walls surrounded a pink checkerboard floor that wasn't swept and there was a smell that might have been over-ripe fruit. Or, as I looked around, dirty dishes. They were piled in the sink and on top of an aqua blue stove that was probably way older than Dad.

"I was supposed to do the dishes this morning..." her voice trailed off.

I'd never been in such a crazy house. It wasn't like a hoarder's house. The piles were neat, and you could walk through without a problem, it was just, colorful, and *lived in*.

Daisy fit right in.

She hip-checked me out of the way and I bounced against the wall by the fridge. It was pink and maybe as old as the stove. And *small*.

The whole house was small.

But the fridge held a deep-dish glass container with the best-looking homemade macaroni and cheese I'd ever seen. Damn.

"Told you," Daisy said with a grin, leaning one hip against the counter. "Sure you don't want to have some?" She waved the dish under my nose.

Oh, man. This was wrong.

I needed to get back. But my mouth said something different.

"If you're sure it's okay with your mom."

"She's cool if I have a friend over. And I have to feed you if you're here. It's like a rule. Not that I have any Twinkies. My mom doesn't allow that stuff in the house."

Mom didn't either. For anyone else. But Mom and Daisy's mom? Nothing in common.

Daisy popped the container into the microwave. When she pulled it out it smelled like heaven.

She rested one foot against the cupboard, her elbows on the counter. I didn't think her clothes could stretch like that...

Hold up.

"Daisy, you're soaking wet. You need to change." Hadn't she noticed?

"Yeah, yeah, you're not exactly dry as a bone. I'll change in a minute." She looked straight at me, "I've been thinking. You should probably know there were rumors about you before I laid one on you at that party."

"What do you mean? What rumors?" The kitchen suddenly felt smaller.

"Come on, Haven, you were all over Alice from the beginning of the year…"

"I was not! We weren't even friends then." Not at the beginning.

"You were all up in her business."

I wanted to disagree.

"It wasn't like that." I didn't need Daisy all up in my business either.

She straightened up, a Cheshire Cat smile on her cherry lips. "Why do you think I kissed you at that party?"

Good question. "You said you just felt like it."

She crossed the tiny kitchen, and she was right there, just air between us and it was very awkward and what was she doing…

She placed a hand on the wall on either side of my head. "I wanted to see what you'd do."

I stood up straighter. I should have known. She'd messed with me just to get a reaction.

"And I wanted to kiss you."

I had just enough time to mutter, "But you're straight," before she was a breath away.

"Not that straight," she murmured, and leaned up and kissed me again, pressing her whole body against mine. Fuzzy sweater. Damp jeans. Skin.

She was warm and soft, her curves unavoidable and her hands were in my hair, pulling me closer and it scared the shit out of me and I should move away I should push her away I should tell her I'm not like that I should tell her to stop all I'd have to do is turn away and she wouldn't be kissing me anymore.

I didn't turn away. I didn't think I could.

She slanted her lips, and she was moving her mouth and oh my God she was kissing me and holding me and my hands didn't know what to do and my mouth didn't know what to do and I should run away from her.

I didn't.

My hands moved to her waist, sliding up enough to touch the ends of her thick wet hair. And then she did this thing, and my mouth cracked open, and she was breathing me in and oh my God.

I felt it to the tips of my toes.

I pulled my head back. No. No. Too much. Wrong. Right. No.

I didn't want to hurt her feelings. I didn't want to give her the wrong idea. I didn't want to be Daisy's experiment either.

It didn't feel like an experiment.

I turned my head. She moved her lips under my jaw, below my ear and I almost lost the use of my legs, slipping down against the wall, my hands sliding down to her waist. Wow. Just Wow. But.

I firmly pushed her back and she let me, pulling her arms from around my neck and letting them hang by her sides. She looked up at my face with those ridiculously large brown eyes, and it was hard to find words. Her lips turned up again. Not as red as before. Was it on me? I put my hands to my face, wiping away the kiss.

I couldn't wipe away the feeling of it.

"Now that was a kiss, right?"

I didn't know a voice could be like that. Like a touch. *My* voice was nonexistent. I didn't know what I should feel. Should I be outraged? Embarrassed? Pretend it never happened? But oh boy, it happened. I focused on the macaroni and cheese on the counter. It had to be cool now. It had to be fourth period now. I was in so much trouble.

"I should go." I felt kind of awful. I did offer a ride there and back, sort of. It was implied when I walked in the door, wasn't it?

Her smile fell. "Don't be like that, Haven. Stay and eat with me. I won't eat you."

God. Why did she say stuff like that? And how could she act like everything was normal?

"I don't get it, Daisy. Why? Why did you do that?"

"I thought we covered that. And you kissed me back."

"No, I didn't." Yeah, I did.

"Whatever you have to tell yourself, babe. Want some?" She pulled a fork out of the drawer and poured half the mac and cheese onto a plate and handed it to me.

I looked at the plate and at her, totally confused. "Thank you. And don't call me 'babe'."

"Why not?" she leaned against the counter and ate from the container.

"I don't get it. You go out with guys." There. She couldn't argue with that.

I thought.

"Eh, they don't want to be *with* me, just hook up." She shrugged.

"But..." I shook my head. I still didn't get it. Why wouldn't they want to be with her?

"And it feels good. No strings attached."

"Is that what this is? You're trying to hook up with me? You could have any guy you want, why mess with me?"

This was unreal. She was totally composed while I was freaking out.

"You're cute." She tossed it out there like it was nothing. She thought I was cute. "And you're nice. I like that. A lot of girls are assholes to girls like me."

I was kind of an asshole. Didn't she see that? And what did she mean by "like her" anyway?

"I am an asshole," I admitted, staring at the floor.

"You *want* to be an asshole, but it's not in you, even if you do think I should cover more skin."

Umm. The floor. Keep my eyes on the floor.

"And I don't want 'any guy'. Not to keep. You," she put her hand over my heart. I looked at her cherry red nails. They were short. "You are a keeper. You have the bluest eyes." She moved even closer. Peering into my face.

My heart thudded against her palm, my legs felt funny, like I wasn't getting enough oxygen, which was probably because I was holding my breath. I drew in air, panicked and frozen.

"Hey, we should get back," she took the plate out of my hand and set it in the sink, like nothing had happened. Like my whole world hadn't been turned upside down.

Because I liked that kiss. Too much. Too much to ever admit.

We walked back through her living room, and I barely noticed a thing. Not while she disappeared to change, not while we walked outside, not while we crossed the tiny front yard.

I swung my leg over the bike and Daisy followed. The sky was blue and bright now.

It could have been my imagination, but it felt like Daisy was holding on tighter than ever, her dry jeans against my legs, her front leaning into me, and I felt her breath on the back of my neck, and it was weird that I didn't mind how she invaded my space.

But I didn't.

Not at all.

CHAPTER SIXTEEN

"I Don't Know Anything Anymore."

I opened my mouth to give my standard speech to the freshman on the chair next to me in the library. Totally going to suggest joining a team or a club or an after-school activity and... stopped. Was that always the go-to? Just because I'd been on fast forward all my life didn't mean it was a one-size-fits-all cure for loneliness and adolescent angst.

And suggesting he become a joiner in May? Why had I never seen that that was insulting? He wasn't stupid. He'd had almost an entire year to decide whether choir or Science Club or the Dragon Boat Team was going to be a life changer for him. Or any of the other activities advertised on every single surface inside Willamette High and praised to high heaven during morning announcements.

Maybe *I* was having adolescent angst. I was pretty sure all those teams and clubs and after-school activities wouldn't put me together again. I was questioning everything, especially why I thought I could or should offer *anyone* advice.

I felt like smacking myself on the forehead because I'd done this Sister Mary Sunshine shit to Alice in the fall, following her up the hill toward her work one day, pushing team sports when that wasn't what she needed.

And this poor kid was staying silent, waiting for me to say something, because Ms. Lamb thought he could use some peer counseling. He probably couldn't wait to get away from me. Or—I looked over at him again and noticed his eyes had circles under them, like he wasn't sleeping and should maybe lay off the *Mountain Dew*—he could use an actual expert.

And that wasn't me.

"Rick, I have nothing to offer you besides saying you seem like a good person, and I wish you were happier here," he sat up straight, feeling the rejection coming, "You're not as alone as you think. We're all figuring it out. In fact, I'm not sure I know anything right now."

And now I'd really confused the guy.

"Let's go see if your counselor is available, Ms. Lamb, right?" because he had no idea that she'd been the one suggesting I talk to him, and Ms. Allen was just the messenger when she sent us out of Ecology to 'talk'. "Ms. Lamb knows everything."

He looked stunned that I'd given up on him so fast. Maybe my blunt admission of ignorance was confusing? But then he nodded, like he understood I was out of my depth, and it really wasn't personal.

"But if you just want someone to talk to? Let me put my number in your phone. If you want." I shrugged my shoulders, not sure if he'd *want* to talk to me considering how useless I'd been. But he handed it to me. And while we walked to the office, he *did* look happier than before.

We caught Ms. Lamb as she finished an appointment, and she ushered Rick into her office right away. Mission accomplished. I thought I was off the hook.

Not so much.

She doubled back. "Five things, Haven, have you figured them out?"

Needs. That was what Ms. Lamb was talking about. She gave me homework.

Uh oh.

At that moment all I "needed" was to not be late to Latin and get to my locker for my textbook before class. But I didn't think that was what Ms. Lamb wanted. I tried to pull answers out of the air. Not starting with I need to figure out what I'm going to do about Daisy.

"One, how about one," she pushed.

"I need to figure out who I am," I blurted, and I met her eyes, hoping she'd let me go at that.

She studied me for about thirty seconds before saying, "Good one," giving me a thumbs up and heading back in to figure out Rick.

I just got my textbook as the bell rang between classes and started down the hallway when I heard her. Great.

"Haven, wait up!" she called.

I half turned to watch Laurie running up the hall, waving at the security guard who opened his mouth to tell her off but closed it again. The click-click-click of her ridiculously high boots were rapid-fire. She sure knew how to run in those things.

I'd be flat on my face in three steps max.

"Can it wait? I need to get to Latin."

True story. My locker was on the second floor and Latin in the basement so it would take almost five minutes to wade through the throng. I didn't need a tardy note to add to my crimes.

Detention Tuesday was plenty for one week. Henderson didn't take kindly to skippers, and I'd been late for AP Calc. Then there was the awkwardness of sitting next to Daisy for a whole hour after school. I couldn't even look at her I was so confused by what happened at her house.

"No, it can't! I'm pissed, Haven. All I hear from Coach Morgan is how you've let the team down. She won't let it go. She's driving us crazy."

Yeah, and guess what? If you knew what Coach Morgan really felt you'd be seething.

But I didn't say it. Because she'd be hurt as well as angry.

"This is Daisy's doing, isn't it? Your new BFF or whatever, since you insist that you guys aren't together." I could feel the air quotes around 'together'.

And my mind was on Tuesday again. Daisy maybe did want to be together. I think that was what she was saying. Sort of. Maybe?

"Does she not want you to go out for sports because she doesn't do any? Does she want all your time? Since when are you someone's lapdog?"

There were so many things to say. Some of them included the b-word. I don't know why I led with, "Derby is a sport."

She rolled her green eyes. "Give me a break. They skate in circles. Big deal. Don't you get it? We need you and you ditched us! How are we supposed to win state without you?"

"With you! And Reya and Becca and Gwen and Celeste. I'm not the only one in track; it's not like there isn't a whole team to take us to state."

"But none of them are you!" Something like desperation tinged her words.

"You don't need me. You're good! I know I haven't been there but it's not like I don't know how you've done at Meets. And I'm allowed to do other things with my afternoons and weekends besides running in circles."

Laurie's eyes narrowed, her face screwing up. "Do your dad and mom even know what you do with your afternoons?"

"My mom doesn't tell me what to do." Not anymore.

Okay, so she laughed.

"Just stop. I already told Mom. Weeks ago."

And she told Dad and they both thought I needed to see a therapist because why would I not want to compete? Especially because I wouldn't give them what they considered a good reason. They only dropped the therapist thing because no one they called was taking new patients and they wouldn't want to ask a friend for a referral and reveal that, gasp, Haven was human.

Not that Laurie needed to know any of that.

"Isn't it enough that Latin is kicking my ass? Don't you ever want to just step away from the a cappella group or volleyball or track and have a life?"

"That *is* my life, Haven, and since you seem to have forgotten, that was *your* life, before you decided to become a quitter." She sneered at me like I was something truly disgusting. "At least if you finally decided you *were* a lesbian you could hook up with someone decent and not someone who's blown half the boys in school."

What?

The fuck.

I was stuck between "lesbian" and "blown" when she flew out of the side door, not neglecting to crash the door against the brick outside. I had enough focus to think that they seriously needed some doorstops on those things, then was right back on "blown".

I stared after her as she disappeared into the Art Building. I've known Laurie since kindergarten. I shared my lunch with her. For years. I'd been delusional to think she'd ever be cool with me if I wasn't her definition of "normal". And I'd been way too slow on the draw because dissing on Daisy was *not* okay.

And I should have told her so.

By the end of school, I had enough of the heavy, deep, and real conversations.

First Knox had been in my face again at lunch about some stupid thing. Ms. Allen had been on about the inevitable destruction of the world through microplastics in fifth period before she sent me out to talk with Rick. Ms. Lamb had put me on the spot. Then the stupid conversation with Laurie.

And I was two minutes late for Latin and Ms. Sulliger might have let it slide, but she called on me for conjugations twice as much as anyone else in the class.

At least things were mellow in seventh period Constitution Team because we'd already taken Nationals again; without me being on the stage, thank God, because I bowed out so Connie could go. Because being up there would not have gone well when Daisy was freaking out about The Hug and everyone had something to say about The Kiss. And the gossip didn't need to overshadow something we'd been working on all year.

And what did I even feel about the new kiss that no one knew about? I couldn't forget a second of it and her and that she was *right there* leaning into me, pressing against me, and I didn't know what to do with *that*.

Thank God Mom was taking Paul home. Daisy and the derby girls had a ride with Daisy's dad. And I was out of there.

Almost.

I got all the way to the parking lot before Daisy caught up with me. And when I turned to see her, she didn't look happy. What had I done now? All I could think of was that I didn't sit with her and Paul at lunch for two days or text her since

Tuesday or linger long enough outside class to have a word between periods.

Crap. I'd ghosted her.

But now, facing me with her hands on her hips, she didn't say a word about any of that. What Daisy said was out of nowhere.

"Are you still in love with Alice?"

What?

"I thought you had a ride to practice," I said, sidestepping the question. Because Daisy could not be waiting for me after school to ask *that*. That would be weird. And I thought we covered the Alice thing. That there *wasn't* an Alice thing.

Daisy watched me for a second and then sighed. "Never mind. I got it. You can't help who you..."

I stopped her as she started to turn around. "I didn't say I still loved Alice. I didn't say that I loved her at all. We're just friends. I mean, she's straight, right? It's not like she's been short of boyfriends ever since I met her."

At the school health clinic. Getting birth control. And I, like an interfering jackass, berated her for being responsible. She thought she was in love. I thought she was stupid. We were both right I guess, considering how *that* worked out. But Alice *like* me? As if.

Daisy shook her head. "People aren't always as straight as they seem, Haven. Just because she dated guys doesn't mean she wouldn't be with a girl. It's not always simple, you know?"

Didn't I ever.

"But what she feels isn't the point. Are *you* still in love with *her*?"

"I'm not in love with Alice..." I muttered. Why were we having this conversation in the parking lot anyway?

"But were you?" she insisted.

"I don't know, okay? I don't know what 'in love' is. What do people even mean when they say that?" I took a deep breath before continuing. I didn't need to be freaking out on her. "So, I used to think about her. Kind of that way. She was so vulnerable and so strong at the same time. Different. Homeschooled. Not into sports. Bad taste in guys."

"Basically, nothing like me. Except maybe the last part." Her smile tipped up on one side, but there was none of her usual spark. "It's okay, Haven, you can admit it to me. Not like I'm going to judge you. I just thought..."

"Anyway, I'm not gay," I said, before she could get more words out, tired of being put on the spot. I was nothing like CeCe and her friends. Maybe I kind of liked Alice, it didn't make me gay. Maybe bi-, but I wasn't going to say so.

"I don't believe you." Daisy looked at me straight on. No games. No attitude.

"I think I know myself better." I hated being told who I was. Who I *should* be.

"You kissed me back." She said it softly, like she was vulnerable for once. Not Daisy King the Derby Queen. Not Daisy waving like a parade princess while she walked by the students who mocked her and called her a slut. Not Daisy standing in her kitchen, telling me she wanted to kiss *me* that night. Not just anyone. Not just because I was there. Because it was *me*.

And I remembered the feel of her wet sweater against my T-shirt and her hands around my neck and oh boy I didn't need to think about this now. Nope.

"Nope." It was all I could think of to say. And then I was a chicken and ran away from her.

Literally ran. In my flipflops. Away from the conversation. Away from my thoughts. Through the park and away from the school and the Volvo and my feelings. Because she was right. I kissed her back.

CHAPTER SEVENTEEN

"What Am I Supposed to Do? Lie?"

After I went around the block to make sure Daisy and her friends were gone—I was such an asshole—I walked barefoot back to the Volvo, my broken flip flop dangling from my finger.

Those things are not meant for running in.

And now I had blisters between my toes, and I totally deserved them.

What kind of person does that? Walks, no *runs*, away from someone asking them a question that personal. And looking so vulnerable. How on earth was I going to make it up to her?

First thing was to stop hyperventilating so I could use my brain, I could manage that much. Maybe. I played the Just Because I'm a Woman: Songs of Dolly Parton tribute album in the car, but it didn't help. So, I bandaged up my toes when I got home and went for a real run with real shoes.

And I almost got there. Rational. Ready to tackle the mess I made after a run that took everything out of me. I pushed myself hard, sticking to the sidewalks, focusing on my body and not my thoughts until I was out of breath and soaked with sweat. Then I took the shower of all showers. Scrubbed. Shampooed. Shaved legs. I could breathe again for a minute before my cowardice came flooding back.

The floor. I felt grounded on the floor. The tufted Persian rug right in the middle of the living room was calling me. I dropped down wearing my fresh Adidas T-shirt and shorts, grateful that it was Mom's vacuuming day and my wet hair wouldn't pick up fluff and stretched out my arms and legs in each direction. And closed my eyes, gripping the rug with my fingers.

The weight of the world dropped away and there was only me, held up from below, by the rug and the floor and the earth underneath. I could almost let everything go, everything but my problem, how to fix things with Daisy...

Mom's screech from the kitchen sent my heart racing. I sat up fast, sending my head spinning, and twisted my body to see. No Mom. Just her voice from around the corner. I moved to stand up until I heard her words.

"How long has this been going on?!" she shouted, after her initial cry of, "Terry Cooper called!"

Uh oh. The President of the Willamette High School Booster Club. The whole Club was like Hydra. Not the mythological beast, the Marvel universe neo-Nazi organization undermining the free world. They see and hear all. But Terry Cooper was the worst of the bunch.

A bunch of parents who cheered me on to victory for the last three years and helped pay for the entire athletic department. I should love the Boosters, not fear them, but between their entitled tirades when their "talented and gifted" kids had to share a classroom with someone like my brother, and their dedication to sharing gossip at lightning speed, I wasn't a fan.

And whatever Terry Cooper shared could. Not. Be. Good.

"How long has this been going on?" Mom screeched again from the kitchen.

I wanted to yell "define 'this'". There were a whole lot of things 'this' could be.

That I didn't want her to know about.

I flopped back down on the rug. I was *such* a liar. Now. Hiding things from her was becoming a lifestyle. I used to be able to tell her everything.

Almost everything.

I wasn't sure whose side she was on anymore. Mine, Paul's, or Terry Cooper's.

Especially right now, I realized, looking up at her face looming over me. That glare. She was pissed. I gave Mom my best "huh?" look as a hail Mary.

"Don't make that innocent face at me, Haven." Her whole body was tense. "Since when do you skip-out after a fire drill?"

Oh... She heard about *that*. I jumped to my feet ready to evade.

Because I wasn't going to own up to anything until I knew what she knew.

"What do you mean?" I asked. Like an idiot.

"You know perfectly well what I mean. Terry Cooper thought I should know he saw you leaving campus during a fire drill the day before yesterday. He knew it was you because of that damn motorcycle. *And* he said you had someone on the back, too. In the rain, Haven? What were you thinking?!"

Oh, shit. I forgot about that transgression. Skipping, detention, *and* riding in the rain with someone on the back. Did he at least mention she was wearing a helmet?

"The school left me a message that you had a detention Tuesday, but I knew it had to be a mistake because you *never told us*. I had to hear about it from Terry! You know that's going to get around the community. Why would you do something so stupid? When were you going to tell us, Haven?"

Never. If I could get away with it.

"This is not okay. The first detention, okay, the text was about Paul, and it made sense you took out your phone to check. I get that. But quitting track and now leaving school grounds during class? You're supposed to set an example! You're a leader not a loser."

The look on her face. *That* was why I had to be perfect.

I had to at least try to give her a reason.

"The girl I gave a ride to, she had to go home suddenly and asked me for help."

"Help" should be the magic word. Wasn't helping people what we were all about? It was practically a Unitarian commandment.

"She had no right to ask you to skip school. She should have gone to the office and gotten a slip and followed procedure. Her parent should have picked her up if she needed to go home that badly."

"Her mom was at work."

"So? And the girl couldn't call her? What was so important that she had to go home right then? And get herself, and you, in trouble for it. And in the rain, honey! How could you take that risk?"

Yeah. All kinds of risks. Mom didn't even *know* what happened at Daisy's house. Not like I could tell her what happened then. Or today. What did Daisy even want from me?

Then Paul showed up behind Mom. He was quiet like that.

His brows were scrunched together and his head jerked to one side in agitation, almost banging his shoulder. "You're yelling. I don't like yelling."

Thank you, Paul, for the distraction. But then I hated myself for thinking it; he didn't need the agitation.

"You're right, I shouldn't be yelling," Mom's voice was suddenly sweet as a Ding Dong, "I was just asking about something that happened at Haven's school."

"My school," Paul said. "It's my school."

Go Paul, I thought, the derby girls were being a good influence.

"My mistake. I just, I need to talk to your sister." She was smiling like it hurt.

Paul studied her, then looked at me. "Did your friend get home okay that other day?" Had he been listening? What was he doing? "Your friend who was sick."

He was lying. For me.

"Yes," I told him, nodding slightly, "I got her home before she threw up again."

He looked me in the eye for half a second, then jerked his head away to study the skylight, his headphones almost slipping.

"I was worried about her."

Mom turned from Paul to me. "She threw up? Oh. Dear. Why didn't you tell me?"

Because I didn't think of it. Paul was a genius. A genius who turned the way he came. I could hear the whisper of his steps as he headed back down to the basement after saving me.

I needed to finish the job.

"It's still not okay to skip class. I know that. It's just she was getting sick and it was embarrassing with everyone around us on the football field and I couldn't get to the office because of the fire drill and it seemed like the right thing to do and it took a while at her house before she stopped vomiting and I didn't want to leave her until she got hold of her mom."

And I talked way too much when I was nervous.

And lying my ass off.

Instead of telling her it took a while to get back from Daisy's house because she stepped across that pink checkerboard floor and gave me the second kiss of my life and confused the hell out of me.

"But you got a detention," Mom said softly. She wasn't angry anymore. This was good.

"I made my choice, and I had to take the punishment. It's only right since I broke the rules."

Take that, Mom.

"Okay," she nodded, "I'll have to talk to Terry. He shouldn't be spreading rumors about the students. He had no right to act like you were a juvenile delinquent when you were just helping a friend. I'm going to go call him right now."

As she stalked off, I took the stairs to my bedroom three at a time. I had to reach Daisy to corroborate my story. Now. Hopefully, Terry Cooper wasn't telling Mom *right this second* that he saw both of us come back on my motorcycle. The guy couldn't be *everywhere*.

And Daisy wasn't picking up.

Or texting back.

And why would she? She asked me a question, and I *think* I got what she was really asking, but maybe I *don't*, and I didn't even give her a chance to explain. I just booked it.

I'll be lucky if she ever speaks to me again.

All I could do was pace. *And* wish that my bedroom carpet wasn't so uncomfortable 'cause I'd be calmer flat on my back instead of doing laps around the room.

And then I realized there was hope yet.

She was at practice. Duh. I rechecked my phone. Practice wasn't done until after seven.

Was her dad going to stay to watch and drive her home, or was he going to work and she'd need a ride?

No. He'd stay. Daisy talked about him like he was a good dude.

But it didn't matter. I knew where to find her now, before she left.

I dove into my homework, trudging through Latin conjugation, an Ecology report on the evils of microplastics, and my final paper on the health benefits of community. It was amazing what I could get through while distracted and anxious.

Though the kinds of things I used to get anxious about, I glanced up at the row of Softball and Track trophies on the shelf above my window, seemed pretty useless. No, not useless, I reminded myself, I'd had a lot of fun competing, making my folks proud. I made friends with good people.

But it wasn't exactly life-altering.

I texted Daisy again.

I need to talk to you.

Please.

I finished my footnotes.

No text from Daisy. Which made sense. Her phone would be with her stuff on the bleachers.

Emailed the paper to Ms. Allen.

It was six-thirty. Still nothing.

Of course there was nothing. It wasn't seven, was it?

There was no logical reason for going there. No reason to head out in heavy rain, the sky darkening. No reason to pull to the side of the road and text her again when I was halfway there and about to merge onto 99 South by Goodwill.

Can I drive you and Birgit and Sophie and Ellie home? Or will your dad still be there?

And there was absolutely no logical reason to wait in the parking lot like a stalker after arriving at the Hangar.

I'm outside. Could you at least talk to me for a minute before going home?

I couldn't even explain to myself what was going on in my head. I just knew I had to be there.

When Daisy was suddenly in the half-light pouring from the open Hangar door, fresh from practice and looking for me, something snapped. My brain went offline and something else took over. I didn't wait for her to come to me; it was too important to talk *now*. The closer I got to her the more I lost my mind and forgot to ask how practice went, forgot I was supposed to be apologizing, forgot everything.

I just looked into her eyes from across the parking lot and kept coming.

She recognized something in my face because she stopped pacing. Stopped shifting in place. Went perfectly still.

I was going to do this.

I shut out my remaining thoughts and tried to just let myself feel the beat of my heart, the lightness in my head, the pressure of my flip flops on the wet asphalt. I kept walking until we were toe to toe, breath to breath, our bodies touching when we inhaled and separating with each hurried exhale.

No more thinking.

I kissed her. Any aim for finesse was out the window. Over-thinking would wreck it. I didn't know if she'd back away, look at me like I was crazy, even though she'd kissed me twice. Maybe she'd only been joking. Toying with me. Oh, look at the silly jock who has no idea what she's doing.

No. I increased the pressure and tilted my head, the motion opening her mouth so that our breaths mingled and the kiss was something else and my brain just turned off.

It was my body that was on a different circuit. Voltage ran through me with a shiver. She *was* kissing me back. And Wow. She held onto my shoulder with one hand, the other holding my cheek. It felt good. Like it was real.

A wolf whistle jolted me back to time and space and I moved to jump back but Daisy held tight for just a second before letting me go and she was the one to step back. Waiting. On me.

Two girls were standing inside the door of the Hangar, lean-ing their heads out to watch the action. Birgit and Sophie. What were they going to think?

"Haven, don't..." Daisy began.

"Don't what?" I tried to focus on her eyes but kept noticing her mouth, the smooth skin of her neck, the dark damp hair clinging just below her ear.

"Don't tell me this was a mistake. Don't run away." She was almost pleading.

I wanted to say the words. No, this wasn't a mistake. I won't run.

And then the thoughts seeped in. Do *you* want it to happen again, Daisy? Do you want me? Or am I still a joke? I pushed back that last thought. I wasn't a joke to Daisy. She cared. Could she care about me that way? The kissing way. And not just because she was bored?

"Do you want me to run?" is what I said, insecurity flooding me now that I'd put it out there and couldn't take it back.

"Please don't," she whispered.

"Maybe we should talk," I muttered, shy about our increasing audience.

She put her hand on my shoulder and stroked along my sleeve and arm until she reached my hand. "Maybe we shouldn't. Maybe you should take me home and we don't do any talking at all."

I didn't even know what to say. So, I said something dumb.

"What about your dad?"

Daisy smiled at me. The imp one that curled up her closed lips.

"He had to go back to work and one of the coaches can drive Sophie and Birgit and Ellie home. You're not getting out of this that easily."

I didn't want to.

CHAPTER EIGHTEEN

"Seriously, Dad?"

Daisy's dad had other ideas.

"What is he still doing here?" Daisy whispered as the tall, lean dude I had to assume was her father strode across the parking lot. Like he owned it.

In a freakin' suit. Greenish gold. With the sheen of gasoline. It caught the light coming from the open doorway as brightly as his teeth. Who wore stuff like that?

Not. What. I. Was. Expecting.

Then again, he did own a tiki bar.

"Sweetheart, daughter of my dreams, who is this delightful young lady you are standing awfully close to in a public venue? Something you want to tell me?"

He was still grinning, showing *all* those white teeth. This was surreal. Weren't dads all protective when it came to their daughters? Because he would have seen *everything*. And with a girl? Daisy had said he was Persian, born in Iran, and the man standing there with thick hipster glasses and slicked back black hair and only a trace of an accent was *not* what I was picturing.

Daisy shook her head at him, not embarrassed at all.

"What are you doing here, Daddy? I thought you had to go back to the bar?" Daisy skipped over and started to throw her arms around him but stopped short, "Oops, kind of sweaty."

He just winked at her, still grinning as he turned to me, and pointed like God in that Sistine Chapel ceiling they made us study in Art History.

Hardest class EVER.

The chapel image went poof when I realized he was lowering his extended hand for me to shake. Umm...

Mind blown, I was fortunate that years of training kicked in, and I took his hand, feeling like a boy in some old show, picking up the girl holding flowers, and shaking the father's hand.

"I'm Haven Alexander, Mr. King," I said, swallowing after he released my hand. Was I imagining that it went on a second or two longer than necessary?

But he was still smiling. "Oh, Frank, please! Everyone calls me Frank. Except you, young lady," he pointed at Daisy, "The day I stop being Daddy is the day I'm spending your college fund in Vegas."

I was beginning to see where Daisy got her boldness.

Not that her mom was shy.

Daisy poked him in the side but let him sling an arm across her shoulders.

"So," he said, pointing to me and then her, "is this a thing? Should I be saving for a wedding or what?"

Oh. My. God. He must have noticed the look on my face because he waved away my distress.

"Oh Haven, don't pay any attention to me, I'm just kidding around. You guys are way too young to get married."

I. Had. Nothing.

"Daddy, I think you're putting Haven into shock. You take some getting used to."

He chuckled. "That's what my customers say. And my last wife. Bless her heart."

"Don't even *try* your southern gentleman impression on me." Daisy patted him on the shoulder. "Maybe we should let Haven get home and you and I can talk in the car."

He raised one thick brow. "After you change, I assume," he said, glancing back at what I realized was a Jaguar.

A Jaguar.

"Shut up. I'll be right back," Daisy said, and she lunged at me and gave me a quick kiss on the cheek. "And we can text later, cool?"

"Cool," I muttered, watching her vanish into the Hangar, leaving me alone with Daisy's *dad*. Awkward.

I noticed how he mirrored my stance, his hands in his pockets, no longer smiling. He'd mastered inscrutable. I shifted my weight from foot to foot, remembering the lyrics of *The Clash* song again, "Should I stay or should I go?"

Then his eyes crinkled up at the sides. "Go on, scoot, escape, depart, scarper. I'm not going to interview you as a candidate for my daughter's affection. As she'd tell you herself, I'm not the boss of her. I'll interview her instead. I'll know all about you before we leave the parking lot."

I didn't know whether I really liked him or was terrified of him. He was like Daisy that way. Terrifying in a good way.

"If you're sure, sir." I edged toward the Volvo.

"Not 'sir', Frank, please. You'll be seeing me again soon. Unless she gives you the boot. You never know."

This was one of the weirdest, and best, nights ever.

And yes, I had to agree, as I unlocked the car, you never know.

I was *almost* recovered from meeting Daisy's dad by the time I got home. Just inside the door I decided I should text Daisy right away.

And it suddenly wasn't so simple. Was I texting I was home safe? Or Holy Shit I met your father?! Or pretend it was no big? Should I be serious? Try to be funny? Not like I'd have any idea how to be "romantic". And to mention the kiss or not to mention the kiss...

Aargh.

I just asked the question I had to know the answer to.

Did I pass inspection?

She texted back right away.

You have the Frank King conditional stamp of approval.

Thank God.

I can't believe that happened. He's something else.

Wait, that came out wrong. I typed some more.

In a good way.

She was right with me.

I hear you.

I typed again.

He loves you.

Your folks love you, babe.

She was right. They did. Conditionally...

But could she stop saying that word!

Why do you call me that??

You know why.

Umm... no. But I was too slow.

And thanks for the kiss. Sweet dreams, babe.

Was I supposed to say, 'you're welcome'?

Sweet dreams, Daisy.

It was all I could think of saying. I was still in shock. I. Kissed. Daisy. And she kissed me back. In front of her dad! I stood in the entry, facing the mirror above the shoe basket. I didn't look any different. But I felt different. Way different. Mind officially blown.

I kicked my flip flops into the basket, thinking of a pair of batwing boots that had been there four days ago.

And heard Mom and Dad in the dining room.

Oh no. I froze and checked my phone. Seven-fifty. Woo! I didn't need to think up an excuse, so long as I was home before eight o'clock, I was okay.

"I think we should invite this girl over for dinner," I heard Mom say.

"This girl" had to be Daisy. That's what Mom kept calling her. This could be good. Maybe they'd see how cool she was if she came to dinner. Maybe they'd see she was important to *me*. If Daisy's dad was okay with *us*...

Us.

Mom and Dad could be.

"Why should we do that, hon', don't we want to get it all behind Haven?" Dad said.

All what?

"What do you mean, David? I was thinking about Paul. He likes this girl."

Oh.

"Are you sure? Maybe, he has a crush on a different roller derby girl. You told me he's having lunch with four girls."

"He invited her here. That girl. Daisy something."

'King,' I thought. Daisy King. I stood frozen in the entry.

"I don't know, Kathleen. I think you're betting on the wrong horse. I told you Lily said this Daisy kissed Haven at some party when she was drunk."

Dad and Mom knew? And never said anything?

And Dad had more to say, "Haven's been getting hell from her peers for that. What kind of girl is that to have around Paul? Let's just let this die a natural death."

"How could she do that to Haven? Why pick on our daughter? As a dare? I guess she *was* drunk."

This time when I blew out a sigh of frustration, I didn't care who heard me. The only reason anyone would kiss me was on a dare or because they were really drunk. Thanks a lot. And for your information, Mom and Dad, she was barely buzzed.

"So, you're going to let this go?" Dad said.

"I know she's not ideal, David, but he really seems to like her."

Dad smacked the table. "Kathleen, let it go. You don't want to push him on a girl who would do that."

"That." Kiss his daughter. Wow.

"Well, I think if he's interested in her we should encourage him to spend time with her. It's good for him to try new things."

"New things"? Oh my God.

I came in hot and threw myself into a dining chair, nearly breaking it by the sound of splintering wood. *Now* they shut up.

"What's up?" I asked, "Carry on, please. I'm fascinated."

"I didn't know you were home, honey. Do you have homework?" Mom asked.

Unbelievable. Was she really going to try and bluff this out?

"Finished it." I tilted my head at her. Try again.

And Mom did. "How did school go today?"

"You mean," I stared her down, "was I swamped with catcalls, homophobic slurs and asked innumerable details about that kiss that had to have been a dare or a drunken mistake?" Then I shifted my stare to Dad.

I felt guilty calling it "that kiss". Like it was a crime. Not the start of something major. Maybe.

Daisy would tell them everything. She'd lay it all out there. I wasn't that brave.

But.

"Daisy wasn't drunk. And yeah, we got hassled a little at first, for a couple days. But it was no big deal. No one cares. Okay, Knox maybe. And Laurie's not so happy with me." I added. Like a fool.

"But Laurie has known you for years—she knows you're not a lesbian," said Mom.

Am I? The words hung there, just below the surface.

"Why are we even talking about lesbians? Forget about the kiss. This is about Paul. And that girl."

Forget about the kiss. Never.

"Daisy, her name is Daisy, and you know that. You met her, Mom!"

"Okay, Haven, no need to get sharp about it. I've got it. Daisy."

"And she's not into Paul that way."

Mom looked startled. "How do you know that? Why else would she come over here?"

Right. Of course. Whatever. They had their universe. I had mine.

I shoved back my chair as I got up, hoping it would fall backward and splinter into a million pieces. I wasn't that lucky.

"I'm going to bed."

Mom called out, "It isn't even nine o'clock!"

And I could feel Dad watching me walk away. Didn't he have something to add? Or did they know they'd said plenty.

In my mind I stomped up the stairs, but my body wouldn't do it. I felt the weight of gravity so bad.

When I got to my room, I lay down on the scratchy carpet three feet in, trying to find my happy place. Forget Mom and Dad. Remember Daisy. Remember tonight's kiss. Remember kissing her. Remember making that choice to walk toward her when Daisy stepped out of the Hangar. Looking for me.

Looking for *me*.

But no, that happy place went poof because Dad wasn't through. It wasn't fair how quietly he walked; Paul got his stealth from him. I was suddenly aware that he was looking down at me from my open doorway.

And that something was off. Was something wrong with Paul? Or Mom? Or him? Did Uncle Jackson's cancer return? I sat up, bracing for bad news.

Dad squatted so we were face to face. "Look Haven, I wasn't going to say anything in front of your mom, but I talked to a friend a couple weeks ago. Mike Lopez. You know who I mean. On the fundraising committee."

Sure, I knew him. His son Mason climbed into classroom cupboards in third grade and terrified the teachers by jumping out at them.

"He told me about the incident at the party right after it happened. Long before Lily told us about what was going on at school. He showed me the video."

Oh, my God. He'd seen the video.

I'd refused to look at it, but Dad didn't.

"He thought I should know."

I bet. Mason Lopez had been getting into a ton of trouble forever. He'd thrown scissors in fifth grade and barely missed a girl. Gotten caught with weed in middle school. Wrecked his first car in his sophomore year. Barely redeemed himself this year by keeping his exploits on the down low. Of course, Mr. Lopez wanted to talk to Dad about my scandalous behavior.

It probably made his week.

But Dad raised a hand to stop me before I could say a word.

"I don't need you to explain, Haven. He told me all about Daisy King. She's got a bad reputation at school. And no wonder with how she dresses. I know who's to blame for this mess."

I felt like throwing up. He judged Daisy based on the word of Mike Lopez? Instead of his daughter? And because she wore clothes that stood out, Daisy was automatically bad? What happened to my *dad*? He was the mellow one. The one who was cool with everyone. He'd been brought up on the first Principle: the inherent worth and dignity of every person. Dad had no excuse. He knew better.

I opened my mouth to remind him of the values he'd taught me from toddlerhood, of the diverse and flamboyant kids in

Youth Group *he'd never said a bad word about,* but he interrupted me.

"The important thing is damage control. Your mom doesn't need this stress."

"What do you mean by 'this'?" I asked, already hating his answer.

"I know these girls are helping Paul develop socially. That's amazing. I don't care if they wear tutus and go bowling or participate in naked bike rides through downtown, they're being good friends to him."

Damn right they are.

"But you need to distance yourself from this girl, Daisy. Make it clear to everyone that the kiss was a prank. If she was a nice girl and she liked you, then maybe I would suggest a different approach. A softer let down. But you know she doesn't."

Because no one—except stupid Knox—could possibly be into me. I was that unlovable. I wanted to crawl into a hole. All I could manage was, "You're all wrong about Daisy."

Dad just shook his head. So certain he was right. Asshole.

"And you know what, Dad? Even if Mike Lopez says Daisy is trouble with a capital 'T', who the fuck cares? She's a person, not a reputation. She's more than how she dresses. We don't have to be alike to be nice people."

"You're right. I was being harsh. And she's being a good friend to Paul."

I couldn't let that stand. "She's *my* friend, too."

More than a friend.

Now.

I thought.

Dad stilled and looked me in the eyes. "What about that Alice girl? I thought she was your friend." I could feel the air quotes. Was he saying what I thought he was?

"Alice? She is my friend. A good friend."

Dad leaned back against my wall, sitting on his heels.

"And now Daisy is a friend?" This time he did make air quotes.

Yes, Dad. She's a friend. More than a friend. But I didn't say it. This wasn't the time.

He was suddenly fascinated by the line of trophies over my window. "The way I see it, you're a peer counselor. You're going to come across kids who need some guidance. You can't tell me Alice doesn't have issues."

Now he was ragging on Alice? "Her mom died! Of course she has issues!"

"And this girl, Daisy, you've only got to look at her to know she's got issues."

"You've never even met her!" I practically yelled.

"Quiet down, Haven, I don't want your mom to hear us. I saw the video. She's not a good friend for you."

He looked at me for a long time.

"Friendships don't always last, Haven. She's going to decide she'd rather hang around with girls like her, or more likely boys who *like* her."

Wait, what was he saying?

He sighed and stood up. "Honey, this is a normal phase. You're pushing boundaries. Maybe you're doing some experimenting. But it's time to cut it out. You *are* going to cut it out. You are not going to do this to your mom, she'd worry herself sick if she thought you were gay. All she wants is for you to be happy."

Happy?

Dad muttered, "I'm sorry," as he walked out of my room.

Seeing Daisy at the Hangar seemed like a million years ago.

CHAPTER NINETEEN

"I Couldn't Do This"

"**U**ncle Jackson doesn't come over much. He looks bad. The chemo is kicking his butt. And he can't control his laugh."

Daisy leaned toward me, her brown eyes confused, her shiny, red lips open in anticipation of my explanation. Her shirt gaping at the neck...

I looked away and shivered. *This* was the girl Dad expected me to slough off like dead skin. Before she did the same to me.

I could have shown him the zillion texts "that girl" and I sent each other Friday and Saturday while she was away for a surprise weekend with her dad. Or given him a blow by blow of that last kiss, and the one before that and the one before that. But he didn't deserve to know that much about me. Not anymore.

I hadn't seen her since Thursday night after derby 'cause we were off Friday for a teacher planning day. My first glimpse of Daisy in Health class was a kick to my system I really needed. And when our eyes met during U.S. History it was like we were connected across the room. But now I was feeling awkward. I should have told Dad the truth.

But what was the truth? I was beginning to doubt myself even though Daisy and I were a foot away from each other. And I could almost feel her reach out to me. She hadn't texted me at all Sunday and I couldn't help wondering if she was backing away when I didn't get a response to my "good morning" message before school.

I was being ridiculous.

I was no better than the girls I'd criticized for agonizing over whether a guy likes them or not.

And that was when I realized that four sets of eyes were still trained on me, and that there'd been a big pause after "laugh". I rushed to fill the silence. Paul was rarely sick, so for once we could talk about him.

Not that discussing Paul's idiosyncrasies felt great. It was talking about him behind his back, and shouldn't he be explaining himself for himself? But I'd started the conversation, so I kept going.

"Uncle Jackson's laugh is particularly startling, it's like this full on hyaena thing, but all laughter is tricky. That's why we don't have people over much. Why I can't invite you over," I flicked my eyes to Daisy's for a second, "All at once anyway. Paul can't take loud laughter. Or raised voices. Or sadness. Or any big emotion. Not well."

He picked up on everything. There was this stupid idea that people with autism were oblivious to social expectations and didn't read feelings. I knew it was just the opposite. Paul felt every emotion around him. Spoken or not. Half the time neurotypical people said things that didn't match their feelings. Paul didn't know what to do with that. He didn't do dishonest.

Even if he'd saved my butt by lying that one time. Thank you, Paul.

I had no idea how he was handling the lunchroom. Maybe he'd made a huge developmental leap. Maybe it was turning eighteen. Maybe the girls were magic.

Daisy was.

"That's rough, Haven," Sophie said, leaning on her bulky forearms—Jesus she was strong, "What happens if he's exposed to that? I think we should know, since we're around him."

Like every school day. Since April.

I wanted to shrug and change the subject. I'd covered the basics with them that first day when they asked by the pool house. I'd "explained" Paul to friends and family, judgmental strangers and confused grocery clerks and new caseworkers. Somehow it was me doing it half the time even when Mom and Dad were there. He must be so sick of it.

"You know. Rocking. Grunting. Twisting his head. The worst is when he hits himself in the face." I looked down, hating that it had ever been my fault. But it had. I'd made mistakes that he paid for.

I felt Daisy touch my hand, just fingertips at first and then my hand was firmly held. I didn't draw away, even though instinct told me to. Her strength flowed through her skin to mine.

"I'm sorry, Haven," Daisy whispered.

No.

I recoiled, every molecule on the defensive. I tried to pull my hand away, but she wouldn't let me. Not without hurting her. "Don't ever be sorry about Paul. He's my brother, and he is no one to be sorry for."

Daisy let me pull away.

"I know that. I'm sorry. Argh. I did it again. I'm saying it all wrong. I didn't mean it that way." Her face reddened and two tears rolled down her cheeks.

I made her cry. Great. I was an asshole.

I laid my head on the table. Wanting to feel the cool surface against my face. It was the next best thing to lying on the floor. "I'm sorry, too. I'm just sensitive. People act like he's a mistake. Like there's something wrong with him. I hate it. But you didn't mean it that way. I know you're his friend."

Daisy watched me like she was expecting something else out of my mouth. Her arms wrapped around her middle before she finally said, "Yeah. I am."

The bell for fifth period drowned out the sound of Daisy, Ellie, and Sophie, and finally Birgit, pushing away from the table with their stuff, leaving me alone to shove my lunch in my backpack. They didn't wait. even though we all had the same fifth period. Huh. I had a bad feeling that coming to the derby girls' table was going to bite me big time.

Fifteen minutes into Ecology, I knew I was right.

"I should have hung out with you and Finn at lunch."

Alice stood up with handfuls of ivy, roots and all, and turned to me with a raised eyebrow. She didn't say anything, just looked at me like she could read my mind. Then threw the ivy into the bin with the other invasive species we were ripping out to die, die, die. "Seriously?" she finally said.

I gripped a long tangle of ivy and pulled hard, uprooting about ten feet of it, and stuffed it in the bin, looking away from her.

Yes, seriously.

"You can barely stand to look at Finn some days. He bugs the crap out of you," she said, elbow deep in native salal. *That* we weren't ripping out.

Her combat boots were a good idea for wading into ivy at the edges of Willamette Park. My flip flops were a fail. Not that I cared. Scratched up feet were not my biggest worry.

The derby girls hadn't shown up. Not even late. Even I knew that was a bad sign.

"So, he's annoying. It's that stupid hat." I grabbed more ivy. "He's not awful. And," I paused while one of the hipster twins squeezed past, "He's got two moms, right?"

Alice nodded to my left. "Yeah. Peggy and Jo. They're nice. Jo makes great puttanesca sauce."

I nodded, as if I even knew what puttanesca sauce was. "They're high school principals, right?"

Alice glanced at me. "You know they are. Not like you forget stuff."

Yes, I remembered. Peggy gave birth to Finn with someone named Sarah, but she died when he was a baby. Then Peggy married Jo and they had his sisters. Alice had filled me in. And no, I didn't forget.

"Did he get hassled for having lesbian moms?" There. I said it.

Alice shrugged like she had no idea saying "lesbian" freaked me out. "He says not. He says it was post-gayby boom by the time he was born, and there are two-mom Mother's Day cards at Hallmark. No. One. Cared." She looked directly at me. "If that's what you're asking."

I wasn't sure what I was asking. Two adults getting together was a world away from being in high school and people thinking you're a certain way just because you like someone and that you're not you anymore.

Not that I knew who that was anymore either.

Then I thought of what Dad said Thursday night about Alice.

"When we first met, you never felt like a project, did you? Like I was your peer counselor?"

The two-second pause told me everything.

"I'm sorry," I said. For a lot of things. Especially for being a know-it-all who thought she had all the answers. "I didn't mean to be such a condescending asshat."

Alice stepped carefully through the ivy to where I was standing and bumped my shoulder with hers. "You weren't trying to be. You thought you were helping. And it means a lot that you kept trying, even when I pushed you away. Like a million times."

"Do you think I'm a condescending asshat to the derby girls? And Daisy?" I could barely say Daisy's name because what if Alice said I was?

Instead, she laughed. Laughed! "No. You're not like that anymore."

Really?

Alice went on. "Besides, they got under your skin long before Daisy saved Paul in the lunchroom. It was at the SlutWalk. You totally wanted to run away but you didn't. Even when Daisy gave you hell about your shorts."

I looked at my legs, crisscrossed with red lines from branches. "There's nothing the matter with my shorts."

"Exactly, Haven. That was the point."

I wasn't sure I got the point at all. But I did know one thing.

"I don't know what to do about Daisy." There. I said it. "I think I messed things up, and I don't even know what I did."

Other than making her cry.

Which was a lot right there.

Why doesn't life come with instructions? Why don't *girls* come with instructions?

And that was my out loud voice. Shoot.

Alice laughed next to me.

"Just keep trying, Haven. You can do this."

Easy for her to say.

Not like Daisy made it easy to keep trying.

She wasn't at her locker after seventh. Or by the pool house with Sophie, getting in a last cigarette. Not in front of the building where she usually waited for me. None of the derby girls were. Had they gone to practice already? Was Dad right and she was done?

But she held my hand at lunch. Before I hurt her feelings.

She couldn't be done.

I could beat them to practice if they got a ride with someone else; I wasn't giving up. I sure wasn't done. I just needed her to give me another chance.

When I got to the school parking lot, I saw that no, they weren't at practice. None of them. But I only gave Sophie, Ellie, and Birgit, sitting on the curb facing me with their backpacks, a second's glance because I was too busy wondering why Daisy was posing like a hood ornament in front of that damn vintage Impala.

Grey's boyfriend's Impala.

I stopped in my tracks. Grey's boyfriend Will was talking to Daisy and they fit. Her retro rockabilly thing, according to Alice, his dude in black with silvery gray hair thing. It was all kinds of wrong. I. Did. Not. Like. It.

Then I saw that Grey was behind the wheel. And started breathing again. It wasn't like Will was here to see Daisy.

Grey was revving the engine on the Impala, then letting it idle. She looked frustrated, pushing her copper hair away from her mouth. Will went around to the driver's side and leaned through the open window. I could hear him as I got closer.

"It's running rough. The idle shouldn't be sounding that way. Go ahead and turn it off," he said, then added, "Please," and kissed her.

He didn't pause before kissing her. He didn't wonder who was watching. He didn't have to care. I watched her swing the heavy door open and wrap her arms around Will. Grey was all copper hair, big men's dress shirts, and shoes like Daisy's. They looked happy.

I couldn't fathom that Grey was moving in with him as soon as she graduated in June.

Daisy turned around to admire the Impala, not sparing me a glance. Even though I was *right there* ten feet from her.

What had I done wrong?

Alice said to keep trying. I could do that. Even if I made an ass of myself.

I came around the hood of the Impala and reached out a hand to Daisy. She looked at it suspiciously. A beat went by. Another. Was she going to leave me hanging? I was putting it out there.

And then Daisy put her hand in mine. It was a start.

"Are you going to practice today?" I asked, hoping hard that she was.

"Yeah," she drew out the word.

"Were you making other plans to get there?" I asked, trying to keep it together.

"Maybe" was all she said, her huge, brown eyes meeting mine.

"Why?" I whispered. "What did I do wrong?"

Daisy looked down at our joined hands and then up again, a hint of a smile just lifting her lips. She squeezed my hand and swung our arms like a little kid.

"Nothing now. Nothing at all. Let's go," was all she said.

CHAPTER TWENTY

"I Have a Question. Maybe More Like a Hundred Questions"

"**I**t's weird having Paul gone so long. We miss him."

Sophie was right. It was weird. I'd gotten used to finding the five of them at the table in the back of the lunchroom.

"I think I'll go get pizza at the Blind Onion," said Ellie, tilting her head and trying to give the puppy eyes at Birgit. Did she want her to come with? Did she want all of us to come with?

I looked over at Daisy, standing next to me like it was nothing in the world. I felt a buzz just standing near her. Did she feel it, too? I waited for her response.

Birgit was on it first with, "I'm in."

And Sophie followed with, "I'll never say no to pizza. What about you guys?"

You guys...

It could mean something or not. What did Sophie and the others think when Daisy took my hand on Monday? Not that there'd been any more hand holding, except sometimes on the way back from practice, when I stayed. If the other girls had rides. If we were alone. And I could almost not breathe from the tightness in my chest and the questions racing through my mind.

Questions I was afraid to ask.

"Are you going to get out of the way or what?" a senior said, shoving by us to enter the lunchroom. Shoving me into Daisy.

We were kind of blocking half the doorway.

"I brought a lunch," I said.

Even if I hadn't, cramming into the Blind Onion during the lunch crush was not appealing. I wouldn't be able to hear myself think, much less anyone speak.

Though being unable to think in circles had appeal.

"Me, too!" Daisy said, swinging her messenger bag.

Wait, did she want to have lunch with me? Just me?

Which is kind of what I said out loud.

"Totally," Daisy chirped, her voice higher than usual. Was she nervous about something? "Let's go to the park."

"Well fine, ditch us why don't you?" snapped Ellie, but she didn't mean it. Even I could tell that.

"You guys suck," Birgit said, giving me an elbow jab that nearly knocked me into Daisy again. She *should* go out for crew, I thought, ready to suggest it, words already forming, but stopped myself. She could make her own decisions. I didn't want to be my mother.

God, I didn't want to be my mother.

Mom was *still* pushing me to apologize to Coach Morgan. So that I'd be guaranteed a spot in Cross Country in the fall. Guaranteed to be Co-Captain senior year. And I wanted it bad; I loved to lead. But not at the cost of making nice with *her*.

Laurie would make a great Captain.

"Haven?"

Daisy. Oh. We were still half-blocking the doorway and I'd spaced out.

"Right. Lunch. The park. Let's go."

We got some looks for sure, but no one said anything, besides Aaron. Though he basically mumbled a "Hey" as we walked by the pool house. A couple of people disappeared back into the school. I guess my narc reputation still stood. As well as my new reputation.

Lapdog. Laurie said it every time she passed me in the hall.

She'd still make a great Co-Captain.

"Haven, you keep going into your head." Daisy nudged me with her elbow.

Maybe it would go away if I told someone.

"Can we sit on the grass by the track? I want to talk about something."

I saw her go stiff. What did she think I wanted to talk about?

"Okay," she drew out the word as we settled ourselves on the west edge of the track, on the empty bleachers facing the field for Lacrosse games. "Spit it out."

"I overheard my coach, my new coach, talking on her phone just after Track began."

"What?" she said, "Holy whiplash Batman. We're talking about Track?"

I'd totally confused her.

"I'm telling you why I quit track."

"Oh," she said, "now we're on the same page. What did she say?"

I still wasn't sure I wasn't being a petty bitch, but I had to tell someone. And Daisy was *someone*.

"She talked about me like a horse. Told her friend I'd win her the Triple Crown."

"Hold up, Haven, I don't speak horse."

I looked at the grass, feeling stupid. "Uncle Jackson used to be big on racing so I could understand what she was saying, even if anyone else nearby might not. She meant that I was a three-year-old—a junior—who would win *her*, Coach Morgan, a district, regional, and state win. She said I was an easy winner and she was going to 'run me for all I was worth' so that she could get a coaching job at University of Oregon."

Daisy looked like she was getting it.

"She called me a shoo-in, a legacy, a nepo-baby who was actually earning her stripes, even if I owed my genetics to my sire," and I'd lost her, "meaning that I was good because my dad had been good and almost made the Olympics and is winning Masters competitions even now."

She mouthed "oh".

"It was worse than calling me a horse," and how could she know that I already felt like a 'show pony' for my mom, "it was that she was entering me in all the events she could, so she'd be guaranteed a win. But not for the team, for herself. For her resume. And I couldn't take it. She wasn't going to give anyone else on the team a chance to compete.

"Is that allowed?" Daisy asked tentatively.

"Technically. But it isn't good sportsmanship. Or coaching. She's supposed to be supporting the whole team's opportunity to win, to place, to get noticed by scouts for colleges. She didn't care."

Coach Morgan also said she was going to "ride that filly all the way through college." But it was too embarrassing to tell.

"What a bitch. That's no way to talk about a student, a human being, or to treat the other girls she's supposed to be coaching. I don't care who she was talking to on her own time..."

I laughed. "Oh no, it was during practice. She was standing far enough away that no one was supposed to hear."

"No wonder you quit. Why didn't you report her? What did your parents say?"

I laughed again. But it wasn't funny. "They wouldn't get it. Dad is all about winning. I mean, he's a good sport, he says it's important, taught me it's important. But for them, any opportunity for me comes first. I guess that's what parents are supposed to feel," Daisy was shaking her head, "but it's not fair to my teammates. And I can't take the pressure anymore."

"Oh honey," and Daisy scooted closer, so we were hip to hip, and slung her arm around my shoulders.

I was at war with myself in a heartbeat. My usual discomfort with touch versus the appealing warmth of Daisy. Choosing fear or choosing comfort; was hugging like this even safe these days? And the big question—was this a "friend" hug or a "girlfriend" hug.

The first bell rang. I couldn't help feeling saved by the bell. I wasn't ready to find out.

Neither of us ate lunch.

But the questions weren't over, once Daisy jumped into the passenger seat of the Volvo after school. I hadn't even put it in drive before she started in.

"Why did you start running in the first place?"

Oh boy. I considered how much to tell her while I navigated the parking lot; students dashed out from between cars and drivers backed out at light speed. Talk about a boss level obstacle course. It was like one of Paul's games.

"Come on, spill, Haven, it's not like you woke up one day this bigtime runner."

"I'm not a bigtime runner," I grumbled.

"Oh, I googled you. Your coach isn't wrong about you being a shoo-in, even if she was a bitch about it."

"No one is guaranteed a win. Everyone has bad days and good days." More pressure.

Daisy met my eyes when I glanced over. "I know that. But let's go backward. Little Haven starts running when?"

I couldn't help a smile when I thought back to when I used to run away from Paul's tantrums—which I now knew were meltdowns—and needed to escape. I'd run down the street as fast as I could, and Dad would chase after me, and we'd end up worn out when he finally got in front of me far enough so I could run into his arms. It was time for just me and Dad. He'd smile and tell me how fast I was, and that we should start timing my distance.

I told her all of it.

How Mom and Dad had their hands full, usually Mom, with Paul when he was younger and we didn't know as much about accommodation and co-regulation and how to look at the world through his eyes. We made a lot of mistakes.

I made a lot of mistakes. And I wanted my big brother to be different. More like me. He wasn't autistic, I insisted when I was five, he was just spoiled. Why didn't he have to follow the same rules I did? Why was he allowed to hit Mom without being punished?

"It kills me how selfish I was," I added.

And I let Daisy take my right hand.

"So, I ran. And ran. And Dad liked it. And it made things easier for Mom so she could focus on Paul. And they knew I'd never break a rule or go off the block, so they didn't worry when I took off suddenly."

"It was survival. You know that, right?" she said, squeezing my hand.

"For him. He needed that level of support. He needed Mom interpreting the world for him and interpreting Paul for the world. He was struggling, and developed tics, and had seizures. I was fine. I love my brother."

"I know you do. And you're also allowed to choose your own life."

And there was that word again. "Choose."

Choose.

I watched Daisy whip around the derby track again, do a crossover, weave, dodge and cross the line, adding another point to the scoreboard. I wanted to cheer. But it was practice, so I didn't. I just watched some of the time, from the back bleacher, away from the coaches and the players taking turns during drills.

Choose.

Okay, I thought, getting out a notebook and a pen, Ms. Lamb said to choose five things that I needed and I'd given her one: I need to figure out who I am. For the rest I started with the easy stuff. I wrote:

1. I need to choose how I dress and cut my hair.

2. I need to choose my own friends.

3. I need to choose how I use my body (sports, running, riding, more?)

I stopped writing. Not going to touch "more". I sighed, looking at my short list, and I needed to do those three things without losing Mom and Dad.

Sophie came barreling my way before I could think of a fourth and went down, skidding into the bottom bleacher.

"You alright?" I called out to her.

Sophie grinned up at me, lying on her back. "I'm great!" and she bounced up and skated off.

It must be cool to be able to skate at those speeds. Like running. Like riding. The wind hitting your skin, the pounding of your heart, and... I was a spectator. And that was weird.

I looked around the Hangar. I wasn't the only person on the sidelines, a spectator, and maybe something else and it was a little weird and a little okay. I usually waited in the car. I *was* waiting in the car, but I came in after five minutes to "do my homework". And getting out a notebook and a pen to make a list was the closest I'd gotten to it.

I realized I needed something else though, that I needed to make another list.

"I have questions," I blurted, as soon as Daisy dumped her backpack in the backseat and climbed in.

She laughed. "Give a girl a second, babe, I think I'd better buckle up before you get started because you look like I have the answers, and you know me and my mouth. I want to be prepared for sudden stops."

Ouch.

"No, Haven, I'm sorry. I was playing with you. You're so intense. What's got into you?"

I glanced over at her, then looked forward again as I started out of my parking spot. "First question: do you like ice cream?"

"Yes," she shot out, "Are we getting ice cream?"

"Do you want to get ice cream?"

"Are you going to only speak in questions? Of course I want ice cream. Where are we going? And don't you dare ask me where I want to go."

If she was standing, she'd have her hands on her hips, I knew it. It was in her voice.

"What kind of ice cream do you like?" I shot out, followed by, "Yes... no... maybe... Almost everything will be a question." Then I added, "Okay?" just to be a jerk.

Hopefully a lovable, I mean likable, jerk.

"Do I have to answer in questions?"

"No." And I didn't add anything.

"Salt and Straw. I like their ice cream best." Daisy pulled one knee up and leaned her back on the door to look at me. "I think I'm going to like this game."

"What is your favorite flavor of ice cream?"

"Salted, Malted, Chocolate Chip Cookie Dough."

"That was specific." I patted the steering wheel, thinking about my next question.

"You asked. You should try it."

She was smiling at me; I could see her rosy cheeks in my peripheral vision. Still red from strenuous skating.

"Okay. I will. And I don't know if it's okay to ask this next question. Does your dad get any shit for being Iranian? Do you?"

I would never have guessed from her looks. Was I oblivious? Should I have known because she had the biggest most beautiful eyes I'd ever seen?

"Dad did. Does. He told me it was hell after 9/11. Every middle eastern man was a terrorist suddenly. It didn't matter that he'd been in America since 1978 and owned a decidedly non-Muslim business. I don't think running a fake Polynesian bar—serving alcohol—is exactly Sharia."

"Ooh, I know that one. Like adhering to Muslim law," I interjected, grateful for all the world religion teachings at Sunday school.

"Dad's family barely got out before the revolution. They just knuckled down to be 'the best damn Americans America has ever known' according to my grandpa. And my Aunt Roksana, she went by Roxy, had a record store—actual vinyl—before she died last year. That's why I got this." She pulled the neck of her shirt to reveal the heart tattoo and looked at the car roof for a second.

I think she was blinking back tears.

I nodded like I got it. Though maybe I did a little. A tattoo to mark something important like that made sense.

"And," she went on in a sing-song voice I figured was to mask her emotion, "I got my fabulous sense of style from Roxy. She could do victory curls you wouldn't believe and sharp, man, she had some serious pin-up dresses to die for."

I held my breath. Did she know what she said?

"And I inherited some of her wardrobe.

Okay, maybe she did.

"And she knew where to get those suits for Dad. They're getting rare, sharkskin suits."

Sharkskin...

"So now you know all about me," Daisy announced.

Not quite.

I found a spot just a block from Salt and Straw, but I stopped her before she swung open her door.

"Daisy, this is probably a stupid question, but did you really do that with that guy at the party? Before you kissed me?"

She raised one eyebrow at me. It disappeared into her bangs. "You're going to have to be more specific."

"Did you do oral sex on him?"

She groaned. "You were at that stupid party. It wasn't like there was an inch of privacy."

"But ever?"

I had a feeling ice cream wasn't going to make everything better based on the look on her face.

"Once. Ever. And he got to third base with me. Enough detail? Or do you need visuals."

My "no thank you" came out before I could think. Also "Why?"

"Look, I was a little drunk one time and he put his hand in my pants and got me off and I was returning the favor. It's not like there was anyone else there."

I wasn't sure it made it better.

Yeah, it did.

"But he's an asshole," I murmured, ready to get the ice cream show on the road, half hoping she didn't hear me.

"Sometimes," she shrugged. "There are worse. But he's a damn good kisser when he's sober."

Oh. My lips formed the word, but no sound came out. I never saw it coming when she launched over the console and kissed me on the mouth for a microsecond.

"But you're better," she said. With a grin so wicked I could feel it all the way to my toes.

I did not get Daisy.

CHAPTER TWENTY-ONE

"I Was Only Trying to Help"

It wasn't like I *planned* it. It just happened. One minute he was upright, swinging his arm, the next he was face-down on the table, unable to struggle, his arms across his chest and hands pinned to his shoulders.

He got a couple of good kicks in when the security guard grabbed me. Fair.

Not that I actually *hurt* him...

I was only just smart enough not to say that out loud as I was "escorted" from the cafeteria to the principal's office. For the first time. In twelve years of public education.

Would I get a lighter sentence because I was a first-time offender? Through the office window I could see Principal Hayes talking to the security guard, and figured the answer was "no" because I got the big gun, while Josh only got Vice-Principal Michaels.

That was messed up.

"He started it," I muttered, throwing myself into the chair placed strategically in front of Hayes's huge desk. I never thought I'd be someone using those words. I avoided Daisy's accusing eyes.

"You didn't have to go all Neanderthal on Josh."

On tone alone, I was pretty sure she rolled her eyes, but when I looked at her directly, she had a strange look on her face. It didn't match what she said, or the tapping of her thick-soled shoe. If only *she* was an open book.

Like she was yesterday before ice cream distracted us.

"I didn't go 'all Neanderthal' on him, Daisy! He was in your face, and I couldn't just stand there," my voice became a whine.

Probably not helping.

"You *weren't* standing there, Haven. You were at *your* table, with *your* friends, and couldn't hear me. You didn't need to run at him like my life depended on it."

"But I heard him."

I thought words like "fucking bitch" and "you have it coming" and "I'll find you alone" accompanied by a raised fist were bad enough to run.

Maybe I should have gotten there sooner, moved between them, or told him off or something. Because the first and only time I used my NCI restraint training it pissed off the person I... don't really want to piss off.

"It's not like I *hurt* Josh. He was just temporarily disabled. I mean, he might be a little sore in his rotator cuffs..."

"And where his face hit the table," she interjected.

She had me there. And I wasn't proud of it.

"If it was anyone else," she said, "would you have done this?"

Pretty sure that was a trick question.

I went with, "What do you mean?"

"You know what I mean." Her usually wide eyes narrowed.

I didn't. Did she mean would I have taken anyone else down if they harassed her? Or Josh down if he harassed anyone other than her? Umm... Intervene yes. Taken down? No. Maybe?

I wanted to say it had nothing to do with it being Josh. The asshole from the party. Who called her a skank. Who didn't deserve to breathe the same air as Daisy. Much less make out with her against a basement wall or have her mouth anywhere near his junk. And considering that, I'd taken it easy on him. It was only a safe restraint. This was getting blown out of proportion.

Not that I told Daisy that.

Or said anything else because I was saved by Principal Hayes. Who didn't think I'd taken it easy on Josh, at all. He made that *very* clear and then told Daisy to go back to class and if he needed anything from her, he'd let her know. When she left his office, he let me have it.

"I never expected this of you, Haven! Attacking someone? How are you going to explain this to your parents? And two detentions and *now* a suspension? I'm disappointed in you."

He looked disappointed in me. But I wasn't sure I was.

"Ms. Michaels is talking to Josh now, and a couple of students came to Ms. Lamb with details of the incident. It sounds like there is more to this story. But. Rules are rules. And 'no fighting' is a serious rule. We will not tolerate it. I should suspend you for a week. I still might."

I nodded. I had it coming. So, did Josh. He better get suspended, too.

But I kept my mouth shut. No need to make it worse than it was about to be. Because Principal Hayes told me he'd called my folks.

Daisy was still in the waiting area of the main office when I got there. She hadn't gone to class. And it wasn't because she was eager to see *me*. She was just standing there. Not looking at me. Or talking to me. For what felt like forever.

I didn't expect her to break her silence with, "I still can't believe this."

Really? That was what she had to say?

"You know what?" I started, "You didn't shove him away, or yell, or kick the shit out of him." Which she totally could have. "All I could think at the time was 'not on my watch.'"

Ms. Marquez shushed us. I was kind of yelling.

"I don't need to justify myself to you, Haven. If I'd needed help, you'd have fucking known it. I didn't lose my shit because I didn't want to be sitting right where you are now, facing suspension and your parents' disapproval."

"Since when do you care about anyone's approval, Daisy?"

She looked at me for a full minute. "That's not fair."

What did she mean? She was Daisy King. Bravest. Girl. Ever.

And probably right about everything. I needed to chill. Now.

"I'm sorry about not trusting you to take care of the situation. It got out of control fast. I know better than this." I blew out a breath that emptied my lungs. There was hardly time to suck in a new one before I heard another voice.

"You *do* know better," Mom's shriek was partly muffled because 'oh no, we wouldn't want to make a scene'.

But when I looked at Mom, she wasn't just freaked out or angry, she looked brittle. I reached for her, "I'm sorry, Mom, I'm so sorry." She let me hug her. She had the best hugs.

Almost the best, I thought, with a quick glance at Daisy.

"I always thought when this happened, if it happened, it would be because you had to protect your brother."

From himself.

She didn't have to say the words. Even though there hadn't been even close to a need for that in years. If you didn't count the whole classroom window episode, it had been a decade, almost, since he was out of control enough that someone else had to lay hands on him. His sensory defensiveness and reactivity had gone down so much after he'd started talking at seven.

But...

"I know what you mean. But what if I *was* protecting Paul, from someone else, would you be this mad at me?"

She sputtered, "No, of course not," then stopped, visibly pulling herself together, "I mean yes, I would be. It's never okay to lay hands on another person. I just never thought you'd use your training on anyone but..."

I stopped her. "I know what the training is for, Mom. But Daisy was being threatened by someone a lot bigger than her. Was I supposed to turn a blind eye?"

Mom was a good person. She'd get it. See something, say something, right? I didn't exactly use my words but still.

She didn't say what I expected when she turned to Daisy. Something like: Are you okay? I'm sorry you were put in that position. Did the bastard get what was coming to him?

Okay, maybe not that one.

Mom waited a long time before she spoke. Daisy stood there, still as a statue.

"You're that girl."

Ow. She wasn't Paul's "friend" now. She was "that girl" who kissed me, "that girl" Dad said would drop me in a heartbeat. Not "that girl" who had a flash of fear cross her face right before I reached Josh.

"Mom..." I reached for her hand.

Before I touched her, Principal Hayes was there.

"How about you talk to Haven at home, Mrs. Alexander? We're finished here. Josh's parents will be here soon, and I don't think you want to cross paths. They may not see the incident in the same light as you do."

Maybe. I didn't know *how* Mom saw "the incident". She was still looking at Daisy.

Ms. Lamb showed up beside me. Man, she was quiet. "Haven, Principal Hayes and I decided that as part of your punishment you won't be a Peer Counselor for the rest of the year."

I wanted to cheer. But it wasn't the time.

"And after your suspension there will be community service hours to fill after school," Ms. Lamb went on.

Oh. "But Ms. Lamb, you know I've been driving..."

Ms. Lamb interrupted me before Mom could. "How about I walk you out, Mrs. Alexander?" She used her hypnotic voice. She could calm a raging bull. "And Daisy, get attendance to give you a late slip for sixth period. I'll excuse fifth period, too."

I saw Ms. Lamb give Daisy a subtle nod. Ms. Lamb would *never* advocate violence, but I had a feeling she kind of understood where I'd been coming from. Maybe.

"Doesn't she get some punishment for this?" Mom pointed at Daisy.

"What? Why? She didn't do anything wrong," I moved between them. Mom was not doing this.

"But if she encouraged this boy in any way, baited him or egged him on."

Before Daisy could explode, I did. "Oh my God, you are blaming the victim. He was threatening her. I didn't *want* to physically intervene," mostly, "and it's not like I hurt him." Much.

Mom snapped her mouth shut. But at least she was directing her anger back at me instead of picking on Daisy. Who did *nothing* wrong.

"Please, Mrs. Alexander," Ms. Lamb glided smoothly between me and Mom, waving Daisy off.

"I agree," Principal Hayes herded us toward the doors closing behind Daisy. I watched her disappear down the hall. "This isn't the time or place to work this out, unless you have time in your schedule, Ms. Lamb? You're Haven's counselor."

This was my chance to talk to Mom with back-up. To really tell her about Daisy. That she wasn't "this girl". She was important. To me.

"Let's do it, Mom," I said. And I thought for sure she'd go for it. She was big on counselors and therapists, for Paul, and this wouldn't be like talking to a stranger. Ms. Lamb already knew I was screwed up. This could work.

But Mom shook her head, looking down now, instead of at me. "Maybe when I'm calmer, Ms. Lamb. I don't know what to think right now."

I groaned. And I didn't care who heard it.

Ms. Lamb walked us out. With her there it didn't feel so much like a perp' walk. More like protective custody. I'd have to text Daisy later. If Mom and Dad didn't take my phone. And lock me in my room. Like a criminal.

At least Mom saved the shrieking for home. Shrieking and pacing. Neither of us could hold still. We circled each other like boxers.

"What is wrong with you, Haven? Ever since you've known that girl, you've been letting us down, letting yourself down, letting Paul down."

My mouth dropped open. What?! "Let's leave Paul out of this."

"He's in it, honey. So long as he's spending lunchtime with those girls, which I hear is *still* going on, he's in this!"

"You were excited he has friends. You were practically making an arranged marriage between Paul and Daisy. What's changed?"

But she ignored me. "What's in it for those girls anyway? Are they getting community service credit? Is this a volunteer thing?"

Oh. My. God.

At least I knew Paul was still at school!

"Can't it be enough that they like him? Paul is sweet, and quirky, full of random facts, and doesn't judge people. They *get* him. And he's opening up more than ever. Asking questions. Having conversations with more than one person. Laughing. Sharing his artwork."

Mom cringed.

And that pissed me off. He. Was. Good. Even I could tell that and the only thing I knew about art was from Art History class and Alice. She told me there are tons of graphic novels with a similar style. Open your mind, Mom.

Not that I said that out loud.

But I wanted to.

Deep breath.

"They're good for him." I walked toward her across the living room slowly. "Remember how we were talking about states of grace at church? And moments of grace? Those girls be-friending Paul? It was like divine intervention. Right place, right time, right people. Can't you think of it like that? You believe everything happens for a reason."

She stilled. No one likes their words being used against them. She took a big breath.

"What's that got to do with your behavior today?" Mom backed away from me and threw herself down on the couch. It slid into the wall. Why did we bother leaving space behind the furniture? I looked at her, her arms crossed, totally closed off. Where was my *Mom*? When I really needed her.

Nowhere.

So fuck it.

"You know what? Nothing. They have nothing to do with what happened today. You want to know what's wrong with me. The answer is I'm human. I make mistakes. I make choices."

She eyed me curiously, as if she was seeing someone she didn't quite recognize. I bet she didn't. I threw myself down on the other end of the sofa and turned to Mom.

"It's okay that I'm not doing Track. Or doing extracurriculars until I throw up from exhaustion. Or betting all my marbles on an Ivy League school." I had no idea why I threw that in. "And I'm not giving up," Daisy, "any of my friends, including the derby girls."

She just looked at me. "What happened to Stanford or Yale?"

That's what she was going to focus on?

"Nothing. There's nothing wrong with them. And there's nothing wrong with me either, Mom. I'm good with the way I am these days."

Confused. Hopeful. Happy.

"How can you say that? You're not yourself! This isn't you."

What do you even know about who I am, Mom? But I didn't say it.

"Don't let these past few weeks destroy your dreams. Your school record is a little tarnished now, but we could probably claim extenuating circumstances. Your GPA is good, your ACTs are excellent, mostly, and you can do more extracurriculars in the fall to make up for this quarter. And for your essay, writing about being the sister of someone with a disability..."

And it was all about Paul again.

"Could give you that edge."

"No. Just no." That much I said.

But she was on a roll.

"And your athletic rankings are excellent. You're a top athlete. You've got this. You don't have to compromise."

"No, Mom. I'm not like Dad. I'm not trying out for the Olympics. And I compete in a sport that brings colleges zero money. I'm not a racehorse. Or a shoo-in. I'm just your daughter."

And then she was on the move, across the couch, wrapping her arms around me. *This* was Mom. The Mom who made treats for Cross-Country meets and cheered me on and gave hugs. Maybe she'd understand why I couldn't compete this spring for Coach Morgan.

"You are my daughter. And I love you. And, honey, you *are* a racehorse. A winning one. All you need to do is try harder and train harder and work on your diet some. And," she kissed my hair, "focus on what's important."

I disentangled myself from her hug.

She looked at me with such love. One hundred percent sure she was right about me, my future, my dreams, what was important to me.

"Friendships are important to me, Mom. Family is important to me."

"If family is important, why are you continuing to let Paul go to lunch with those girls?"

Wow.

I stood up and crossed the room to face her with some distance between us.

"I'm not 'letting' Paul do anything. If he wants to have lunch with friends, he's allowed to do that, right? Decide who he wants to hang out with?"

She. Was. Speechless. For a minute.

"Yes, but you introduced them in the first place. You vouched for them."

"No, they met each other all on their own. Weren't we just talking about this? Right place? Right time? Daisy helped him out in the lunch line, remember? When Luce left him alone?"

"But that was before today. It should never have happened."

But everything happens for a reason, Mom.

Patience, Haven. Breathe.

"True. Assholes shouldn't harass people."

"Language! You shouldn't have gotten involved. You wouldn't have if not for that girl."

And we were yelling.

"Because friends let friends get bullied? Not very Unitarian, Mom. Not very Christian. Friends are we, etcetera?"

"Give me your phone. I'm done talking about this."

She held out her hand.

"With you. I'm calling your dad."

CHAPTER TWENTY-TWO

"Real Mature, Mom"

Mom wasn't speaking to me.

Friday night, it seemed like the end of the world or something and the Mom I knew had Mr. Hyde-ed out of existence. That hurt, and Dad joining in just made it weird. The only person talking to me on Saturday was Paul. And there was no way to contact Daisy until after my suspension since they took my computer, too. I thought about asking Paul if I could borrow his phone. But that would make trouble for him.

And he didn't deserve that.

There was *one* upside to being ignored. I did *not* have to stand around like a show pony during coffee hour on Sunday while Mom talked about Paul and made shit up about me and Knox. She didn't even mention me to anyone. Not a peep.

Yay me.

But I'd *almost* swap being ignored for a place beside Mom as she wove la-la land tales of romance if it meant she loved me. That was seriously up for debate with her back to me, talking to Mrs. Landry about her husband's surgery. Mom hardly said a word beyond the necessary "oh, no", "I'm sorry", and "hope he gets better soon".

It was as if the whole world had pissed Mom off. She didn't even say "Hi" to Liz when they dropped us at Youth Group before service. She and Dad left without a word to me *or* Paul.

What did *he* do?

Youth Group was cool. Most days. Liz, the facilitator, was bad with conflict. She tried, but with a handful of teens with only church in common there's going to be conflict. Paul went right to the school desk at the back of the room and pulled out his phone and headphones. He still heard every word. He had superhero ears.

I wedged into the circle of chairs and desks Liz had set up. Sitting in a tight circle past kindergarten felt a *little* weird, though face it, it was Sunday School. But now I had to somehow sit with everyone crammed in around me and zero room to spread. I'd end up kicking Liz for sure.

The circle got even tighter as Dylan and Trinity pushed in, grabbing the last two chairs.

"Does anyone have something they'd like to talk about before we begin today's discussion?" Liz's flannel sleeves almost covered her big hands, her knuckles white from gripping her knees. She wasn't shy about her anxiety disorder. We all knew she struggled. I think it made it easier for some people to talk about their own.

But I wasn't one of them.

No one jumped in with a burning question. All Liz got were half a dozen shrugs and a few blank faces. Ray and Maia were on their phones. Andrew had grabbed a desk from the corner and dragged it, screaming against the linoleum tile, back to the circle and sat *on* it, swinging his legs. Shay was faking sleep, flopping forward in her chair.

She did that every Sunday.

Elizabeth looked uncomfortable, jiggling her leg like a maniac. And Elaine was right beside Liz, paying attention like a good girl.

She *was* a good girl.

While Liz waited us out, I looked around at the quotes from Martin Luther King, Jr., Gandhi, the Dalai Lama, Buddha, the Koran, and the Talmud. Studied the painting of a chalice Elaine did—art was not her strong suit—and a poster of the seven principles of Unitarian Universalism.

Not like they were a surprise after a decade of going to church on Sundays and waiting around when Mom had choir practice Wednesday nights for years. But the first principle hit me hard after what Dad had said about Daisy: The inherent worth and dignity of every person.

The other stuff made sense: truth, justice, the search for spiritual truth, respect for nature, blah, blah, blah. But the inherent worth and dignity of every person sounded so right. Where had Mom and Dad gone so wrong?

And Liz was talking. Oops.

"You guys are a tough crowd today," she continued, attempting to comb her fingers through her vivid red dreadlocks. Not happening. "So, since June will be here before we know it and I won't be seeing you until September, and we won't be here when it's most topical in July..."

Oh, she was going there. Portland did Pride in July.

"Let's talk about the difference between tolerance and acceptance and how it plays out in real life."

Liz was big on "real life."

Shay popped up as soon as Liz paused, like she always did, ready to rant. When Sean came back to Youth Group as Shay after summer break it was easy to adjust. Maybe because I'd known Shay since we were six? And she hadn't been subtle about wanting to transition.

I felt bad that nonbinary just glitched in my brain. Male and female, I got, gender on a spectrum, I got, but neither or both just didn't make sense to me. Not like I was going to bring *that* up now.

"Tolerance sucks and acceptance rocks," said Shay, tossing her black hair. Growing it long had taken almost a year.

I fingered the blunt ends of my hair. I wish Mom would let me... wait, no, she didn't get to decide that. And what was Mom going to do if I told her no? Tell me she didn't know me anymore?

It was her parting shot Friday afternoon.

"It's like, one is barely letting you exist, and the other is 'let's party together!'"

"That's what you always want to do, Shay. Party," Elizabeth said, tugging her skirt down over her skinny thighs.

She was such a hypocrite. Hopefully rehab' was working.

And I was a jerk. What did *I* know about addiction?

"Tolerance is saying it's okay to be prejudiced, just don't hurt anyone," said Andrew. "You could say White Supremacists are tolerant by that standard. So long as they don't blow anyone away."

"Except they do want to hurt BIPOC. And take away our civil rights," Trinity said. I had to strain to understand her. Her Peruvian accent was still strong.

"What's it like for you, Haven?" Shay said, turning to face me.

Me?

"What do you mean? I'm *so* white bread."

Shay blew out a breath like she was praying for patience. "I mean as a lesbian. I know what it's like being Hispanic and gay and now a straight Trans Woman, and that it's scary out there..."

Even I knew that. There were more reasons than ever for Trans Day of Remembrance. But that word. The "L" word. My brain was glitching again.

"But you've got to have struggled with the tolerance-slash-acceptance issue?" she finished.

I shook my head so hard my hair whipped my cheeks. "I'm not a lesbian. Where did you get that idea?" It wasn't a lie. Just because I liked Daisy didn't make me a lesbian. Maybe I was just like Daisy. Not *so* straight.

"Oh, come on," said Dylan, "You're not fooling anyone. You couldn't be straight if you tried."

Everyone laughed. *Laughed*!

Liz held up her hands. "Hey guys, you let Haven speak her truth. You speak yours. She gets to choose her identity..."

Did I?

"Internalized homophobia in action," Shay said, "I know all about it. Well," she stopped for a second, "Actually I don't. I was always into dick. If you have a problem with pussy just say so."

Oh. My. God.

"Come on, Shay. This is supposed to be a safe space. And if Haven doesn't identify as gay, that's up to her don't you think."

Thank you, Elaine.

"Why did you say 'pussy'?" Paul asked from the back.

Shay opened her mouth. And stopped, looking from Paul to me to Liz.

"Cat got your tongue, Shay?" Dylan smirked.

"Haven is allergic to cats. I'm allergic to cats. Pussy is another name for cat. We have a problem with pussy," Paul said.

Pretty sure he knew exactly what he was doing. Good redirect, bro.

Everyone else thought that was hi-la-ri-ous. Andrew practically fell off the desk.

"Let's get back to acceptance versus tolerance. Some folks tolerate people on the queer spectrum, in the dictionary definition way of 'putting up with', or in the anti-authoritarian 'live and let live' way. Some folks accept queer people and queer*ness*, as in embrace individual differences from straight people and within queer culture."

Were we talking about the purple-haired pierced people? Because that was *not* my culture.

Nice as they were.

And I *think* I just exemplified the lesson. I'd been "putting up with" them. Not accepting.

"Embrace it, Baby," Shay interjected. Looking right at me.

"There are coming out parties. People celebrate transitions," Liz said.

Elizabeth laughed. "I used to think a 'gender reveal' party was that. Like yay, this is my real gender everyone. What is with people and the gender of their baby? Like it's this huge thing that dictates their whole future and what they'll play with and date and everything."

Dylan drooped. "Sylvia is like that. She painted Phaedra's room pink as soon as she knew." He didn't want his little girl to grow up to be a stereotype.

"And some people don't even tolerate queers like us," Shay said. To me?

"Shay," Liz said. A warning. "That's enough."

"I think she's a big old dyke and just doesn't say so because her parents don't want her to be," Shay blurted.

"Why are you doing this?" I stood up, sending my chair skidding behind me. "Just leave me alone. I'm just me, okay? I'm just normal."

There was a collective "ooh," and I knew I'd said the wrong thing.

"Typical. Boring. Average. Nothing special. I didn't mean that anyone different than me wasn't normal. I'm sorry Liz, I'm gonna go. Paul, you can stay if you want to."

"Haven, are you okay?" Trinity asked.

I nodded. I'd said enough. Everyone had said enough.

"I want to go with you." Paul unwound himself from the desk and the narrow hall echoed with the tapping of our feet on the old linoleum as we made our way to the basement.

"Why were you arguing with Shay?" he asked. "Don't you like him?"

Paul was still working on pronouns. He liked consistency.

"We were just talking." I wanted to sling my arm around his waist. Knowing he wouldn't like it. Then I remembered that Daisy had. "Paul," I got his attention, "Can I put my arm around you?"

He kept walking. "Why?"

"Because I love you."

He stopped and looked down at me. "I guess so."

I wrapped my arm around his waist, leaning into him, smiling so hard it hurt.

"Thanks, bro."

"I love you, too," he said, just over a whisper.

As I watched Mom talk to Mrs. Landry, Paul suddenly got up and walked straight across the room and up to Mom and Dad. I followed Paul slowly, keeping my distance. I wasn't about to try to force Mom to talk to me.

Not Paul. He got right in her space, avoiding eye contact, despite breathing the same air. "We talked about cats in Group and Shay said 'dick' and can we have Daisy over when we get home? I was sick this week. I missed her."

They were the most words Paul had spoken at coffee hour in years.

So happy he said, "cats" and not 'pussy'. "Dick" was bad enough.

Dad reached out to clap him on the shoulder. Paul twisted to avoid contact.

Dad muttered, "Sorry, Paul," before grinning at Mrs. Landry for some reason.

And Oh Joy, Knox's mom decided to join the party.

"David, you were supposed to email me the volunteer sheet for the Fun Run," Lily started.

But Paul interrupted her. "Can we have Daisy over? You didn't answer. Why didn't you answer?"

Paul had struck my parents speechless. Go Paul.

Knox must have said something to Lily, because she said, "Do you mean Daisy King?"

Like it was a bad thing. She and Mom had that in common.

"Daisy is my friend," Paul said, avoiding Lily's eyes.

Mrs. Landry beamed. "A girlfriend?"

Seriously? Way to be heteronormative.

But Mom pounced on it. "Yes, they sit together at lunch every day."

Lily opened her mouth. Looked at me. Shut it. She was Mom's friend. And dying to deny what Mom was selling.

"Daisy is Haven's friend, too," my brother added.

"That's right," I said, straightening up, "She is. She's a great person."

Knox's mom didn't know what to say. It wasn't like she could slander Daisy at church, right in front of Mrs. Landry.

Dad ignored me. "I'm glad you've found a friend at school, Paul. But I don't think she should come over. But good try."

And he winked at Paul.

What the ever-loving fuck?

"No," I chimed in, joining the group, "I think it's a great idea, Paul. We should have Daisy over. Maybe for dinner."

Take that, Mom and Dad.

"Maybe," Mom said, after a long pause. Meaning no way in hell.

Paul rocked his body forwards and back, "Dinner with Daisy. We should have Twinkies for dessert. She likes Twinkies."

Uh oh. I'd forgotten to refill Mom's stash. Mom threw me dagger-eyes. Lily excused herself and Mrs. Landry found another person to tell about her husband's operation.

Paul told Mom and Dad what he wanted on the menu when Daisy came for the hypothetical dinner the whole car ride home. Score one for Paul. He would totally text Daisy when we got home. And I bet he'd let me join in. I couldn't wait.

CHAPTER TWENTY-THREE

"Would I Be Here if I Didn't?"

Daisy texted me right before I got inside the building and had to turn off my phone.

If you're going to be jealous of Josh, you're going to have to deal with the consequences.

As if I didn't already know that.

She was looking right at me when I got to Health class, chuckling.

Laugh it up, derby girl, first time I hear from you in five days, and this is what you have to say?

If Paul had texted her as planned, I could be laughing *with* Daisy instead of being laughed *at*. Mom played dirty after we got back from church and offered to watch him play *Portal* and how could he resist Mom being interested in something *he's* interested in? She wasn't above using his AuDHD to distract him and divert his focus.

Particularly when that focus was on having Daisy over.

Dad just went for a run. And did not ask if I'd like to join him.

I had no idea what was going on in Daisy's head, besides this ludicrous accusation of jealousy. I had been in total isolation since Friday afternoon, stuck in my room except for meals—fun meals held in total silence—and the occasional knock on my door from Paul, who would come in, sit on my bed, tell me some fun facts and then leave. Church was my only outing and look at how *that* turned out.

Though the part where Paul said "dick" to Mom and Dad? Priceless.

Instead of being able to get online, get the assignments, and keep up in classes, I got to hope I could predict what chapters we were supposed to study so I could be ready for a load of work when I got back to class. I finished the last chapters in all my textbooks in three days. And took notes.

It was boring. And you can only do so many planks to refocus your brain. I was bored and boring, my mind kept telling me, and oh so white bread and nice, neutral, modest and free moving.

And I missed Daisy.

Who was none of the above.

And didn't waste any time before giving me shit about Josh just as soon as I *had* my phone back. Her timing was perfect, like she'd been leaning out the classroom window watching me walk up the front steps before hitting "send".

Then she didn't even make eye contact with me for the rest of Health after practically laughing in my face, or in History, or catch up with me in the hall.

Fine.

Not like I could text her back at school.

She was ignoring me, so I would ignore her. I didn't sit with her at lunch. Which was a mistake because all I could think about was what she was saying, and thinking, and had I taken this too far and was she just teasing me or was she still mad at me and what could I do about it if she was? She didn't even look my way.

Because I was checking.

No, she was having a blast talking to her friends, and Paul, and why did I have to mess things up so much?

And *my* friends had texted me for days, they were telling me, and had a lot to say about taking down Josh.

Grey wanted to know how to do it and where to get the training because she was working with high needs developmentally disabled middle school students in the summer and was supposed to know how as a last resort. Dog Meat wanted to know what on earth I was thinking. Maddy said I was a beast, then amended that she meant it in a good way.

Trent and Knox weren't saying anything about the "incident" and talked Baseball and Track when they could get a word in.

Knox ignored me just as much as Daisy did.

Besides this stupid cold war going on with Daisy, the only changes since Friday were that Josh gave me, and Daisy, a wide berth, and that the whole lesbian bashing or teasing or whatever was back. I guess the idea was that I must be in love with Daisy to go to her rescue. Like it wasn't enough to just help someone being hassled.

And I got high fives from some girls and a few of the guys for taking the asshole down.

I only felt a little guilty about that.

And a lot guilty for not sitting with Daisy.

Not that Daisy shot me evil looks or anything in Ecology. She was focusing on her work, as far as I could see, same as me. I was trying to understand the illustrations Alice made of the micro-fauna and -flora from our Eco site. I had to label them and had *no* idea what I was looking at. When Ms. Allen stopped lecturing, I was going to have to grill Alice on the details.

I was trying to listen and label when I suddenly felt Daisy focus on me. I looked over at her table, and she was looking at me. Trying to communicate psychically or something? I finally found out when she waited for me at the end of class instead of skipping off.

She smiled wickedly—I missed that smile—before saying, "Do you know what Paul asked me today?"

Did. I. Ever.

"Do you want to come over for dinner?"

She grinned wider, her lips shining red, her big eyes narrowing with lines slanting up at the side. "He sure did. Third time this week. Handsome devil."

What?

"Not you, too. I'm so sick of this stuff. Paul doesn't mean it that way..."

"Haven."

"First it was Mom. Then Dad. Then Mrs. Landry at church..."

"Haven, stop," she waved a hand in front of my face. "I think I know Paul. He didn't mean a date. And neither did I. Are you still up for driving me to practices?"

"Yeah. Definitely. I'd love to." And that was too much. I could have stopped with "yeah". But I'd been worried that I'd be phased out since Ellie finally had her license long enough to drive them all.

Shit, I was getting paranoid.

"Meet you at the usual spot?" I said, when we reached the hallway.

"You bet, Babe," she called out with a wave. I froze. Half the hallway heard that "'babe".

But beyond a few smiles, a palm held up for me to slap from Trent—who'd been looking happier lately, I noticed—and a muttered "lesbo" from a guy pushing by who I thought was on the boys Track Team, nothing. I was making too big a deal out of this. Why was I so worried about what people would say?

But when I thought about it on the way to Latin, maybe I always had. Worried about what other people would say. I'd thought I was this totally cool-with-myself girl, so not hung up and distracted by a stupid guy, my head on straight. Priorities on track. I was so wrong. I wasn't even sure I was cool with myself or ever had been.

What I'd been cool with was being whatever Mom and Dad wanted me to be. Whatever Knox wanted me to be—except his girlfriend—and whatever Paul needed me to be. I'd wanted to be a good enough friend to Laurie that she'd like me even if she knew me, but that didn't work out. I wanted to win the district, regionals, the state championships in whatever was asked of me.

I loved running. The winning was for them.

And then Alice didn't want anything from me. She wasn't even sure she wanted to be a friend. I kind of made her be my friend. And that opened the door.

To Daisy. Who didn't care about my grades, or my wins, or how fast I could run, but *still* liked me. Why?

I was still asking myself that question, "quare?" in Latin, when I met up with Daisy in front of the school. Not another derby girl in sight. Which was cool because she was enough all by herself.

And not just because she'd changed into some kind of red bra shirt that matched her lips and black volleyball shorts. Though there was no missing them on her. Daisy King was distracting me more than any *guy* could. I was pretty sure.

And there was Shay in my mind, saying I was a "big old dyke" and Dylan saying I "couldn't be straight" if I tried. Were they right?

It was weirdly quiet in the Volvo on the drive to the Hangar. Daisy usually gave me hell. And there was plenty of material. What I did to Josh was still on my mind. It had to be on hers.

I watched her during practice on and off, slogging through my missed assignments on my laptop. I couldn't keep my mind focused though. It kept wandering to Daisy weaving through the other players, bodychecking and taking narrow turns without going out of bounds. Except once when I almost threw my laptop to the floor, I got up so fast, because she fell and her helmet bounced off the floor, and she didn't get right up.

I was frozen, not even breathing, until she lifted one arm for a hand up.

I figured that was why she was quiet on the way home. Being sent home early from practice because of concussion protocol. I hated it when I got hurt and couldn't finish practice. When it happened back in September when I hurt my ankle I was pissed. She probably wanted to be away from humans and chill.

But when we got to her house, Daisy suddenly announced that she should put ice on her head. And that I should stick around for a while in case she really had a concussion. Check if her eyes were tracking. And she didn't pass out.

We didn't make it to the freezer.

She stopped me by saying, "Babe."

And it wasn't her usual tossed out "babe" either.

"I think I should lie down," she said, backing toward the couch. "And you should, too." She caught the end of my fingers and pulled gently.

Oh.

She stretched out on her side and left just enough room for me to sit at her feet. The couch was deep, and dark purple, and felt comfortable under me. She leaned on one arm and reached out to my left hand.

"You can't check my pupils from over there, Haven."

Oh. And I said it.

"Oh," she repeated after me, and scooted into the back of the couch, leaving room for me to lie down facing her. Face to face. Breath to breath. My body sinking into the cushions, pulled by gravity in her direction.

I looked at her pupils but didn't linger, they were too intense, too dark, too holy hell a close-up Daisy was even scarier.

And beautiful. She was beautiful. Not only her huge, chocolate brown eyes with the line she drew lifting at the outer edges, but her full tinted lips, the length of her nose, her warm, tan skin, midway between her mother's pallor and her father's olive coloring.

I was practically writing poetry in my head about her skin.

And her hair, how soft it looked, glossy and brown but almost black pulling away from the sides of her face and coming down straight as a line mid-way through her dark brows.

Arching brows tamed and shaped and ending in narrow line to perfection.

And other parts. That were right there in front of me. So close. A perfect curve from shoulder down to her waist and up over her hip and down to her bare feet with red toenails.

When had she taken her shoes off?

And I remembered her slipping out of her buckle shoes by the door, setting them neatly alongside my flip flops.

Her chest was rising. Falling. So was mine. It was like they wanted to meet in the middle.

I reached out with my left hand, my head on my right, and stroked the skin of her cheek. It was just as soft as I thought it would be. Soft, and warm, and right there. So beautiful.

And I said it out loud. On purpose.

And before I could think maybe I could kiss her, she kissed *me*.

Full on lip assault. Mouth, hands in hair, scooting closer, mouth, kissing, hands on her waist, scooting closer, tongue, there was tongue, and Wow. Wow. I lost my freaking mind. Feeling it all to my toes and along my body and strangely in my breasts and Wow.

Daisy broke away long enough to say, "Mom's working a twenty-four-hour shift."

And my mouth was on hers again, more relaxed, more tense, more, more.

I hooked my leg around hers and pulled her away from the back of the couch, kissing her the whole time and she felt so good I just wanted her closer and I pulled her closer and she was almost under me. Scary. Good. Wow. Soft and strong and curvy and smaller than me and Wow.

When we took a breath and stared at each other she caught me off guard.

"Are you absolutely sure you're not still in love with Alice?" she said in a breathy voice.

My heart was pounding and all I could think was how could she ask that? Now?

I tried to pull out of the tangle of limbs on Daisy's wide sofa. Where were those words coming from? Not from the tiny space between her lips and mine. But there they were, floating in the crackle of energy that was always between us.

I struggled harder to pull myself away and Daisy shifted, pulling her arms from around my stomach and sliding her hips farther from mine. I could only look at her, my mouth probably open like a fish.

"Are you, Haven?" Her brown eyes were looking at me in this weird way I'd never seen before. Not the Daisy who was afraid of nothing. Not the derby girl who hip-checked her opponents off the line at every bout. This Daisy was different. A little like the Daisy who confronted me in the parking lot before I took off that day, running in flip flops like an asshole. But more.

"I was never in love with Alice," I started, "I don't even know what 'in love' is."

So *not* the time for this conversation. Couldn't she see that?

"You know what I mean," she said, looking away, toward the poster pinned up beside the window. Some lady leaning on her palm with swirls surrounding her, her eyes staring at me like Daisy usually did. With confidence.

I looked at Daisy, sure maybe for the first time. The "No" was ready to jump out of my mouth. But Daisy deserved a thorough answer, considering what *this* was between us. I *had* liked Alice. I could admit that in my head, though it was weird to think that about my friend now. My unlikely friend.

I looked at Daisy's profile. If anything, Daisy was an even more unlikely friend than Alice. With her bluntness that out-shone mine, though her bluntness had style while mine just fell over its feet, and her whole pin-up thing.

And there was so much more than her appearance.

But while I studied her face and felt the warmth of her soft body still radiating inches from me, her scent familiar and new at the same time, the fact was, I did know.

No, I wasn't in love with Alice. Maybe I was a little in love with *her*.

Daisy looked back at me, something like shyness spreading over her, and I knew it was because of me. How long had I stayed silent?

"No. Definitely not," I said, finding myself whispering it.

"Oh," she said, her boldness taking over again as she slid back into place, click, like a piece of me. Only better. "Do you like me, Haven Alexander?" She drew out the "er", making a game of it but she still looked serious.

Did I like her? I knew better than to say "duh" but yeah, would I be here if I didn't? Okay, I said the last part.

Daisy sighed, flopping onto her back and away from me.

"Why are we even doing this? If you can't even admit you like me?"

I pulled back, barely on the edge of the sofa. Landing with a thud would be so uncool. "How can you think I don't like you? We kiss." It was so much more than a kiss, but the word said it all to me and it felt vulnerable to even say the word out loud, like it was a fragile bubble that would pop if spoken. I liked the bubble just the way it was.

"Do you want to hang out with anyone else?" she asked, staring at the ceiling.

"Do you?" I mirrored her, our bodies crammed in side by side, studying the cracks in the plaster overhead like they would provide insight into what the heck she was getting at.

It wasn't like she could think there was anyone else I wanted to hang out with like we did. But then, she'd been with other people, with boys, maybe all this was because she wanted to hang out with someone else. Too.

I lay perfectly still. "Do you?" I repeated.

Crickets. Shit. I felt my whole body go heavy. And not in the good, let gravity hold me down way. This was like falling. Then I heard her move, and Daisy's chin slipped over my shoulder while her body inched behind mine, arms wrapping around my middle. She squeezed me so tight I fought for breath.

"No, Babe, I don't want to see anyone else. But I kind of want us to be a thing. I want to hold your hand at school, you know, without you freaking out."

I swallowed. Yeah, there had been that one time, by Grey's boyfriend's car. But that was it. I didn't even know what I thought about that.

Could I do it?

Was there a reason not to, if it would make Daisy happy?

We'd already been labeled since the night she kissed me at Carter's party. Even before we were "hanging out". Would it really matter if people were right about me? That I liked Daisy. And she liked me. Like a girlfriend?

Yeah, I wasn't planning on saying those last three words out loud.

But I did.

"Like a girlfriend?"

And then a key turned in the lock on the front door. We had about two seconds to leap apart. I barely made it upright with some space between us. This had seemed like a good idea when her mom was supposed to be at work for twenty-four hours. Now, not so much.

"I thought you said she was gone 'til morning," I whispered in a rush.

"Not always," Daisy hissed back. "Sometimes there's a lull in the labor room."

Oh. I swallowed hard as Daisy's mom swung open the front door, an enormous purse over one shoulder and a big leather bag in her other hand.

So many thoughts crowded my brain. First and foremost: Daisy's mom walked in on us, Daisy's mom walked in on us,

Daisy's mom walked in on us. I jumped up, tangling my fingers together because what was I supposed to do? Stick one out to shake hands when those hands had been on her daughter moments before? I didn't think so.

Ruby King didn't look happy to see me.

"You're quite the troublemaker, aren't you?" And she gave me an obvious once over. Was this how boys felt when dads checked them out before the big date? I never thought I'd be on the receiving end of one of those looks. From her mom...

And "troublemaker"?!

"Down girl," muttered Daisy. Not looking in any way bothered that her mom had walked in on us practically making out all over her couch.

"Nice to see you again, Mrs. King," I said, suddenly sure this wasn't the right thing to say. Whatever I said would be the wrong thing to say.

"Ms. King," she said, not breaking eye contact. But she sighed and the tension eased out of her body. "No, call me Ruby. I just had a rough one, breach and five days overdue. That sucker had a sixteen-inch head."

"Are they both okay?" Daisy asked, standing up.

"Yeah, yeah. Jesus, longest transition phase I've ever had, and Mom had refused medication. I think she was hallucinating she was in so much pain. She kept saying 'the birds, the birds'."

She threw her purse and bag onto the floor by the door and slipped off a pair of bright pink Keds. More like kicked off. They landed in different parts of the room. I guess Daisy wasn't wrong when she said her mom didn't mind her dumping her things all over the place. I couldn't so much as set a sweatshirt on the arm of the sofa at home without Mom picking it up and putting it in the coat closet.

"Did you eat already?" Ruby called over her shoulder as she strode past, heading to the tiny kitchen. Out of the corner of my eye I saw her stop and shake her head. "Wait, don't answer that."

I was going to die.

"Carry on. I'll just be over here stuffing my face and then planting that face on my mattress until the next baby's arriving."

I was relieved that Daisy stood as still as I did while her mom rattled around the kitchen, came out waving a microwave burrito, stomped down a hallway I'd barely noticed before, and slammed her door. I blew out a breath; that could have gone worse.

But "troublemaker"?

Then again, she hadn't thrown me out for maybe having sex with her teenage daughter. And then she acted like we were going to go at it again or something. What mom was okay with that?

I think I was in shock.

Until Daisy's hand wrapped around my forearm and pulled me toward her. I looked at her and gestured toward the hallway where her mom went.

"She's already dead to the world. Come on, lay down with me." The sparkle in her eyes was hard, impossible, to resist.

What was I doing? When she got me like she wanted, our bodies facing each other a breath apart, she went on. "Where were we?"

I just looked at her. I remembered exactly where we were. But I wasn't going to be the one to say the words.

"Like a girlfriend," Daisy said, and there wasn't confidence in her eyes, the sparkle dimmed.

Maybe I should have said the words. This time I did.

"Like a girlfriend."

I could feel her nodding against my shoulder, her soft cheek rubbing against mine with every bob of her head. She smelled so good. "Yeah, like a girlfriend."

Did I want Daisy to be my girlfriend? To have a girlfriend? Could I do it?

And then I imagined Daisy being someone else's girlfriend and hell no. Yeah, she was my girlfriend.

"I want that."

CHAPTER TWENTY-FOUR

"I Don't Know If I Can Do It."

It wasn't lost on me that the person I *needed* to talk to the next day could have been the last person I'd *want* to talk to. But she wasn't. Not anymore.

I only hoped I'd persuaded Daisy that it was true.

I *knew* it was true.

But I had to get through school first.

Luckily, for me anyway, Daisy had a dentist's appointment. She texted me first thing in the morning. She was getting cavities filled. And told me to "have a fabulous day" followed by a daisy emoji.

I liked the daisy emoji.

She missed classes in the morning and was a no-show in Ecology. Maybe she couldn't sleep any better than I had last night and was taking a nap. I could sure use one, I thought.

Latin couldn't be over soon enough. I kept screwing up and even though it was a rough class I *never* screwed up. Ms. Sulliger was not happy.

Constitution Team was a breeze since competition was long over. It made debating private school vouchers tolerable, because there would be no chance of having to do it onstage. No way could I have even written arguments in favor, much less spoken the words, if we'd been asked to take that on as our debate. Private schools weren't exactly inclusive.

And now they didn't have to be. Stupid politics.

I couldn't even believe Celeste found any arguments in favor of paying the jerks to cherry pick students from public schools. I still lost. I was too tired to fight.

I couldn't sleep for a second after squeezing in the door just barely before seven last night. I was feeling tired, yeah, and a whole lot shell-shocked. I. Had. A. Girlfriend.

I needed today, without Daisy at school, before this reality shift became official.

I headed to Paul's classroom to pick him up. Taking the steps two at a time, I thought, 'I'm going to do it."

No. I shook my head, denying my own thoughts. I wasn't going to *do it*, the idea was terrifying. Just... live the life. Be out, as whatever I was, bisexual, gay, a lesbian... I didn't want a label. I just wanted to be with *her*.

What was Daisy going to say *she* was?

She'd say something. Being with Daisy wouldn't exactly be subtle. And I'd made a lifestyle out of being just me. Average. Boring. Responsible. Normal.

Not a word I was going to use out loud around anyone else EVER again. Youth Group last Sunday was going to stick with me forever.

Not that being with Daisy would be a big PDA fest probably. I'd never noticed her making out in the hallways like I'd seen Renee do with Malik on the regular. And Alice at least once when she was with Rowan the thug.

Alice. I needed to talk to Alice...

Paul was waiting by the classroom door.

And I felt that other kind of jolt. I always felt it when I first saw him, that combo of love, protectiveness and a yearning I only admitted to once, years ago, in family therapy when Paul was home with Dad. A yearning for a big brother who could take care of me, too.

Mom had flipped out that day—cue the guilt and anguish and self-reproach—she was all sorry about Paul not being the brother I needed. When all I needed was to be *heard*. And move on. Instead, I felt guilty for ever saying it aloud, for ever thinking it, for ever wishing Paul wasn't *Paul*. It made even feeling it wrong.

"Hey," I said, when he joined me and we headed downstairs.

"Hey," he said, looking anywhere but at me, his headphones firmly in place.

When I'd asked Alice in the morning if I could drop by Comikaze to talk to her later, she was all, "What time should I have his double-tall extra-hot mocha ready?"

And I fumbled for an answer.

She stopped me with a raised pierced eyebrow. "Kidding, Haven, just kidding. You're being kind of intense."

Intense. That was a good word for it.

Now I was thinking, do I really want to talk about this in front of my brother?

Before we could get out of the front doors, I heard my name from behind us.

I turned toward her, then turned back to Paul, "Do you want to meet me at the car?" I dangled the keys. He shook his head like he always did when this came up, and a tic lifted his right shoulder to his chin. I turned back to her. When did she have time to change in the three minutes since we were in seventh period?

"What's up, Celeste? And hey, you were amazing in the 100-meter sprint last week."

"You were there?" she looked shocked. And ready to run another sprint, considering the spandex. She must be on the way to Track practice.

"I watched it on YouTube." I wanted to cheer on the team but that could be weird for everyone, if Coach Morgan said anything. "And I'll be rooting for you next week against Lincoln. I know you'll do the team proud."

It felt awkward telling her that, like she wouldn't already know how important she was to the team. But she lunged at me and hugged me like a vise, so I guess it was okay.

"Thank you! I never thought she'd let me off the bench. If you hadn't dropped out..."

I didn't want to, I thought. But it was the right thing to do. "You deserve the spot."

And she hugged me again. I held my arms out to my side, not sure what I was supposed to do with that. Not like I was going to hug her back. Or would anytime. But if I was Daisy's girlfriend did a hug count as cheating?

There needed to be a rulebook.

"We're stopping here?" Paul asked. For the third time since I began parallel parking. It was a close fit. I had to finesse it four times before getting the distance just right. Being an exhausted nervous wreck didn't help. When I pulled the parking brake and turned off the engine, his body slumped, tension easing out. But just as quickly he was up and out, paying zero attention to where he was pushing the passenger door.

Parking with Paul wasn't a no-brainer. He'd hit his fair share of bike racks and parking sign poles. The Volvo could take it.

I slid in the door to Comikaze behind him. He headed straight for the comic book side and crouched in front of the new release shelf before I had time to even look for Alice.

Not that I had to look far.

"Double-tall mocha for Paul, coming up," she practically sang it—*she* was sure having a good day—and got to work cramming coffee grounds into the cup-thing. "Do you want something?"

"You know I don't do caffeine." I drifted over to behind Paul, my eyes sliding over the covers. Boobs and gore were the prominent themes. The issue of *Harley Quinn* was gruesome. I leaned closer, suddenly and uncomfortably aware that I wasn't really checking out the issue as much as checking out the lace-up corset thing she was wearing.

And thinking that Daisy had one similar.

I was so in over my head.

And, my luck, just as Alice brought over Paul's drink and her boss, Tim, took over the café register for her, the door jangled again and we were in the presence of Finn the knit-hat wearing, not-supposed-to-be-a-boyfriend-yet boyfriend.

Great.

"Here you go, Paul." Alice put the drink beside his hand. He didn't like to be handed anything. When he grabbed the paper cup she stood and faced me. "What's the deal, Haven? Tim said I could take my break if I want..."

I couldn't even wait for her to stop speaking.

"I don't know if I can live the life, Alice. Like, walk the walk, you know, be with Daisy." If I said it any faster, it would have been a whir of words.

Her pale eyes lit up. "Are you *with* Daisy?"

Alice didn't muck around.

"Yeah, I guess I am, I mean, I am," I was so full of questions it didn't quite register that Finn was hanging on my every word, too. "We're like a thing, like girlfriends, I guess."

Thanks Alice, you can stop looking so smug now. But I didn't say it.

"*Like* girlfriends?"

"Yeah, yeah, okay, yes girlfriends, and you can be like that all you want but it's one thing to admit how I feel to you but another thing to admit it to God and everyone. And I mean *everyone*. Everyone will have something to say and some of it is going to make me want to punch people. And Mom and Dad are going to find out for sure. And the Boosters already have it in for Daisy."

I thought of Dad coming to my room. All I needed was Mike Lopez telling tales again. But Dad coming in and telling me this was just a phase? Not going to let it happen again. Screw that.

Finn opened his mouth to speak but Alice put up her palm to halt him. He closed it and bounced on his toes, bursting with things he wanted to say.

"Just let him," I said, rolling my eyes already, and he hadn't even spoken. "Bring it on, Finn."

He let out a big breath and settled back on his feet. "First, you're not that interesting, Haven. There are bigger deals to talk about than you being with Daisy. Second, everyone knows already. Third, you could always talk to my moms. It's not like they came out now, but they've been through the whole coming out thing."

The "whole coming out thing" was terrifying.

And "everybody knows"? Okay, he might be right about that one. Except...

"My parents don't know." Not for sure. Maybe Dad, kind of. He said "experimenting" but we both knew what he was talking about.

"It's really not a big deal anymore," he added with a shrug.

Easy for him to say. It was to me. And it would be to them. Especially Mom. She'd made her feelings crystal clear. She thought it was a "choice". And yeah, it was, in a way. Did I just pretend I didn't feel that way? Pretend Daisy didn't feel like she did. Give up caring. About her. About me.

"I don't know..." I said, checking behind me to see that Paul was occupied. I wasn't sure how *he* would feel if I was with Daisy.

That I *am* with Daisy.

It was going to take some getting used to.

"But what if I'm not enough? And Daisy gets sick of me. And I go through whatever's next for nothing. Or someone comes on to me now that people know that I'm going to be... out?"

Alice's brows scrunched. "Come on. Give it a chance. You want to. Or you wouldn't have said you would. She won't get sick of you."

I wanted to say 'how do you know that? This is Daisy we're talking about. She's smart, sarcastic, and yes, sexy. Why would she want to stay with me?' Suddenly, *I* felt a little sick.

"And as far as come-ons go," Finn added, "I assume you're talking about girls. You should be so flattered. Or not. Same as with guys."

Which I had no experience with, except Knox. And he read that on my face.

"Just say no. It's easy."

"Do you think I can do it?" Be with Daisy? Be girlfriends with Daisy?

And thank you Alice for not taking the words "do it" the wrong way.

"I think you can."

I'm glad she had confidence in me. I sure didn't.

"What if I mess it up?" The idea made me feel even sicker.

She smiled at me and said two words that didn't help at all. "You will."

Paul and I were halfway home before he said, "You like Daisy."

Okay. We were going to talk about it.

"I do, Paul. A lot."

"I like Daisy."

"I know." Did I need to spell out the difference? Did I want to, when he wasn't going to lie if it came up with Mom and Dad? Would I want him to lie?

Maybe I didn't.

"I like Daisy," he added, "But you like her more."

I wasn't sure I wanted to say it, but I did. "I *like* her like her. Like a girlfriend. Do you like her like that?"

He was silent for a long time. "No. I like Erin. I want to be in the classroom at lunch with her."

What? For how long? But that's not what I said.

"Why don't you?"

He rocked in his seat, looking out the side window. "I don't want to hurt their feelings."

God, he was a cool dude.

"You should spend lunchtime with Erin. The derby girls will understand."

He paused until we were almost home.

"Will you tell them?

I almost touched his hand. "I totally will."

CHAPTER TWENTY-FIVE

"Some People Are More Equal Than Others? What Is This, Animal Farm?"

I don't know what I was expecting. Maybe the boys a cappella group singing about love, like in a movie, or whispering in the halls, or some dramatic change in my social status—recoiling students who knew *for sure* and appalled friends. Maybe a welcome banner over the school entrance thanks to the purple-haired pierced people. Or a secret video going around of me whispering the word "girlfriend" to Daisy on her couch.

It didn't happen. On Friday I went to Health class, she went to Health class, she sat by Sophie, I sat by a silent Knox. I didn't even move to her table at lunch, and it seemed to be okay with Daisy. I could see she'd shared the news with her friends because of the way *they* looked at me. I wasn't sure what they were feeling, but it wasn't overjoyed. And it wasn't because Paul chose to stay in his classroom for lunch.

Why were they looking at me like I was on probation, and they thought I'd reoffend? It made zero sense. 'Cause they were practically cheering when I kissed Daisy at the Hangar.

Was it because Daisy and I were so different?

Which would be super weird because wasn't it their point that daring to be different was good? But was I too different? Did they think I wasn't good enough for Daisy? I looked back into their eyes, and yup, totally judging me. *Was* I good enough? We were "girlfriends" for like a minute, and I was already second guessing myself.

Second. Third. Fourth.

Did it mean anything that Daisy and I *weren't* acting different? The "girlfriends" part was all non-verbal as far as I could tell, no attempted handholding yet, so no one probably knew.

But I knew. It was in the way she looked at me. Focused. On. Me. In Health and U.S. History and Ecology. I could get used to that. I hoped she could read my face and see that I liked it.

A lot.

At the end of the day, she waited for me by the outside door, as if she was waiting for a ride to practice, but there was no practice today. And *that* was when she took my hand. In the parking lot. With everyone streaming by. And the world didn't end.

Maybe even it was just beginning.

"Hi," Daisy said when she was settled in her seat.

"Hi," I said, meeting her eyes.

And she leaned in. And I leaned in. And we met in the middle.

When she pulled back after the most lingering kiss on the lips I could imagine, she sat back against the passenger door, her left knee pulled up on the seat.

"Want to go somewhere?" she asked. Almost purred. And then gave her trademark wicked grin.

Yeah, yeah, I did. I totally did, do, can, and will.

I think I only nodded, but that was enough.

Where to go wasn't so easy. Her house was out because her mom was home and not at work or faceplanted in her room.

Daisy checked.

And my house was obviously out.

Though... Mom had taken Paul to Occupational Therapy. And it was half an hour away, and took an hour, so the house *would* be empty. There *might* be a neighbor who'd mention me bringing someone by the house, but why would they?

My house it was.

My heart was thudding in my chest, my lungs reminding me that I was forgetting to breathe as I took Daisy around to the side door after pulling into our driveway.

It was happening.

Daisy was coming over with *me*. Not Paul. And this was *us*. I felt a little like throwing up when I opened the door to the mud room. And we took off our shoes, and practically tiptoed through the kitchen, the living room, up the stairs and to the bedroom hallway.

Was my bedroom clean? I hadn't made my bed, I knew that.

Daisy forged ahead to the only open door, peered in and glanced back at me, biting her lip and I think one eyebrow went up. Hard to tell with those bangs.

"This is your room, isn't it? Are you serious with the blue-and-white cottage core? You didn't choose all that, did you?"

I could only shake my head.

Daisy. Was. In. My. Bedroom.

I followed her in, and she was looking at my trophies over the window, glancing back at me once, then looking at the top of my dresser. Why? There was almost nothing on it. Except that stupid jewelry box Dad gave me on my sixteenth birthday, all emotional, like he was gifting some imaginary future to me. I could practically see his father-of-the-bride aspirations in his eyes.

Ugh.

And she was eyeing my bed. The only place to sit. Or whatever.

Remember to breathe Haven.

"You're nervous, aren't you?" Daisy's face softened, the light mockery leaving her. "I'm not going to jump you, you know. You don't have to be afraid."

I'm always afraid around you, I thought. And realized it was my out loud voice. Oh, no.

"I know what you mean," she said, coming closer, "You know, you're a little scary, too."

"Why do you think that is?" I said calmly, but I was buzzing inside, standing at the foot of my bed.

"I think it's because we like each other, Haven. And, I know for me, it's because any time I'm near you I can feel it. Can you?"

Oh, yeah. I nodded. I didn't know she felt that, too. That awareness. That thing in my stomach that started when she was close by, and when I saw her, anywhere.

"Is it okay if I sit down?" she asked, talking quietly, like she was afraid to spook me, another kind of afraid.

Enough with being afraid.

I grabbed her around the waist and tossed us onto the bed sideways, so we bounced on the messed-up duvet and ended up facing each other.

And ended up with the duvet on the floor, her hand on my butt, and mine awfully close to her breast and our lips so melded there was no space at all between us. No space but us. And our clothes.

And my watch timer went off.

I pulled away. Her cheeks were red and her eyes huge and the sunlight made her even more beautiful. I wanted her to stay.

But she bounced upright and out of the bed, straightening her T-shirt and shifting in place. Her "we'd better jet" was a bummer.

But she was right.

I followed her out, pulling my shorts straight, and we hustled out the door, making it to the car without anyone looking over the hedges by the garage, and hustled to Daisy's house to drop her off.

There was a lot of hustling that week.

Saturday and Sunday took *forever*. Mom watched me like a hawk and Dad kept suggesting we go for runs. Was he trying to run the gayness right out of me?

Paul and I skipped the last day of Youth Group before summer. How could I go there now? When I basically proved them right. We walked over to Peets and got him a real coffee before we faced Coffee Hour.

With Mom ignoring me again.

Paul didn't ask about Daisy coming over.

I lived for afternoons without practice. Even though going to practice meant holding hands in the Volvo and kissing in front of the Hangar before she started and when I dropped her off, lingering together for as long as we possibly could, and hurrying home by eight. Birgit and Sophie rode with Ellie all the time now. And barely looked my way. I wished they'd just say what was up.

Not that I asked them. I was afraid of what they'd have to say.

On no-practice days there was time. Time before I had to be home. Time her mom might be at work. When our moms were home, it was like a game, looking for somewhere safe to go. To get out of the hot car and walk and talk and hold hands when and where it seemed safe.

I was crazy. There was no other explanation. Because I seriously decided Friday afternoon to take Daisy up the mountain to our family cabin. I told Mom I was going to the Track Team's meet in Salem. That gave us time.

I wished I could ride my bike with Daisy on the back. The road was beautiful, running through the trees on Highway 26. Past the Dairy Queen. Past so much history. My history.

At the cabin I wrestled the lock open and got to see it through Daisy's eyes. The plaid wool blankets folded over the back of the sofa, the spiders that rappelled down from the rafters every few feet, the swinging chair that hung from a crossbeam so Paul could sit in it while the rest of us were in the living area or the kitchen. Centrally located but soothing.

He hardly used it anymore.

The afternoon light barely crept in the small-paned windows. I thought about telling Daisy how seven of them had been broken over the years by flying cups when we pushed Paul too far and realized it too late. Dad used to say he could deal with a broken window and have it boarded up in under thirty minutes.

But that was years ago, before he was verbal, so I didn't tell her.

Daisy was taking it all in, the old red carpet, the log walls, the stone fireplace you could roast a whole pig in. And then I saw her glance at the stairway to the second floor. I wondered if she was as nervous as I was. We were alone. No parents possibly coming home. No sneaking around. No one. But us.

Was I really considering whether we would use the bed?

No, I told myself, we only had about ninety minutes 'til we had to make the hour drive back. Couch. Couch it was.

It was cold in the cabin but not under a blanket, tangled up in each other.

I was startled when Daisy spoke, her words warming the skin at my neck. A place her lips had been. Her head on my shoulder was like the most natural thing in the world. I shook off the Daisy-fueled fugue I felt around her when her words registered.

"What was the other school like?"

It took me a minute to figure out what she meant. Then I saw the handout on the coffee table. From Lewis and Clark School. For a second I thought about asking if she really wanted to know. But Daisy wouldn't ask if she didn't.

"Honestly, it seemed like a bizarre place for Paul when he was sent there in fifth grade. *Reassigned* was the word used by the district psychologist and his principal. When Mom and I toured the school and saw the staff wearing thick fingerless gloves," I looked at the ceiling, noting the spider making his way downward, "It weirded me out. But there were all grades there and the gloves protected against biting students."

Daisy's "Oh" made her mouth become a kiss.

For a second I forgot what we were talking about.

"Biting students?" she prompted.

"The principal there was nice, and the staff didn't freak out even if Paul did. They understood his sensory defensiveness. He struck out because the brush of fingers felt like an assault. I guess it's amazing that it took until fifth grade for him to make contact. Other than with family. And he didn't hurt anyone, really."

Daisy didn't comment. She just listened. I liked that about her. Usually, it felt weird talking about this stuff. I was betraying Paul's privacy. But I knew he trusted her.

"He went back to the autism classroom at his regular school after four months. And then came ninth grade and a high school staff who didn't get him. He tried typical classrooms, and it didn't go well. It was less than two weeks into the year before he was reassigned again. That time his new class was mostly girls."

"That was a good thing, right? He likes girls." Daisy smiled.

"There are fewer girls there, so it was weird, until the classroom therapist told us they were almost all cutters. Some needed a break from getting harassed at their home schools. Others were too fragile to go back."

"Did Paul know?" she asked, nestling closer, curling her body around mine, only denim and my shorts between us. Hard to stay focused when her breasts were right there!

"I don't think so. He transferred back to Willamette after his forty days of good behavior. He never knew that one of his classmates didn't make it to the end of the year."

Not just his classmate. His friend. We never wanted him to know Elena took her life.

"When he went back to Lewis and Clark in September after punching Naomi, Mom and I were freaking out that someone would mention her death."

Daisy sat up. "Hold up, punched?"

"Umm, yeah. One of the para-educators. His favorite." Hadn't I mentioned that? Now that she knew Paul had hit someone recently, would she feel differently about him?

"What did she do?" Daisy demanded.

Maybe I *did* love her.

"He must have felt terrible!"

Oh yeah. The head-banging had been extreme. And stopping him only made it worse. If you physically intervened in any way you became a hindrance to his self-punishment and might get hit, too. The biggest problem was the combination of head-banging and epilepsy.

I let out a huge sigh. "He did. He ended up having a seizure."

And then Daisy was holding *me*. It felt wrong for about eight seconds and then it didn't. "That must be so hard, Haven."

Her face was soft, her makeup rubbed off, naked and Wow.

"You're pretty amazing, you know that?" I said, running my fingers through her loose hair and kissing the tiny heart on her shoulder.

Her lips curved up. "I know. You're amazing yourself," she paused for a second, "And you have the most beautiful breasts."

Oh. I looked down at where we were smashed together, skin against skin. I'd never appreciated my breasts before. I sure appreciated *hers*.

"What are you going to tell people?" I whispered, finally bringing up what had been nagging me. "About you. Your orientation," I added, in case I'd already made this more confusing than it had to be.

"I'm your girlfriend," she said, kissing my chin.

"I know. And that's mind-blowing, Daisy," truth, "but are you, we, gay?"

She laughed and I could feel it. "Signs point to yes," she said, looking down at us.

"Ha. But this isn't a Magic 8 Ball. How do you identify yourself? I think I should know 'cause I'm going to be asked, and I have no idea."

"It's not that complicated," then she sighed, "But I know what you mean. I'd say I'm pan. It's the person, you know? Not that I've been with a girl before."

Oh. I'd been afraid to ask.

"Do you want to be with a guy?" she went on.

My "no" was instantaneous. I guess I had my answer.

"Oh shit. I *am* gay."

The purple-haired pierced people were right all along. CeCe was right. And my parents were going to be pissed when they knew. For sure. That I was gay.

I'm gay.

If only things were different. "I wish you *could* come to dinner at my house. My parents couldn't help but love you when they got to know you." If they have half a brain. Maybe I could try? "I'll work on them."

But would I? Could I? Looking at her amazing skin and those big brown eyes that saw everything, and *still* wanted to be with me, maybe I could.

Daisy looked at me for a long time. "I'd love to, Babe. But. I need us to do something first."

CHAPTER TWENTY-SIX

"I Don't Know What the Hell to Think About That."

A date. I have a date. What am I supposed to do on a date?

If only I could ask Mom. This was her cue, right? Help her daughter on her first date. It was like in the parenting contract. But I couldn't ask her. Unless I lied about who I was going out with.

It was enough making up something convincing so I could go out at all. A party. The basketball team. Renee and Anna and I were going.

Right. Neither of them had spoken to me since Daisy and I became official. I know where Anna stood, but what was up with Renee?

Mom let me drive Daisy in the afternoons only because she and Dad thought I was driving Sophie, Birgit, and Ellie, too. Even Mom conceded they were "good for Paul". And we should "be nice" to them.

No shit.

She had no clue he was hanging out with Erin at lunch now.

I searched through my dresser first and then rifled the closet. Nothing but stupid girl sweaters in the wardrobe and mostly my sports T-shirts in the drawers. The Eddie Bauer debacle was no help at all.

Hmm, since I didn't have the bike, I could wear shorts.

Or should I wedge myself into a pair of jeans? I hated how they felt.

No, Daisy wouldn't care. Or would she? Did I need to show her I thought she was special by dressing up somehow? Mom would think I should.

I dumped T-shirt after T-shirt onto the carpet. Most of them had logos, which was cool with me, but did it say "date"?

It wasn't like I didn't know if she liked me. We were solidly on second base so no pressure to like, do the goodnight kiss thing; there *would* be a goodnight kiss.

Hey! A black T-shirt. I could wear that and my bomber jacket. It was a cooler day. I'd be missing my bike the whole time I had it on, but Daisy liked how the leather smelled. I did, too. It smelled like *us*. Riding the bike. Her arms around me. We hadn't had enough of those rides before my bike was yanked until July.

Still, I kind of deserved it for "going all neanderthal" on Josh.

Crap. It was almost seven. I stuffed all my clothes back in the dresser. I'd deal with that later. I had to get out of the house before Mom and Dad got back from dinner. And asked me why I was leaving so early.

To pick up Daisy, that's why, what are you going to do about it?

Easy to think. Not so easy to say. I swung by the basement before heading out. Paul was drawing with his headphones on, so he didn't hear me come down the stairs. I walked into his line of vision and said, "Hey."

He looked up at me, away from me, halfway between. "What?"

"I'm going out. Just wanted to say hey." And get what? Affirmation? A compliment? A you go, girl?

"You look different."

I stuffed my hands in my pockets. "I do, kinda."

I felt different. Happy. Hopeful.

And he was back to drawing.

When I got to Daisy's, I slammed the car door, feeling empty-handed. Like I should be bringing flowers or something.

Which was super validated when I rang the doorbell, and she answered and Wow.

She was wearing a dress. Black, with cherries all over it and this skirt that went poof, and the neck was almost like normal. Like, not a whole lot of Daisy showing. But this was even better. She looked... sweet.

Daisy looked sweet. She did her hair differently and didn't wear as much makeup, and it was better. Softer. Like she was *right there* with me. I wanted to kiss her in front of her mom and everybody. She was my girlfriend.

My girlfriend.

I took her hand.

And I barely let it go all night.

Not while driving, not while walking to the Hangar, not while I went to pay for both of us and the woman giving out tickets waved us through.

"Thanks Rexie," said Daisy.

Rexie?

Daisy knew everybody.

The coaches, Elise and Rebecca, the referees, Dale and Sid, the guy at the concession stand when we got sodas. We kept passing people who stopped and said hi and each time she held onto me as if I'd slip away if she let me. I didn't want to.

I wished I could do the same with her, only at church, to meet people I'd known forever. Pastor Sabin would love her. And Pastor Tom and Christine. And they knew me, no matter what stories Mom spun.

Not that I'd had much time after sliding in just before seven last night and doing homework and running with Dad and taking Paul over for a mocha and missing Alice by fifteen minutes, because who else would I ask about what to wear?

Daisy didn't let go of my hand until we got to the bleachers. We needed both arms to balance as we climbed them. They weren't exactly rickety, but they shook *a lot* as everyone climbed up and sat down. Daisy's dress dropped open under her legs when she took her seat and immediately read my face.

"I've got this covered, babe," she said, flipping up her skirt to reveal biking shorts.

Oh. She did that. And oh, she called me "babe" surrounded by strangers.

Before I could think of something stupid to say she dropped her skirt over her legs again. I needed to get over myself. It was okay to be together. It was okay for Daisy to call me "babe". It was more than okay. I could do this.

The announcer boomed a welcome and the last people hurried to get a seat, and the teams started for the floor, each player announced.

From watching derby practice, I thought I knew the game. I was wrong.

"Holy shit! Can she even do that?"

Daisy laughed. "She did do that." I could hear the smile in her voice. "I told you they're good."

Wheels of Justice. The five-time world champions. Damn. I can't wait to tell Dad, I thought. Then not.

Why couldn't Mom and Dad be more like Daisy's parents? I could tell them I loved this sport even though I didn't even understand it yet. I could tell them about going tonight and the crowd and being with Daisy. Most of all being with Daisy.

I scooted closer so I could hear her over the crowd. Closer for a lot of reasons. The press of her arm against mine. The smell of her skin, her cherry lip gloss, something she did with her hair...

Then I heard him.

"You're Killer Queen!" He almost shouted it he was so excited.

Dude, chill out. But I didn't say it. Of course she had fanboys. And probably fangirls, I realized.

Huh. At least I knew she hadn't gone out with any of *them*.

"I saw you guys, I mean you girls, or women, play Eugene last week," the guy went on. He kept running his hands through his curly short hair and leaning closer to her from the next row. Not cool.

And last week? She had a derby game last week and I didn't know about it? Didn't she want me there? Or did she think I wouldn't want to go? It couldn't have been Sunday, could it? That's the only reason I could think of that Daisy would think I was busy. And we texted a lot.

I needed to chill out. I tried to watch the bout. And not the guy inching closer

"Are you a senior?"

Every inch of my skin tightened, and alarm bells went off. He was coming on to her. I knew it. Couldn't he tell she was here with someone?

No. Because it wasn't like I was holding her hand anymore. I should be holding her hand. No. Then how would I cheer on our team? I'd want my hands free. But I didn't like this guy. He should move. We should move.

Only there wasn't room. The Hangar was full. I should tell him no. Daisy would tell him no. No, she wasn't a senior. No, she wasn't eighteen. Yes, she was jailbait. And that he can keep his fanboying to himself.

She didn't. She smiled and nodded and leaned in to say something I couldn't hear. And put her hand on my leg.

Put. Her. Hand. On. My. Leg. Like, my upper thigh. In public.

It worked. He held up his hands and gave her the chin tip and turned away after giving me a once over. Suck it dude.

But now she had her hand on my leg. I looked around. We weren't the only girls holding hands when we walked in, we weren't the only girls *together*. This was not a crowd of Booster parents pretending they were cool with whatever. These were fans of derby, family of derby, willing to wear T-shirts with fists over their boobs. These were hardcore fans.

"Are you okay?" Daisy asked, looking away from the game for a second to study my face. "What's wrong?"

I'm a little freaked out. You have your palm on my thigh, and I don't know how I feel about that, and I'm afraid someone is going to give us shit and I won't respond right. I'm afraid someone will follow us to my car. I'm afraid someone will tell you I'm not good enough for you and you'll see it's true.

Would she accept "I've got a lot of feels going on?"

I didn't think so.

But I could also feel the warmth of Daisy's hand on my leg, and her strength flowing into me, and maybe some of her boldness, because I grasped her hand with my right and held it tight.

"Nothing's wrong." I smiled at her, hoping none of my worries showed.

"You went stiff. I know you, Haven. It's not this is it?" she held up our grasped hands.

I shook my head and nodded.

Not helping. She stiffened for a second, too, then squeezed my hand and tried to let go. I held on. I wasn't going to let her slip away, even if she was doing it for me.

"No, please. I want to, I do."

Just, can you read me now, Daisy? Can you read that I'm new to being out? To being "us"? To being whatever that made me?

She studied my face, and I hoped she could feel it. How much I wanted to hold her hand and how much it scared me. I'd tell her my whole complicated knot of feelings, but we were jammed into a crowd and there were women whizzing by and it wasn't the time. Could she see it wasn't the time?

She watched me for a long time. And set our clasped hands down on my leg. And went back to watching the game. But we weren't cool.

"Daddy!" Daisy squealed, jumping at him in line for a hot dog during half-time.

Frank King. In his slick green suit and everything—he had to be boiling—in line for a hot dog? Not what I was expecting to see. He was standing with a tall woman with long blonde hair who looked like a beauty queen. Only older. Did Daisy have a stepmom?

"Beloved daughter," he reeled from her onslaught. She let go and stepped back.

"You're at a bout! A women's bout! Are you regulars?" Daisy was grinning, taking in the lady with him.

More like studying—I could tell—even if she looked friendly.

Frank took the woman's hand. "Only since I met Frederika. My darling, meet my daughter, Daisy. She is my heart. And this is Haven, who I have heard so much about. You," he pointed a long finger directly at me, "Have made the grade. Keep earning it."

Did. He. Just. Say. That?

"Enough, Daddy, you can be too much. Let Haven be."

"Nice to see you again, Mr. King." What else could I say? I wasn't about to call him "Frank" when he said *that*.

"Hi Frederika. Thanks for getting this guy out to see some derby."

When the woman finally answered it was in a little girl voice. Weird. "I'm visiting from Seattle. I played for Rat City."

"Are you serious? Oh my God! You're Vermin!" Daisy turned to me, "I've seen her play. I've seen you play!" She turned to Frederika, totally fangirling. I'd never seen that side of her.

"Thank you. I look forward to seeing you play as well."

Swedish. I think her accent was Swedish.

"Do you do derby as well?" Frederika asked me.

Me? "No. I couldn't skate a yard without falling on my ass."

Should I have said "ass" in front of Daisy's dad?

"You'd be surprised what you can learn when you try," she said, "I could barely skate when I tried out. I just really wanted it, you know?"

Fair.

When we got our dogs and sodas, Daisy carefully hugged her dad, so she didn't get mustard all over him and herself, and they went to their VIP seats, and we went to ours.

Maybe I should have bought VIP seats for us...

I stuffed my face with hot dog and recovered from the Frank King encounter. And learned something about Daisy. She could consume a hot dog, and not so much as smudge her lip gloss, in one minute or less. She was a real girl. Not a pin-up come to life.

And then I had this brilliant idea. What if Daisy showed Dad and Mom and the boosters, or whoever, that she *was* a real girl?

If she looked like any other teenage girl, would that make a difference? Dad said if she was a nice girl I should let her down easy, so that meant he would feel different about a "nice girl". What if Daisy showed them all she *was* a nice girl? Just for a while. Long enough to have dinner with my folks because they'd have to love her after spending time with her.

I couldn't wait to tell Daisy my plan.

"You don't get to tell me how to dress," Daisy said, planting her feet and refusing to get in the car. She was being ridiculous.

"It's just temporary. And I could lend you the stuff Mom bought me that I'll never wear."

She rolled her eyes, her lashes almost brushing her eyebrows, and crossed her arms. And laughed.

It wasn't a happy laugh.

This wasn't going right.

"Let me get this straight. You want me to dress like what your mom wants you to look like? When *you* won't even where those fucking clothes?"

She had me there. But...

"Well, yeah, for a while. Or maybe just when you come to dinner." If I can make that happen.

The hurt on her face turned flat and determined. "Look, you don't get to make me more palatable and homogenous so your mom and dad will deign to accept me. I don't give a shit if other people have a problem with me the way I am."

I opened my mouth to explain what I really wanted but couldn't find the words. I *did* want Mom and Dad to accept Daisy. But more than that, I wanted them to accept *me*. Couldn't she see that?

Daisy took a step back and held up her palm, stopping me before I could come closer. Show her I didn't have a problem with the way she was.

"Before we even get into what your parents will think, you have to decide if *you* have a problem with the way I am. Because that would be a real problem for *me*."

The ride to her house was silent. And there was no goodnight kiss.

CHAPTER TWENTY-SEVEN

"So, We're All About the Double Standard Now?"

Kids whizzed through the crowd at Coffee Hour, playing tag, happy, innocent. Lucky. The lights flashed off. And getting at the light switch.

"Paul has a crush on someone at school, and she might have a crush back. They've been spending a lot of time together at lunch. In the lunchroom! We are so proud of him."

The lights went back on.

Hold up. *She might have a crush back!* I didn't care that Mom was talking to Sam Fuller, new head of the Sunday School program, she wasn't going to shovel this crap.

"Mom," I tugged on her arm to get her attention. This was getting ridiculous. And he knew what he felt. And it wasn't like that. "Mom! Paul doesn't have a crush on Daisy, and she doesn't have a crush back. No offense, Paul." I smiled at him. He studied the ceiling.

The lights went back off. In the dark, Paul replied, "Daisy is my friend. She looks at my drawings. She likes me."

The lights went on again.

I literally groaned. Not the best thing for him to say in the circumstances.

Mom beamed at Paul, then Dad, then Sam Fuller, then back at Paul, making darn sure they were all paying attention. "That must be pretty wonderful to have a girl who likes you."

The lights flashed off and on again. Once. Twice. Three times. On again.

This was... No. But before I could clear out the bull, Paul decided to get chatty.

"I like Daisy. She likes Haven, too."

Thank you, Paul.

I looked at Mom, but it was like he hadn't said my name. She was laser focused. My temples were starting to throb.

Off. On. Off. A second or two went by, then the lights were on again.

"But you like her, sweetheart?"

Talk about feeding him lines. Why did she have to do this?

"She has big eyes. Like a Manga girl."

He wasn't wrong.

Mom beamed. "You wanted us to have her over for dinner sometime."

What. The. Fuck.

Way to dangle and not commit at the same time, Mom. But enough is enough.

"Hold up. Daisy is Paul's *friend*. Stop playing matchmaker. She doesn't like him that way and he doesn't like her that way. They are *friends*."

"That's how these things start, honey." Mom's smile widened. It was almost manic.

The lights went on and off like a strobe light for a few seconds. I shook off the phantom lights in my eyes.

Was I going to do this? Now?

Yeah, I was.

"Mom, get a grip. She kissed me, not Paul."

Sam Fuller backed up to get a better view of the action. Or maybe to run away.

Mom whirled on me. "And you agreed that she was just messing with you. And why do you even bring that up? Her reputation clearly indicates Paul is more her type than you are. Stop getting in the way of his chances to get to know her better."

Off. On.

Mr. Fuller had the grace to disappear. Pastor Tom, not so much. Though I couldn't blame him, he and Christine were innocently making the rounds. So, they were right there when Paul went on, "I want to get to know her better. She should come over and play video games again."

Surely, Mom could see he wasn't talking girlfriend—she was his *friend*.

Nope. She just chuckled, beaming at Pastor Tom and Christine. "I'd been hoping he'd mature into wanting a relationship," she gushed. "We all know he's having the usual feelings in there..."

I blew out a breath before I did something I'd really regret. I hated it when she talked about Paul like that. Like he was in a bubble. Or didn't understand what she was saying.

"...and he finally has the chance to act on them. You don't get lucky enough to meet a girl who likes video games and D&D every day."

Damn right you didn't! You didn't meet a girl like Daisy every day and the world should know it. I must have looked like I had something to say because Pastor Tom glanced at me, looking for what I didn't know. Confirmation? Denial?

"Haven," said Christine softly. Her hair was blue today. "I haven't talked to you in weeks." It was weird that she just left Mom hanging. "We should talk." Christine looked at me with so much kindness it kind of killed me. She didn't need any of this pretend. Mom was full of shit. Christine could take the truth.

That I'm struggling with who I am and with the girl I like but don't want to like and don't understand why she liked me but now she maybe doesn't because I wanted my parents to like her. To like *me*.

That I drove her to practice on my motorcycle in April and I can't stop thinking about her hands gripping my jacket during the ride and slipping under the leather to grip me across my stomach. That maybe I get kissing now, and why girls smell good and guys don't, and that I really can't live with this lie anymore.

Or without Daisy.

The lights flickered on and off. This was the problem with multiple light switches. You could guard one and a kid could go for another. Then on.

The only part I said out loud was that Mom was full of shit. I swear Christine looked like she wanted to clap. Pastor Tom, too.

"Haven, not now," Dad said.

"No, Dad, now! She's gotta stop acting like Paul has a thing going with Daisy. And that I don't!"

"Haven!" He practically roared, "Not here."

Pastor Tom touched Dad's elbow. "Take it easy on Haven, David. Let her talk."

"I think she's said enough," Mom hissed, glancing around, all eyes on us.

"I don't think she's done yet, Kathleen." Christine said, "Though we can take this to a classroom if it makes you *all* feel more comfortable. And without the light show."

Paul started rocking.

"Look at what you've done to your brother!" Dad barked.

"I didn't do anything," I threw my arms out to my sides. There was a whole world of anything's that I hadn't done. "But tell the truth for once. Paul is Daisy's friend, right Paul?"

"Daisy is my friend." He was rocking on his heels faster.

"But it was me that was in love with her. *Is* in love with her. And you know why she doesn't like me anymore?" Maybe. Yeah, I was booming, "Because I wanted to please you!"

And all hell broke out.

The only thing I noticed was a stillness next to me before Paul went down. The hard linoleum floor flew up to meet him and his head bounced once before his whole body began spasming. All of him shook and, for a second, I panicked and didn't move. And then I reached for him, throwing myself in front of him to protect him. But Mom got there first and knocked me out of the way.

I flew back, skidding on the slick surface, and there were voices and someone calling 911 and Dad was bending over Paul and waving his arms to keep people back. It was seconds probably, but enough for me to hear Mom shriek "This is your fault" before I was swept up in getting Paul enough privacy with my body so no one would see he'd wet himself because he would care when he came to church again.

If anyone would dare say anything to him about it. My hackles were up at the thought.

And then a woman and a man in uniform were there with a stretcher, lifting Paul and strapping his body, wracked with aftershocks, down. Mom was gone before I could say I was sorry or beg her to say she didn't mean it.

Dad had his arm around me and led me to the car, hardly saying a word besides my name. Softly. Like a mantra. To what? Pierce the cloud of words swirling around me? What if Paul hit his head? What if he got a full concussion? What if he broke his nose or his suborbital floor or his neck? What if this was the time the seizures didn't stop with medication and recurred and recurred and recurred, scarring his brain?

My thoughts were the only noise on the ride there except the windshield wipers.

I realized I was shivering as we raced into the main hospital, soaked with rain, steam rising from mine and Dad's clothes, fogging his glasses.

Paul Alexander?

Was he in the ER?

Did he have a room?

Was he getting an MRI?

I groaned, imagining him surrounded by the machine. They wouldn't give him the dye for this one. They'd do preliminary. We'd been through this so many times before.

The waiting room. Mom standing there, clutching her hands together. She looked so small. Not the mighty woman who stood up for Paul anywhere, anytime and didn't take any shit. Not the fantasy weaving woman from church either. She was raw and terrified and resigned to whatever came next.

Probably nothing.

Probably an isolated incident.

Probably unrelated to any other illness.

Probably my fault.

I slowed down. Afraid of what Mom might say. Wanting to go to her and for her to give me a hug and tell me he was okay

and the people in the ambulance had been reassuring and he
was just being checked out, and we could be home in an hour
or so. But her stricken face told me it couldn't be that simple.
She wouldn't look like that. I stopped. Unable to hear what she
might say about my brother. About what I'd done.

From where I stood in the doorway, I heard background
noises and the echoes of voices and the squeak of shoes. And
her voice. Telling Dad.

"They had to sedate him."

"He's getting an MRI. They want to be sure."

"I think they're going to keep him overnight."

"He went unconscious in the ambulance."

Dad's voice.

"Come on, Kathleen, it will be all right. We've been here
before."

"He's strong and healthy except for the epilepsy."

"It's okay to cry, honey."

And after a minute, "You should tell Haven it's not her fault."

And then silence.

More silence.

I couldn't just stand there waiting. I ran out an exit door,
stepping into the wall of rain pouring from the overhang, soaking me to the skin. Cold. Alone.

Alone...

I didn't even stop and think. They should know. *She* should
know. I stepped back under the overhang and pulled out my
phone and typed.

Paul had a seizure. I'll let you know when I know anything.

After Daisy, I group-texted Sophie and Birgit and Ellie and Luce and Grey and Uncle Jackson and Alice. It felt like an S.O.S. But not like I was asking them to come; I didn't want to feel so alone.

But I couldn't just wait outside for who knows how long. As I walked back into the waiting room, I saw Dad put his hand on Mom's arm. To what? Stop her from telling me this was all my fault? Because maybe it was. Maybe it was too much to ask to be happy.

Dad said, "The MRI looks good, Haven. But they're keeping him for a couple of hours. Just in case. But if all goes well, turns out he won't have to stay overnight."

I felt the tears on my cheeks join the rain dripping from my hair.

"Why, Haven? Why? Why did you have to do this to him?"

Everything went cold. Through blurred eyes I saw Dad touch her arm again, but she shook him off.

"I don't get it. Why can't you give him this? This is a chance for Paul to be happy."

"Don't you get it? He's happy. Paul has friends. He has Luce and Grey and Daisy—*as a friend*—and the other derby girls he sits with at lunch." Or did. But that's his business to tell. Or not. "He has his art," Mom cringed. She needed to get over that. Her idea of art was watercolors of flowers, and we all tolerated *that*.

Mom grabbed a few tissues from the box on the side table. Her eyes were red, and her face swollen. "How could he not be unhappy, Haven?"

"Just stop thinking his happiness should look like some pre-mixed cake with icing on top. You don't need to make up some story about his romance with a girl at school."

"You know she's right, Kathleen, Paul has seemed a lot happier the last two months," Dad said.

"He said he liked her! Let him have her, Haven."

It took everything in me not to explode. "Like she's what? A prize that he's won, a thing. She's a person. A person I like! Don't *I* deserve to be happy?"

"Of course you do! I've never denied you anything!"

"Except my own opinion! You know what, Mom? I'm not some icing on the top pre-ordained cake mix either. You think I'm happy? No, I chose to make *you* happy. *Daisy* made me happy! And I wrecked it. I acted like she wasn't great the way she is, bold and beautiful and smart and snarky and... sexy."

Mom gasped. Take that Mom!

"But I thought if she looked different, if she looked like you wanted me to look, you'd like her. I wanted so badly for you to like her that I expected her to change. I fucking asked her to change! And she was smart enough to say no, she wouldn't change, because I was being an asshole."

"Haven! Language!"

Was it wrong that I wanted to say "fucking asshole"?

"Do you not get it? I love Daisy. We were a thing. And I was scared to tell you. Scared you wouldn't love me just the way I am."

"Oh honey, you can tell us anything," but she didn't mean it and we knew it. "And I hear you; you had a crush on her. She's different. And it's not like you've had any other relationships besides Knox, so it's understandable that you be curious."

"I have never, ever, in my life, had a relationship with Knox that was more than friendship. And I don't even have that anymore. We were close. And you and his mom had to poison that by pushing us together. He would have accepted me telling him I wasn't into him long ago if you hadn't kept this farce going. No wonder he was confused. He probably thought I was playing some head game with him."

"Oh, come on, he wouldn't think that. He just probably thought you were shy."

My mouth dropped open. "Me? Shy? Since when have I been anything but blunt? It wasn't fair to Knox, and it wasn't fair to me that I had to keep fighting you to tell the truth. Friendship should have been enough. And being with Daisy was more than a crush. Don't you get it? I was happy, like really *really* happy. And I fucked it all up."

I expected another "Language!" From Mom. Instead, I heard her gasp and a familiar squeak of shoes. And I knew what I'd see when I turned around. *Who* I'd see.

Daisy. Her dark hair dripped. Black stuff was smeared around her big eyes. Her totally stupid inadequate jacket was soaked to her body, and she was carrying a small paper bag. Just seeing her made me want to cry and run to her. At the same time.

Wanted to? Did. I got to her in three steps and stopped inches away. She looked terrified. And I got it. She wasn't there for me. She was there for Paul. And then I really did cry. Big sobs that shook me from head to toe. And I didn't know what to do. What to say. So, just like the coward I am. I ran.

Leaving Daisy alone with my folks.

Wishing she'd tell them she wasn't there for Paul alone. That she was there for me. That we were a *we* and they could just get over themselves. Work some Daisy magic. Magic that made them see how amazing she was. And that I was good just as I am. It would take some magic.

By the time I got my shit together in the ladies' room and came back, she was gone.

And I could see in the wet paper bag that she'd brought Ding Dongs for Mom.

CHAPTER TWENTY-EIGHT

"I Still Don't Understand Girls."

Why did it have to be this hard?

At lunch the next day she was talking. Just not to me. She hadn't even made eye contact in our classes together in the morning.

Trying to sit at her table seemed like a bad idea after leaving her alone with my folks, so I went for my usual.

I looked over to where she was sitting with her friends. Paul's friends. Less my friends lately. Saturday night, our "date", was forever ago. I should talk to her. I should have talked to her yesterday, should have texted her after I took off, should have texted her when I got home. Or this morning. Why didn't I do that?

She can't stay mad at me forever. Can she?

"How's Paul?" Maddy asked, her voice seeming far away.

Paul. Daisy's friend. Daisy who I should be sitting with. Sitting next to. Holding hands with...

"Haven?" Dog Meat.

Oh, right. "He's good. The seizure was from the lights being switched on and off constantly." Not because I told Mom about Daisy. About being with Daisy. And maybe losing her. Though the stress didn't help.

"Paul will be fine," said Grey, "I love seeing him so happy these days."

Me, too.

I looked over at their table again, only to catch Birgit shooting icy glances at me. Daisy's back was rigid as she ate. She was so good to Paul.

She was so good to me.

I was an asshole.

I looked down at what the cafeteria labeled "Salisbury steak" and figured why not? It fell to pieces in my mouth as I glanced from Maddy and Dog Meat to Sarah and Eddie and wondered if it could be that easy. I knew I shouldn't care. It's not like there weren't other same-sex couples holding hands in the lunchroom. And it was super holding hands at the derby bout.

Just not so much the hand on my thigh thing. It was too personal. But I don't think Daisy understood that. Like if I dated a guy, no way would I want his hand on my thigh in public. *If* I dated a guy. Could I even imagine dating a guy? Or another girl? No.

Daisy was it.

I looked at her back, my eyes traveling from her slender neck to her square shoulders and narrow waist and her butt in those jeans and it kind of did something to me... I did like her just the way she was. Outrageous, impractical clothes and all. I liked her lipstick or no lipstick. Either way she was Daisy. I should tell her. After school. I could tell her, and she'd forgive me. Maybe. I hoped.

Knox climbed onto the seat next to me, knocking his tray into mine. My left leg started vibrating. Would we ever get back to being easy friends again? I looked up to say something to him, anything to break the ice, and noticed he was looking over my shoulder. I turned to where Daisy was standing.

She had one hand on her hip, bristling with attitude. "We need to talk."

The table went silent for about two seconds. Then a chorus of "Ooh" broke out. Morons. I shifted nervously under her narrowed gaze. She didn't expect to talk now, did she?

"So, after school gets out?" I tried a hopeful half-smile. I didn't get one back.

"No. It can't wait. Is Paul okay?"

Not what I was expecting.

"Yeah, he's okay. No permanent harm or anything."

Daisy nodded. "Good. So did you decide or what?"

I swallowed. Everyone was looking. Way to put me on the spot. I stood up. "Let's go outside, okay?"

"No, let's not," she said, "Do you or do you not want me to 'tone it down' to please Mommy?" Now she had fists on both hips.

Yes. No. Maybe. No. No. No.

I waited too long to answer her.

"Never mind, Haven. I get it, that's where you're at. But do *you* get it? You want me to be *not me* to please her? Is that any different than what she wants from *you*? Look, this thing with you..."

Thing!

"...doesn't work for me. My friendship with Paul, yeah, it works. He likes me just the way I am."

I tried to ignore the tightening of the skin over my skull. I couldn't take a migraine now. I had to tell her everything. Everything I should have said. But when I opened my stupid mouth, I said everything wrong.

"So, what, you're going to go back to hooking up with guys who treat you like shit?" The words were out before I could stop them. The look of pain in Daisy's liquid eyes killed me. Her face was soft, but her voice was hard.

"Couldn't be shittier than you. At least they don't pretend to be anything but assholes."

I just gaped as she walked back to her table, head high. What had I done?

"You are an asshole. You know that right?"

Yup, even Knox thought I was an asshole.

I dropped back into my seat. "I know. You're right. But you are the last person," I leaned in toward him, my temples throbbing, "That I thought would take her side."

He held up his palms to me. "Hey, I never thought you should waste your time and energy on her. I don't know what your type is, obviously, but she's not it. Doesn't mean you have to be an asshole to her face."

"No, you want me to do it behind her back, like you," I snapped. "And she is my type."

I snatched up my tray and dumped my unfinished lunch in the trash. I was so done with drama.

I skipped lunchroom all week. Went off campus and ate alone twice. Ate in my car on Thursday. In the park on Friday. In the afternoons I just ran.

I started straight from school, changing my shoes at the car and just going.

Up the hill, along Fremont, through the neighborhood, through the park and around. Winding through Alameda, pounding the street and rebounding, raising my leg again like a machine. A machine with a brain on repeat.

Why didn't I just tell her yes, I loved her exactly as she was?

Why didn't I tell her she was important to me?

Why didn't I tell her I didn't care anymore what my family thought, or our friends thought, or the Youth Group at church had to say, I liked her. Maybe I loved her. Because this sucked.

I stopped by the Lutheran church to text her.

I like you exactly how you are.

But no answer.

I made a mistake. I'm sorry I didn't reply right. I didn't mean what I said.

But I had. I'd been a jealous asshole hurting her.

I feel terrible.

That was the only one I got an answer to.

Not my problem.

I thought about listing all the things I loved about her but maybe that was too much. Did I need to not reach out? But her three words encouraged me.

I sat on the curb and typed for like an hour. Typing. Deleting. Trying again.

Dear Daisy, I like you exactly the way you are. Love the way you are, really. You light up everywhere you go. You light me up. I was asleep before you told me off at the Slut Walk. You woke me up. I love the way you talk and the way you dress, even if it's totally wrong for the weather. I love the smell of your hair and the way your ponytail bounces at the end like a girl in a comic book. I love how you talk. How you tell it how it is. I love how you were with me. I think I love you. Haven.

Nothing.

Nothing Saturday, when Daisy's team played in Corvallis.

Nothing on Sunday, when I went to church and sat silent during service, away from my family, though Paul followed me and sat close to me on the pew. Almost touching me. The lights totally stayed on during coffee hour.

Nothing Monday before school. So, I decided to go back to my lunch table—at least I could see Daisy from there—and confess the whole saga.

"You didn't! Haven, what were you thinking? You don't attack how someone dresses."

Of course, Maddy would go straight to that.

"You suggested Daisy King dress to please your mom?" Grey looked appalled.

I knew Grey admired Daisy's "style" because she'd said so, plus she wore the same thick soled girl shoes with the strap thingy. But seriously, she sounded like I ran over Bambi.

"And OMFG," Maddy gasped, "She went to the hospital, and you ran?"

"You did not seriously just leave her there? With your folks?" Grey's incredulous tone did nothing to make me feel better. I already felt like crap.

"You have a lot of making up to do." Sarah nodded her now-violet head of cotton candy hair. I barely contained the "duh" that bubbled up in response.

I couldn't believe I'd spilled the whole stupid story. I told off my mom, and declared my undying love for Daisy, and then dumped Daisy there with my mom when Mom was just acting like an asshat about her. How much did Daisy even hear of her speech? Or mine?

I'd been too much of a chicken to go back into the waiting room as Dad talked to Daisy, giving her the rundown on Paul. He told me he had when I finally came back. After she was gone. After she offered my mother "comfort food" and Mom ignored the bag in Daisy's hand and turned her back.

Of course she left. I couldn't blame her. I blamed *me*.

After finding out Paul was fine, we bundled him home, without another word about Daisy or me or whose girlfriend she was supposed to be.

Mine, that's whose.

Not that she was an object to own, but I did want her to be mine. I think I finally got that. Too late by a long shot. Getting through the next few weeks, and then all next year, with her hating me was going to kill me.

"She's never going to forgive me," I mumbled, shoving away from the table, my chair screeching as it slid. Oh yeah, people looked.

I was beyond caring who looked at what except for the one who didn't move a muscle. But I swear she knew it was me.

Trent leaned into me. "Wait a fucking minute, Haven. You're just going to give up? Like that? I don't believe you!"

He didn't even flinch at my glare. He was right. I shouldn't just give up. Or I didn't deserve her. Not that I ever deserved her.

"It needs a big gesture," said Grey, leaning on her palm to face me.

Great. Drama. I didn't need more drama. I just needed Daisy.

"She's right," Maddy interjected, before I could even think of having my own thoughts heard. "You need to do something huge, like ask her to be yours in roses across the football field." Then she froze, big-eyed, and glanced at Trent two seats down. It was what he'd done for her two years ago. He didn't look happy.

It didn't slow her down, unfortunately.

She bounced in her seat. "I know, I know! You should totally have a makeover and get dolled up rockabilly style like Daisy.

Show her that you get her and put it out there, you know? Like, show your boobs and everything." Her grin was wide and brilliantly white. She was getting way too much fun out of this conversation.

Out of *my* misery.

Saved by the bell for fifth period, I let the table clear while I gathered up my garbage and mucked with my backpack. When I looked up, Joey was still waiting at the end of the table.

I faced them. Not sure if I was in trouble or not. Were they mad at me for messing up everything with Daisy?

"What's up, Joey?" I asked nervously, keeping to my end of the table.

"Do you mind another opinion?"

"It can't hurt."

"I like Maddy, she's fab, but she's totally wrong. Don't dress up like Daisy. She wouldn't like that at all. She doesn't want you to change yourself, that's kind of the whole point. She needed you to accept her as-is. You know?"

I couldn't help but hang my head. I knew that now.

Joey shrugged. "You're not going to figure this out by lunch table committee. Only you know what is special to the two of you."

That was true...

"How did you get so wise?"

"That's what I would want, someone to show me they got me."

I wondered if Joey had found that person. I guess it showed on my face

because Joey winked.

"Just 'cause I don't walk around holding someone's hand doesn't mean I'm alone. Robin just goes to school closer to their house instead of here. Maybe, if you end up with Daisy, we can double."

The idea of a double-date gave me a heart attack—a single date had been a disaster—but meeting someone who was dear to Joey, that sounded like a cool thing.

I couldn't focus in Ecology or Latin, and it probably wasn't even safe for me to use the machines in the weight room during seventh period because we were let out of Con Team early. Maybe I needed to take a dumbbell to the head to get an idea how to prove to Daisy that I really, really liked her exactly as-is. And that I was sorry for running like a rabbit.

I hardly knew I was saying the words aloud as I drove Paul home. My internal voice just popped out. "I really messed up. What am I going to do?"

"Fix it, Haven. Duh."

I stared at my brother. And almost laughed. He was spot on.

"Not so easy to do. It was Daisy I messed up with, Paul."

"At church. You said that at church. You got angry. And yelled. I hate it when people yell."

"I'm sorry. I know you do."

"Is Daisy angry at you?"

"Probably. Yeah. But it's worse. I hurt her feelings."

He glared at the roof of the Volvo. "How could you do that? She's nice. And you like her. You said so."

"I know," I said, my voice becoming almost a howl.

"Then why did you hurt her?" he asked. So rational. So *right*.

"Because I'm an asshole."

He didn't argue. "You need to fix it."

"I want to."

Then he patted me on the shoulder, his eyes steady ahead again, staring at the road like usual. "Then it will be okay. You made a mistake. She is a nice person. She'll forgive you."

"Do you really think so?"

"If you don't hurt her again."

"I will try my best, Paul, I promise you."

"I know. You always do, Haven. Even when you make mistakes."

"Thanks."

"You're welcome. You *are* my baby sister."

And it was so nice to be reminded of that. Especially by my big bro.

CHAPTER TWENTY-NINE

"Yeah, Not as Easy as It Looks."

It seemed like a good idea at the time.

I drove the Volvo Monday instead of my bike, even though I was allowed to use it again after last week. Because obviously I wasn't driving anyone to derby anymore. Mom could see that. I was coming home from school an hour late soaked with sweat from running. And running with Dad in the evenings. I was being a good, predictable girl. Wholesome as a warm slice of wheat bread.

On the outside.

I drove the Volvo because I wanted to blend. No way did I want to run into Birgit or Sophie or Ellie in the parking lot outside the Hangar after school. They were going to kill me. That's what they'd been telling me since the day Daisy broke it off. With gestures. So, I parked far from where I used to and ducked into the amusement park to get to my destination.

Instead of heading to the Hangar to beg for forgiveness.

Because I didn't want to be a stalker.

I glimpsed the Hangar between buildings as I walked down the main promenade. The double doors stood open to let air flow in. And players step out for the port-a-potties.

I couldn't fault the derby girls for wanting to push me off a cliff. No one was more aware that I'm the asshole in this situation than I am. No one knows better that there is no way Daisy should take another chance on me when I let her down so badly.

But I *so* wanted a second chance.

And somehow, I had to prove it.

I slid through a passage between the carnival game booths, swung a left and went up the wooden ramp. And then I was inside. Billy Idol's *Rebel Yell* blasted through speakers as old as the guy at the skate rental counter.

"Size nine-and-a-half men's, please," I said, and took the ancient skates over to one of the benches.

Okay, I reminded myself, my plan was amazing. In theory.

I took off my shoes.

It was like Joey said, only I knew what was important to the two of us. Or, more accurately, what was important to me: our date. When she opened the door, it was like Wham, I knew. Even if I couldn't admit it at the time. And screwed it up in the end...

And then Alice asked later what was important to Daisy, and I said derby. And date plus derby equaled not derby exactly. But close?

Reality blew the whole 'my plan is amazing' theory to hell as soon as I laced my skates and stepped onto the wooden rink. And fell on my ass so hard I saw stars.

Damn the floor was hard. No wonder the derby girls padded up to their helmets before flying at top speed... Wiping out like that seemed mondo risky from where I stepped, rolled, stepped, rolled, inches at a time. Holding on to the wall like a preschooler. The sound of the skates, the smell of nacho cheese from the concession stand, and the whizzing of people passing me were overwhelming.

And the music. Something this century would be great.

Sensory overload. Paul would hate it. But he loved the idea when I told him.

I tried to narrow my view. Focus ahead. Ignore *I Love Rock and Roll* and resist the urge to "Yow" at that part of the song. Step, roll, step, roll. There were little kids going faster than me as they hung on, parents trailing them on the other side of the half-wall. I was holding up three girls in sparkly pink and a boy in full hockey gear who couldn't be older than six.

I let go of the wall. Stepped, rolled, far enough to let traffic through. And kept rolling, my arms windmilling as I tried to get my balance and... Whump. I swear I bounced on my butt. As I got hold of myself to crawl over and scale the wall and think up something realistic to win Daisy back, the lineup along the edge was held up by a soccer mom about Mom's age. She stared at the four kids behind her and obviously pondered her options.

Including letting the kids be the ones to go around her.

She should have. She let go, leaned too far back, overly corrected and her skates shot out from under her and Crack, she caught herself on one hand as she hit. The floor felt like it shook under her fall. But that was nothing to that crack of bone. Or bones. The woman lifted her hand to look at her wrist. It was bent at an angle that made me want to throw up.

I think she almost did. What I could see of her face went white. And a little green.

But she crawled over to the wall using her knees and one hand, dragged herself standing, holding her arm carefully to keep it from being further collateral damage from passing skaters, and leaned over the half-wall looking ready to puke. But she laughed. Pulled herself upright and kept on step rolling her way to the exit ramp, laughing and smiling, her wrist swelling as I watched.

If she could have a sense of humor about *that* I would not wimp out.

Put one foot in front of the other, Haven. You're starting from scratch on this one, I reminded myself.

I pushed off with my toes, rolled a foot, lifted the other, fell on my butt. Repeat.

Bit by bit, I made forward progress, keeping going even though the stress was getting to me and sweat was in my eyes. It helped a lot when a six-year-old told me it worked better if you pushed your skate out to the side instead of straight back.

There were three more hours of open skating thanks to Teen Night. This couldn't take weeks. Who knew how many days I had before some smart person would spark Daisy's interest and wouldn't insult her and she'd hang out with *them*?

The idea made me as sick as the broken-wristed soccer mom.

I pushed off for the thousandth time as the buzzer went to announce closing. I glided a good five feet as I headed to the benches to return my skates. As I unlaced them, the speakers went silent for five seconds, and then the familiar sounds of *Change Your Mind* by The Killers came on. If only I could change her mind. I'd do anything to make that happen.

I went back the next day. With wrist guards.

Five feet stretched to ten and I was beginning to get it and Wham, side-swiped by what looked like a freshman. And my butt was burning on impact, even though I doubled up my shorts. It took a second to get my breath back. But I got up without a wall as support and kept going, more determined than ever to get this down.

As I went around the rink, falling less and less, I sped up, finessing my plan. It was probably a stupid plan. And I'd probably fall on my face in the attempt. And it would take a lot of persuading to get the administration on board. Step one, I decided, pushing off one foot and then the other, getting up speed, was to talk to the athletic director. Step two was talking to the President of the Booster Club.

Step three... I couldn't think about that yet.

But before any of that, I needed Ms. Lamb on my side.

And with only one and a half weeks of school left, I needed her now.

Ms. Lamb was expecting me the next morning even though I emailed her after school hours.

Her first words were "Have you thought of the other four things?"

It wasn't hard to think of some.

"I need Daisy to forgive me. I need to prove to her that I know her and like her, maybe even more than like her, in public, in front of God and everybody including my parents. That part is super important."

She was smiling. "You've got two more."

"I need your help to make this whole thing happen."

And... Was I really going to say something?

"I need to tell you something about Coach Morgan."

It was like she wasn't even surprised about the phone conversation I overheard.

After I filled Ms. Lamb in about that, my mixed feelings about not competing—letting down the whole team maybe versus giving individual members the opportunity to shine—and about Coach Morgan's confrontation in the hallway and that I didn't want *her* to get any kudos from anything *I* did, I felt less crazy.

A little less crazy.

Ms. Lamb shifted in her seat, knocking me in the knee, "Tricky one, Haven. It was a private conversation, so she can be as big an ass... I mean jerk, as she wants to be. On the other hand." She stopped abruptly. Like she wasn't sure, for once, what to do about the problem. "I guess what I want you to do is leave it to me. I can have a private conversation with the athletic director, maybe, or directly with Coach Morgan."

I'm thinking she saw the look on my face because she added, "Don't worry, I won't throw you under the bus. I bet I can get through to her that *every* participant gets to compete."

I bet you can, I thought.

"But back to your other needs. Let's make appointments for you with one vice-principal, one athletic director, and Ms. Martinez. Being an admin means wearing a lot of hats these days and she does do most of the work arranging these things. And we should get Trent to photograph the event. I want this in the yearbook. And I think you should tackle the Boosters."

You bet. They were going to love this. So long as they didn't know I hated them.

Some of them.

"What about my folks?" I asked.

"You can count on me."

And I could. And we'd never mentioned Paul once.

With Ms. Lamb there, the athletic director was onboard in a heartbeat, though we'd left out a few details. Vice-Principal Michaels told us there was only one day left on the schedule to fit in an assembly and it was only a week away, so I'd better get my ass in gear.

Okay not in those exact words.

I told Trent the real reason behind the assembly and he laughed so hard he burped.

Mister Booster Guy Mike Lopez was all over the off-campus teams, and because irony is a thing, he was going to help clean up the mess he started by snitching to Dad.

The mess I completed by letting Daisy down.

Paul said I could fix it. I sure hoped he was right.

I was never so busy. I had skating practice after school, meetings with all the involved parties putting this thing together, homework to keep up on, a speech to write, and photos to wheedle out of unsuspecting participants. In a week.

Most of all making sure I could skate well enough not to fall on my ass. Because like the roller rink, the auditorium stage was made of wood.

Ms. Lamb told me that getting my parents to be there was a breeze. Her words. They were so proud on the days leading up to the assembly they kept telling me it was "such a good idea" and "they couldn't be prouder" and "this will look great on your applications. Of course we'll be there."

And "it's lovely to see you turning your life around" which almost made me cry.

All the parents of student athletes who could make it would be there. And most of the student body.

The ones who didn't skip anyway. 'Cause not everyone is into an All-Athletics Assembly.

I stood in the wings of the school auditorium, so grateful I didn't have to do most of it. The athletic director would make his speech, coaches would thank players, Boosters would handle off-campus athletics, and then it was showtime.

I'd have crossed my fingers *and* toes, but the skates were too tight.

The noise from backstage was muffled by the curtains at each side, but still, I could hear the auditorium seats creak, people talking and laughing, students scuttling hunched over to get to and from their seats without being caught by Ms. Martinez, who stood by the door to let in stragglers and keep escapees in.

That was when I spotted my parents, looking all proud. I hoped they could keep it up. For me this time.

Mr. Everett had thanked his way through the sports at Willamette: Soccer and Cross Country. Football and Lacrosse. Basketball and Baseball. Track and even Dragon Boat. Swim team and Wrestling.

Mike Lopez had congratulated traveling rec teams, especially women's soccer, who had nailed it in the fall. He mentioned the Rose City Rowing Club members. And more.

I made sure my shorts were on straight, questioning for the millionth time whether I should have gone all the way with this. Not just the T-shirt. But Joey said to be myself. And booty shorts were not me. But then again, I wasn't sure who I was anymore. Basketball shorts would have to do.

I peeked around the curtain and smiled big time. He was there. He'd done it. Paul had successfully lured Daisy into the auditorium to be by his side. Birgit, Ellie, and Sophie on his other. I was so amazed she came that it took me a second for it to sink in that *Paul was at an assembly*.

He made me so proud.

If he could do it, I could do it. I'd make him proud or make a fool of myself trying. I guess this was what they meant by a fool for love.

Daisy. Daisy was there. Right in front as planned. Right there when I fell flat on my ass any second. All I was waiting for was the signal from Coach Everett, who had taken over after Mike Lopez waved his way offstage like a politician. Asshat.

"Let's support all of our Willamette High School students as they strive to win and some of them get up at five to practice and make it to school by eight."

Coach Everett raised his eyebrow at Thomas in the second row and cleared his throat.

"Others stay late into the night, representing their teams. We all know the big five: Basketball, baseball, football, soccer, and track and field. Most know we have students who are members of traveling teams and intramural teams. Congratulations one and all."

He paused for dramatic effect and let the clapping die down. "What many of our staff and student community don't know is that we have members of a world champion athletic organization at Willamette who also deserve our applause.

Haven Alexander, co-captain of this year's Cross Country Team, will present our unsung athletes with awards for excellence for representing the Willamette community in the bigger community. Come on out Haven."

That was my oh-so-ironic line because that was what I was going to do. I took a big gulp of breath and thought, 'I've gotta try' and skated across the stage, stopping short just next to the podium where Coach Everett was waiting. Ms. Lamb was there, too, holding the microphone out to me and beaming.

"I think this is a first, Haven." She waved at my skates. "There's a first time for everything," and her big brown eyes lifted at the corners she was smiling so hard, "Have at it."

And I turned to face pretty much half the student body of Willamette High. Six hundred or so. In shorts, knee pads, wrist braces, and a Rose City Rosebuds T-shirt, hoping this could change her mind.

It was like a second of silence hanging in the air, before Sophie laughed and the rest of the student body joined in. Laughing. Catcalling. Cheering even.

Was that *my brother*? Cheering?! I never thought I'd see that.

And reminded myself this was not the time to cry.

I could do this.

"Good afternoon fellow students and parents. As the end of the school year approaches," there was a lot of laughter because we were talking two days, "we should give a round of applause and show appreciation for this school's members of the Rose City Rollers Junior roller derby players, The Rose Buds. Please come on stage Sophie Johnson, Birgit Ziegler, Ellie Montoya, and Daisy King."

It was hard to even make eye contact with the four of them. All I'd been getting were glares for the last three weeks and the cold shoulder from Daisy. Why would it be any different today? They were just as likely to yell "fuck you" as to come onstage.

It was a miracle they were at the assembly. Only Paul could get them to something as unofficially optional and uncool as a school assembly.

But when I *did* focus on the four of them flanking Paul, they were standing up and smiling, even Daisy, though she did raise one eyebrow at me—I was pretty sure—as she edged down to the aisle and gave me a head to toe once over that made me want to die. And beam.

Because she was smiling at me!

Luce moved next to Paul, with Grey coming to sit on his other side seamlessly as the four girls made their way to the stairs at the side of the stage.

My parents weren't smiling anymore.

I could barely breathe. This was it. This was my big gesture as they came to stand on the other side of the podium and I reached across, in front of the podium, and offered my hand to Daisy.

Please take it, I thought, loud and hopeful and terrified. Can you read my mind?

Daisy looked at it, looked at my face, took in the Rose City Rollers purple logo on my shirt and the preposterous matching skates on my feet, and was still smiling when she met my eyes again.

And took my hand. And came to my side of the podium. I held our joined hands high, no longer thinking of derby teams or athletic awards but of us. Daisy and me. We. And maybe, I thought, meeting her eyes, we had some figuring out to do, but this time I wasn't going to chicken out, and if I was reading her mind? She wasn't going to let me.

CHAPTER THIRTY

"Friends Are We, Friends We Will Always Be. See, I'm Not Always a Jerk"

My face hurt. That was how much I was smiling. And if the look in her eyes was the truth, Mom was just as thrilled as I was. Probably more. She watched Paul's every move as he made his way, only lifting his shoulder to his chin a couple of times, to the steps of the podium. He looked at the banner overhead mostly but made brief eye contact when he took the diploma. The principal didn't shake his hand, as arranged, unlike with all the other graduates.

The principal got the memo. And Vice-Principal Michaels, and Ms. Lamb, all there to congratulate each student, not one of them trying the handshake, back pat thing. There were times when I really loved Willamette High.

There were times I loved, period. Like this. Proud of Paul and proud of my parents adapting to the impromptu addition to our gathering of church people, Uncle Jackson, and Knox and family, who were keeping their mouths shut if they had anything to say other than "Go Paul." A "Paul Squad", cheering him on silently, because we weren't supposed to cheer until the end. Proud of the connection running like a current between Daisy and my linked hands.

When it was time, the three girls shouting Paul's name as he faced the thousands of friends, family, and fellow students in the stadium made me feel more than I thought I could. Birgit, Ellie, and Sophie knew how to make some noise. Daisy had one hell of a whistle, too.

It wasn't the time for the "what next" that had plagued Mom all year. Or the whispered conversations that Paul only pretended not to hear. There were decisions to be made about whether Paul would attend Community College in the fall, whether he would live with our folks or spread his wings and accept a place in a Group Home, about what life skills were most important for him to learn for independent living.

Because he wanted to live independently. We knew that much whether it was sooner or later.

I never cried unless I was angry. Who knew that the exception was happiness for my brother? My big brother. My friend.

Paul made his way coltishly to his seat with the rest of the students, Naomi, his para-educator, waiting in the wings to take him somewhere quiet if he needed, and handing him his headphones. He wanted to try to make it through the speeches. Through the ridiculous moving of the tassels and throwing of the mortar board hat-thingy. I'd give him a forty-percent chance of making it the whole way through considering the noise and chaos.

It was that he wanted to do it that counted.

It was his desire for a bigger life that helped Mom and Dad see he had more potential than they'd dreamed of, even if it didn't look like the dreams they'd had before he was diagnosed.

I looked over at Daisy. Her eyes were wet with tears, drops falling from her chin. She was leaning forward with enthusiasm. As excited as I was.

Without Paul I might never have met up with Daisy again after the Slut Walk. Might have passed her in the halls and never spoken. Or hugged. Or kissed. I didn't believe in "It was meant to be" or "Everything happens for a reason". I believed in kindness and bigness of heart and big brown eyes and straight-shooting tell-it-like-it-is. I believed in Daisy, and I believed in us.

And maybe I believed that the *me* that was part of *us* was someone I believed in even more than the me that was part of no one. Friends are we, friends we will always be.

EPILOGUE

"I Have a Lot to Learn"

I t still weirded me out. Sure, I'd seen photos, but it was nothing like being here LIVE.

Breathe, Haven.

The men, okay, that was whatever. If some dude wanted to truss himself up like a leather studded turkey go for it. And the couples were sweet, especially the ones carrying signs saying how many decades they'd been together. I could do without the bare, hairy butts and the oiled abs, but I had to admire the commitment to being buff.

On the other side of the street, Joey was holding hands with Robin, who was just as cute and petite and androgynous and non-binary presenting. Joey's uncle walked with them in his police uniform. A united family.

Seeing Joey reminded me of how I'd misunderstood and judged Joey for being they/them. I'd been like Mom, thinking they were signing up for unnecessary hassle and could have just gone along with she/her. Gone along like I had, refusing to piss off my parents and pretending it didn't matter that I was probably gay, pretending I was happy, pretending to be perfect. Because that was what *I* thought they needed.

Today I didn't have to pretend anything.

Not that there weren't protesters. With signs. It so helped knowing I was going to hell and God didn't make Adam and Steve and even *I* knew they'd been saying that for decades. Get over it already. The men and women two blocks down accusing trans people of being mass murderers because the president said so, that was harder to ignore.

Breathe.

And there were women. Hundreds of women and girls walking by in every outfit known to humanity and a few dressed as other than humanity. Inflatable frogs. Rainbow unicorns. Easily a dozen people in kigurumi animal onesies who had to be boiling on a July day. Some people got around the heat with only those sticky things Daisy said were nipple petals and shorts.

Happy Pride, I thought, still weirded out by all the skin as two girls walked by holding hands who'd skipped the nipple petals...

Was it even all right for me to find it attractive when a girl my age walked by wearing a corset-top thingy and a skirt that skimmed her butt? When I was with Daisy.

As in, right. Next. To. Her.

There was *definitely* a lot more to figure out.

And we were. After two double dates with Joey and Robin, one triple date with Grey and Will, and Maddy with Dog Meat—who were all in line for Voodoo Doughnuts when we passed on the way downtown—and one dinner with Daisy's mom who was maybe starting to trust I wasn't going to hurt her daughter again, we were getting in some practice.

And then there was the evening spent at the tiki bar after hours... The smell alone knocked me out. Add Frank and Fredericka and Wow.

Dinner with my folks was a no-go, even if Daisy was allowed in the house to hang out with me and Paul. Sometimes. Dad even smiled at her.

Mom, not so much.

Which made the next group coming into view much more painful.

The church groups. The Unitarian Universalists at the head of the line. I knew every person holding the hand-painted banner. I went to Sunday school and Youth Group with the kids and filled food baskets for the homeless shelters with most of the adults.

It was the handheld signs that broke my heart. Daisy read my expression as always and rested her chin on my shoulder and wrapped her arms around my middle.

"I love my gay kid", "Proud parent of my trans son", "I love my lesbian granddaughter", "I love my gay moms", they went on and on. Liz and Shay and Dylan and Pastor Tom and Christine. They were a sea of familiar faces. But not the ones that really mattered.

Suddenly, all I could see in my mind were the signs held high, the ones we'd made at home, "We love our autistic son" and "I love my autistic brother", the fundraisers and marches and interviews my parents had participated in to further education about autism. They were great.

But.

Now.

Here.

Nothing.

"Take a picture," Daisy said, "If you want to."

I knew what she was really saying, and I had about fifteen seconds to decide before the church group was past us. Did I dare? I held up my phone. Pressed the screen. And again. And again. And send.

No caption. No "Hi Mom" or "why the hell aren't you here supporting me??" Just the photos.

I watched my phone, intent on the bubbles that started, stopped, started again. And then words popped up.

I just want you to be happy.

It's such a hard life.

Only because you're making it hard, Mom. I looked up to push the tears away and checked my phone again, afraid that was all I was going to get. Then bubbles appeared again.

Maybe next year.

I'm sorry.

I let out a breath I'd been holding.

"Hey," Daisy's voice was whisper soft, "eyes over here, doll face. Look at me."

And I did. At her enormous brown eyes peering over my shoulder. I felt her fingers take mine.

"It's time, babe," she whispered, as Birgit and Sophie and Ellie skated up.

And she smelled like sweet peas and cherry lip balm and Daisy King, Derby Queen. I breathed in her scent, letting it fill me full of her confidence, her bravery, her boldness, something I sure didn't have all on my own. But I was getting there. She came around and pulled me after her as she skated backwards into the stream of people, and I followed.

And I totally didn't have a problem with being "babe".

Playlist

Everybody's Haven

There were a few songs that made Haven come to life (mostly by The Killers) and gave me inspiration.

Change Your Mind written and performed by The Killers

Mr. Brightside written and performed by The Killers

Somebody Told Me written and performed by The Killers

Read My Mind written and performed by The Killers

Smile Like You Mean It written and performed by The Killers

Stop and Stare written and performed by OneRepublic

Apologize written and performed by OneRepublic

Secrets written and performed by OneRepublic

Pushing Me Away written and performed by Linkin Park

An Honest Mistake written and performed by The Bravery

Creep written and performed by Radiohead

ALSO BY

ALICE IN BLACK

A Willamette High Novel, Book One

Sixteen-year-old Alice Carroll is a self-illustrated girl. Grieving her mother's death two years before, hating her father for abandoning her, resenting her grandmother's low expectations, she armors herself with ink before entering a new high school in a privileged neighborhood in Portland, Oregon.

Her entry into that Wonderland of sculptured landscaping and SUVs is complicated by her summer flirtation with Matthew, a nice college boy who comes by her work at Comikaze Coffee, a coffee and comics shop, to walk her home most nights. The flirtation becomes more the night before he goes back to college. But Alice's expectations are low. She's had too many losses to believe that anyone stays, more than anyone knows.

Yet some people ignore her warnings, finding a way beyond Alice's illustrated walls, and she's torn between hoping for more and holding on tight to grief.

PET SHOP GIRL

A Willamette High Novel, Book Two

Seventeen-year-old Grey Evans loves her job cleaning cages each morning at the pet shop before school. She loves the parakeets hanging upside down from her hair, the mice with pinto pony patches and especially a baby guinea pig who trills and purrs when she's nearby.

Even though she's convinced she'll forget to change after work one day and get to school with feathers in her hair and bird crap on her back.

And she loves her flirtatious exchange of notes with a fellow employee she's never met.

Grey doesn't love when her recently divorced mother has a panic attack that sends her to the emergency room. Or the pills her mom is prescribed, making her ricochet from controlling to raging to zombified in minutes.

How can Grey follow her mom's ever more isolating rules *and* have a senior year with friends, college applications, and a cute co-worker named Will?

This Willamette High series novel about family, friendship, mental health, and dating will appeal to fans of authors Kathleen Glasgow and Erin Stewart.

ABOUT THE
AUTHOR

Bebe Duncan is the author of contemporary young adult novels in the Willamette High series, *Alice in Black* and *Pet Shop Girl*, set in Portland, Oregon. Her realistic fiction focuses on social and family issues that teens face, from a first-person perspective, and on developing characters with challenges that resonate with readers.

Long a writer of narrative nonfiction, she was reintroduced to YA by her daughter, and the sense of immediacy, the emotions portrayed, and the action in that genre inspired her to start noveling stat.

She lives in Portland with her family and two humongous goldfish named Richard and Blanche. When she's not immersed in nouns and verbs or reading aloud as she edits, she revels in crime shows, YA fiction, WNBA games on TV, and walking a zillion miles a day. You can visit her online at b ebeduncan.com, on Goodreads, and @bebeduncanauthor on Instagram.

Reviewing this book would be fantastic! Thanks!

COMING IN 2026

A Willamette High Novel

Luce Romano has been in therapy for three plus years. First, because all her mom could think about was getting pregnant, and after charting cycles, taking her temperature, and hormones made her crazy, in vitro it was. Mom was driving Luce just as crazy. Her parents had a kid. Her. Why was it so important to expand her family?

After the twins were born things were just plain crazy, but in a good way. Luce became absorbed in her photography, both escaping reality and celebrating it, one closeup at a time.

And then her friend Grey's mom went whacko on the freeway having a panic attack and almost killed Luce, Grey and herself.

Thank goodness for therapy!

But when the unthinkable happens right on the other side of Luce's bedroom wall, in the neighboring rowhouse, it's crazy in a whole other way, and creates ripples even photographing toys and a weekly appointment aren't enough to handle.

Because not everyone survives the unthinkable, but everyone else has to deal with it. One way or another.